St ....

Texas. He graduated .   .s in

2004. Block's first novel, the internationally acclaimed *e Story of Forgetting*, was published in 2008.

Praise for *The Storm at the Door*:

'Intelligent and empathic, this hybrid book gathers together the best qualities of the novel and the biography.' *Herald*, Paperback of the Week

'Beautiful writing.' *Scotsman*

'Powerful.' **** *The List*

'Compelling . . . and the humanness of the characters is a credit to the author.' *bookmunch.co.uk*

'One of the bravest and most beautiful books I have ever read . . . Block moves nimbly between fact and fiction, history and the imagination, to get at truths that are almost unbearable: that love can fail, that a mind can immolate, and that language can sometimes leave us lonelier than our original silence. This is a powerful, enthralling and unforgettable book.' Karen Russell, author of *Swamplandia!*

'Told with intelligence, a poetic ear for language, and empathy, *The Storm at the Door* is a captivating story about separation and enduring love.' Lisa Genova, author of *Still Alice*

'Lucid, intelligent, passionate . . . The style is masterful. But most important the compassion that reconstructs the painful past and analyzes the uncertain present is unflagging and deeply admirable. Ste: who has turned out   e

by the same author

The Story of Forgetting

THE STORM AT

A NOVEL **THE DOOR**

Stefan Merrill Block

ff

faber and faber

First published in the US in 2011 by Random House,
an imprint of The Random House Publishing Group,
a division of Random House, Inc., New York.

First published in the UK in 2011 by Faber and Faber Ltd
Bloomsbury House
74–77 Great Russell Street
London WC1B 3DA
This paperback edition first published in 2012

Printed and bound by CPI Group (UK) Ltd, Croydon, CR0 4YY

Grateful acknowledgment is made to Farrar, Straus and Giroux,
LLC for permission to reprint "Waking in the Blue," "Epilogue,"
and seven lines from "Dolphin" from Collected Poems by Robert Lowell,
copyright © 2003 by Harriet Lowell and Sheridan Lowell.
Reprinted by permission of Farrar, Straus and Giroux, LLC.

A CIP record for this book is available from the British Library

978-0-571-26961-7

For my grandparents

Listen,
How quickly your heart is beating in me.

—from "Any Case" by Wisława Szymborska

I have sat and listened to too many

words of the collaborating muse,

and plotted perhaps too freely with my life,

not avoiding injury to others,

not avoiding injury to myself—

to ask compassion . . . this book, half fiction,

an eelnet made by man for the eel fighting.

—Robert Lowell, from "Dolphin"

AUTHOR'S NOTE

This book is a work of fiction inspired by my grandparents' true history. This story does not depict my grandparents' actual lives, but it does incorporate some of their real letters and pictures, a few of my memories and the memories of those who knew them, and historical details from a number of books and articles. I use this documented history as a point of departure into the story I imagine. For your patience, generosity, and openness in my interviews, and also for your gift of the freedom to diffract your stories through the prism of myself, thank you Roberta Gatehouse, Melissa Waldie, Lyn Waldie, Betty Hall, Betty Campbell, Sydney Hall Jr., Joanie Singer, and Carol Avery.

In my attempt to comprehend what my grandfather's life inside of a psychiatric institution in the 1960s might have been like, I found the following works particularly useful and inspiring: *Gracefully Insane: Life and Death Inside America's Premier Mental Hospital* by Alex Beam; *Under Observation: Life Inside the McLean Psychiatric Hospital* by Lisa Berger and Alexander Vuckovic, M.D.; *Girl, Interrupted* by Susanna Kaysen; *Life Studies* by Robert Lowell; *Lost Puritan: A Life of Robert Lowell* by Paul Mariani; *Anne Sexton: A Biography* by Diane Wood Middlebrook; *A Beautiful Mind:*

The Life of Mathematical Genius and Nobel Laureate John Nash by Sylvia Nasar; *The Bell Jar* by Sylvia Plath; and *The Mental Hospital* by Alfred Stanton and Morris Schwartz.

The Mayflower Home for the Mentally Ill is my fictional rendition of McLean Hospital, the real institution in which my grandfather resided. Today, McLean Hospital is one of America's leading mental health facilities and its invaluable work has helped many people and saved many lives. My depiction of the treatment of patients at the Mayflower Home in the 1960s does not describe actual conditions at McLean. The poet Robert Lowell was a patient at McLean Hospital, but the Robert Lowell of this novel is a fictional character, and—with the exception of his poems reprinted here—the actions, thoughts, and language I ascribe to him are products of my imagination. The other patients, staff, and administrators who populate the Mayflower Home are entirely fictional and they do not represent any real people.

I wrote part of this book as a Fellow at the idyllic Santa Maddalena Foundation; thanks to the generosity and support of the great Beatrice Monti della Corte von Rezzori.

Bill Clegg, David Ebershoff, and Lee Brackstone: once again, your insightful, creative, and diligent work has gladdened every page. If not for your passion, kindness, and guidance, this book would not exist. Thank you.

For springing me from self-imposed solitary confinement, thank you, thank you, thank you, my brilliant friends, readers, teachers, and publishers.

Mom, Dad, and Aaron: to say how much I owe to you would require a whole new vocabulary.

THE STORM AT
THE DOOR

WE MUST

ALWAYS BE VIGILANT

1

There is the house in the wilderness. The house, Echo Cottage, with the lake spread before it, a quivering lattice of light in the late afternoon. Beneath the mossy portico, a placard displays Echo's flaking name.

An overcast-pale porch rings Echo Cottage, and at its far corner is an aging chaise lounge, rusted aluminum supporting an avocado vinyl cushion. Sticking to the vinyl, my grandmother dozes beneath the brown-gray nest of her hair.

The air along the shoreline is dense with an insectival mist, the gnats hovering. From time to time, my cousins pierce the droning quiet with their yelps, as they tackle one another in the water. Thirty years before, my great-grandmother rested on Echo's chaise; years later, my mother will ascend to the recumbent throne. But it is 1989, and the chair belongs to my grandmother.

My grandmother's calves unsuction from the cushion as she wakes. Her stalwart New England face tightens, the fine wrinkles drawn taut. The translucent shells of her eyelids part to reveal her eyes, which can hold light in a nearly impossible way, as if her irises were twin concavities, blue geodes. My grandmother's eyes look out to the lake; her gaze is as inscrutable as ever.

There is my grandmother, Katharine Mead Merrill. What do

I know of her? That she was so often in that chair. That in the afternoons, she often slept. That, one afternoon, in the summer of 1989, she woke from a nap to make the vexing decision that she made.

2

Katharine has been dreaming. Of what? Of her husband, of Frederick. Though the specifics of the dream recede into the static of wakefulness, a feeling of certainty remains. Not one of anger or sadness, but perhaps born of both. A simple knowledge of what must be done.

Katharine knows, suddenly, the rightness of what she must do.

Still, she takes her time. She rises slowly, pauses to receive the diffracting late afternoon light as she enters the house. Katharine passes through the musty, tenebrous living room, which always seems resentful of sunlight, seems to be the place nighttime gathers to hide out from the summer's unblinking sun stare. As she enters the kitchen, the smell of stale coffee prompts her to empty the filter into the trash. She pulls a box of Lorna Doones from the cabinet, slips one whole into her mouth, as she used to as a child, letting it dissolve on her tongue. Increasingly, in these last months, she performs such behaviors that, if not exactly childlike, are not quite as prim, quite as austere in her familiar matronly ways. On this summer day of 1989, Katharine is sixty-nine; the early traces of Alzheimer's have begun to fray the edges of her attention and intention. For a moment, pausing at the kitchen sink to observe my cousins diving off the dock, she remembers her certainty but forgets its object; for a moment, she thinks she woke, simply, resolved to swim. But, no, no. It was something else; the idea of a swim does not fill the space opened by her resolve.

Katharine reminds herself that forgotten notions can sometimes be found where they were first conjured, and crosses halfway back to the porch. Just before the screen door, Katharine remembers her determination, and its actual object. The actual object is lodged like a repressed memory, like a Freudian scene of childhood trauma, behind and within all the clutter of the years, somewhere deep inside the attic. The actual object she has not held for a decade or more, but she often still finds it holding her. The actual object, or the idea of it, sometimes rises in her thoughts against her will, threatening to ruin all the progress she has made in converting her memories of Frederick to the stories she tells. When she speaks with her daughters and her relatives about her husband, all accept her characterization, without a flinch of doubt. Frederick was an alcoholic, a philanderer, a madman who once exposed himself on the road leading into town. He was insane, and she was sane. He was selfish, and she sacrificed.

Frederick was a man of manic passions. He wrote a great many letters to her, just as he also wrote stories, ideas for inventions, patents, politics, and philosophy. He also wrote poetry, some good, most dreadful romantic boilerplate that leaned heavily into Elizabethan English in a sentimentalizing, embarrassing way. She can keep all of these pages in boxes in her closet, as she usually can keep the memory of him near her in her orderly way. But the actual object, that bundle of papers, is a telltale heart. She buried it long ago, and still it thumps its maddening beat. Katharine finds an ancient, paint-splattered stepladder in the laundry room, and carries it upstairs.

At the top of the cottage's staircase, the entrance to the attic is a heavy door, carved from the ceiling. The heft of the door, along with the dexterous, near-acrobatic maneuver one must perform to pass through it, makes entering the attic an act as burdensome as the mental act that it accompanies. At sixty-nine, Katharine is lightly stooped, her gait stunted with osteoporosis, but her arms are strong from the water, from canoeing and swimming. She hoists herself, tries not to look down.

Inside, the shock of attic, the recognition of this alternate parallel space, always suspended here, above us: a silent, cobwebbed clutter of immutability, a dark antipode to the house below, forever blustery with motion and light, with cocktail parties and children chasing one another in swimsuits. Katharine eyes the piles nearest the door: the old records, the broken gramophone, a box of withered gloves. Up here, without our choosing, things simply persist. Katharine wonders at the mystery of what does and does not survive. There are a great many things she would have wanted to keep that are not here now; a great number of unwanted objects remain. Nearly all photographs from her two youthful, single years in Boston are gone, and yet here are the legs of a mildly pleasing doll she had as a girl. Katharine suspects that the truth of memory is that it works this way too: that if we do not decide to discard and rearrange, if we do not deliberately inventory and organize, unwanted things will simply persist. Memory can be a willful power, but we must always be vigilant. Always, we must choose.

She walks carefully along the beams, knowing that the space between, which appears to be a floor, is in fact the thin cardboard paneling of the ceiling below. Once, while she was sleep-

ing in her bedroom, Frederick, who would spend long afternoons excavating the attic's recesses, fell from the beams and
came plunging down, ricocheting off the side of her bed, landing on the floor. He then stood, holding a milk crate of antique
Christmas ornaments from above. *Ho, ho, ho,* he said. *Merry
Christmas!* That was Frederick.

She knows precisely where to find it, back five yards or so,
in the bottom of the crate that contains the things of Frederick she cannot quite bear to throw away, yet also cannot quite
bear to live with: his naval uniform, a collection of pressed and
dried flowers from their early courtship, the box that once held
her engagement ring. It is strange to put her fingers on these
things; at first they are only common objects in her hands. Yet,
if she lingers too long on any of them, they become sentient
and electric. Through her fingertips, they begin to transmit
something; they begin to transfer their history, nearly bucking
Katharine's determination. And so she digs. She digs and hefts
and shifts until, simply, there it is. For a brief moment, it too is
diminished in its objectness. It is, after all, just ink and yellowed
paper, just paper holding commonplace words, like the words
in which she thinks, writes, speaks. It is strange that this particular arrangement of mere words, of letters of ink, could haunt
her dreams.

For a moment she thinks this whole enterprise, her resolve, is
foolish, or worse. A disrespect, a betrayal. These are only the
words of a man she has not seen for more than twenty years. A
man she loved once in a life she no longer lives. She nearly puts
the papers back, nearly leaves the attic to change into a swimsuit
and enjoy the water at its best hour, as the sun starts to settle. And
then, just for a moment, she lets herself read.

And suddenly here, in her hands, is another place. She knows that she does not believe—not really—the stories she tells of Frederick. She knows she does not believe—not really—the opinions of Frederick's psychiatrists, her relatives, her own family. She knows that she still does not believe it is as simple as others tell her it ought to be, as she tells herself it ought to be: that she was sane, while Frederick was mad; that she performed the heroic necessary work of saving her family, while, in his mental hospital, Frederick *indulged in the escapist writing behavior* (his psychiatrist's words) that is now in Katharine's hands. Sane, mad, heroic, dissolute, earnest, deluded: she knows she does not believe—not really—in those simple divisions into which she has spent the last twenty years organizing the past.

Katharine's determination returns to her.

And still, as she carefully descends from the attic, papers in hand, Katharine wonders: why now? Why all these years later, when everything has turned out, more or less, well? When the fate of her family no longer hinges on the outcome of her marriage's drama? Why now, this certainty?

Frederick so often devised moments of dramatic catharsis, would drag himself bleeding from the night, into the living room, and demand reckoning. In those moments, with all his impassioned urgency, he was always more powerful than she, and she hated him for it. But here, now, is her reckoning, solitary and silent, the way she has always felt that such resolution actually comes. A private feeling; a quiet moment.

Does guilt at all taint her certainty? Katharine tries to encourage herself. Likely, she thinks, these pages would be of no use to anyone. Likely, their power comes only from what they signify to her alone. To others, these pages would likely seem only the madness that perhaps they are. And, besides, hasn't she earned this? After all she has suffered and survived, hasn't she earned this final power?

Katharine is in the downstairs living room now, stuffing newspaper into the Franklin stove, arranging the kindling.

3

Twelve miles to the east along the shore of Lake Winnipesaukee, I'm sitting at the counter of the Mast Landing diner, chatting with a flanneled man in a ski cap. I pretend that my mother and my brother, seated at a table behind me, are not there. I try not to notice the man's gaze meeting my mother's. I'm seven years old.

David and I started a rock shop, I tell the man. *We sell mica. And granite. And quartz. And fool's gold. But mica is the best.*

Mica? the man asks.

Yeah, it looks like glass. What do you do?

Mostly, the man says with a laugh, *I drive a truck and eat junk food.*

That's your job?

Ha! I guess.

Holy cow.

Speaking of which, the man says, consulting his watch, *I need to get going. Anyway, I think your mom and your brother are getting bored.*

I turn back to them. My brother happily swings his legs as he manipulates his Game Boy. He seems grateful for the air-conditioned diner, for the waffles now reduced to a sparse syrupy slop on his plate. My mother watches the scene, my imitation of adulthood, with unswerving adoration. I can see how adorable she thinks I am, and for a second I'm furious about it. I have started to put on these displays of my self-sufficiency every chance I get.

Yeah, I agree with the man. *I should get back to the rock shop.*

On the ride home, my mother maneuvering our minivan along the twists and hills of Route 109, I think about the trucker, the roads, freedom.

I've decided what I want to do when I grow up, I say.

Oh?

I want to drive a truck and eat junk food.

Haha! my mother says. *Stefan, that's the sweetest thing I've ever heard.*

That's retarded, my brother says, not glancing up from the Legend of Zelda. *You can't make any money doing that. And you'll get fat.*

We turn off the paved highway onto the rutted dirt path, marked with the hand-painted sign for Providence Road. Sixty-five years earlier, my great-grandparents concluded their long horseback journey from Concord down the same path.

The jostle of the car catches the attention of my brother, who immediately joins me in our ritualistic competition, to be the first to spot the glimmer of the lake through the dense forest.

I see it! David claims.

No you don't! I yell. *Liar!*

Why is there smoke? my mother says.

A delicate line of white smoke ascends from the chimney of Echo Cottage, just coming into view. I watch the smoke's strange configuration, like a calligraphic word nearly written into the immaculate early evening sky. Nearly written, then vanishing.

Huh, my mother says. *Isn't it warm for a fire?*

From the dirt and pine needle parking lot, we descend the path to Echo's back door. I carry a superhuman number of bags from our stop at the grocery. I want, very much, to impress my mother with my strength.

Mum? my mother calls, once in the house.

In here, she says from her spot near the stove.

My brother rifles through the paper sacks for a bag of potato chips as I follow my mother to the living room.

(My grandmother must have been there for some time, considering. Or could it possibly have been as coincidental as that? That the moment we arrive is the moment she finally holds the papers to the flames?)

What's with the fire? my mother asks. *What are you doing?*

Oh, I thought I would get rid of some things, my grandmother says, as if performing any household chore.

All three of us now turn our attention to the bundle in my grandmother's hands. There, on the top page, are the precise slopes and flourishes of my grandfather's handwriting.

Are those Daddy's? my mother asks.

My grandmother shrugs.

Daddy's, I think. My name for my mother is *Mommy,* but my mother's name for my grandmother is *Mum.* A minor difference, but one that helps me forget that my grandmother is indeed my mother's mother, that my mother was once, like me, a child with parents. But, *Daddy. Daddy* is my name for my father. *Daddy,* like mine, but gone.

· · ·

Awestruck and grim in their recollections, my mother and her sisters have outlined my absent grandfather darkly: adventurous, tragic, brilliant, a case study in the dangers of living too extraordinarily. During our de facto family reunions at Echo Cottage every summer, my mother and her sisters recite the Frederick mythology, stories that seem our family's equivalent of the Trojan epic, the original story from which all our modern stories rise:

Once, when the family was at a beach town on the Gulf Coast as Hurricane Betsy neared, Katharine and the girls fled inland, but Frederick did not join them. Instead, he lashed himself to a tree to confront the storm, face-to-face.

Once, while Frederick was sailing with my mother in the South China Sea, their boat caught on a reef as a storm unfurled before them. The reef was jagged and mottled with poisonous blowfish, my mother was barefoot, and monsoon clouds fell swiftly. My grandfather abandoned his boat, lifted my mother, and carried her a quarter mile along the reef, back to open water, where they could swim to shore.

Once, after a long, boozy summer evening with friends, Frederick ascended Providence Road to Route 109, where, like a cartoon wino, he opened a raincoat to expose himself to passing traffic.

My grandfather, I know, spent time in a famous mental hospital, populated by great poets and thinkers. But a mental hospital nonetheless. I don't know whether to admire or to fear Frederick and his legacy.

My mother often tells me, in her determined way, that I will be nothing like Frederick, but she says this so often it seems more a worried wish than a statement of fact. When her sisters and her cousins comment upon my remarkable physical similarities to Frederick, my mother winces. At seven, I have already developed an interest in my lost grandfather that is something more than curiosity.

. . .

Please don't, my mother says. *Please.*

My grandmother pauses, looking at the pages. The inscrutableness of my grandmother's countenance never vanishes entirely. Always, she meets your eyes to reassure you, to be gracious, but still you sense unreckonable distance, still you wonder her true thoughts, her depths. For a long while she is silent and staring; what does she think?

4

Katharine thinks that her daughter sees this as an uncharacteristically dramatic act. But even her daughter cannot know the importance of the moment, or what the incineration of these pages seems to promise.

C'mon, Mum. What are those anyway? Love letters?

Katharine thinks for a moment now about how to answer. A line she does not know she has memorized, a line from one of the pages in her hands, suddenly exposes itself in some internal, nearly forgotten place, some attic door thrown open. It comes to her, word after word. *I tried,* she thinks. *I tried to make sense.*

Please don't do that, her daughter says. *What if someone wants to read them later?*

Katharine wishes she could explain it. She wishes she could explain all the ways she has let herself be deceived, and the resolution she has finally come to. But, then, maybe what has proved true for her is not true for everyone. Maybe if she had loved differently, or if she had been able to think differently, or if she had been more faithful to her own visions, or if she hadn't allowed herself to get so damned down, so damned angry, her life might have been something else entirely.

All right, you're right, she says evenly, stands from the fire, and slips the bundle of her husband's papers onto the bookshelf. Instead of Frederick's words, she places two logs on the fire, and then helps unpack the groceries. Later, while her daughter and her grandsons go for a swim, Katharine reclaims her spot on the chaise.

And then. When the embers have nearly burned through the logs, she rises again; again, she enters the living room, holds her husband's letters, sits down to the fire. This time, she burns them all.

For minutes, she watches the fire articulating Frederick's words into something else, a plume of white, sucking upward. The transformation is both simple and impossible. A moment ago they were words, considered and set; now they are a rising whiteness. Now they could have been anything.

THE

SADNESS OF

DISTANCE

1

There is my grandfather. My grandfather, Frederick Francis Merrill, at the Mayflower Home for the Mentally Ill, in July 1962.

Frederick awakes in the pale blue of himself, as he has awoken every day since his arrival here, the stupor of last night's dosage of Miltown worn thin at dawn. He will grow agitated and mystified with the day, as he invariably does, but at least for this moment, when he is scheduled to sleep but is awake, Frederick feels nearly lucid. He reminds himself of where he is; the truth of his present still seems ridiculous, impossible. He is a patient in a mental hospital, he tells himself. This is what has happened.

He is a patient in a mental hospital, and so he resolves, as he now resolves nearly every morning, to be what the hospital and its deluded staff require of him. They are deluded, and he is lucid. And so he will play their games and convince them, easily. Frederick tells himself it will be simple: he will be the model of sanity, or at least their model of sanity, for a few days, a few weeks, a month, and then he will be free. He will be free from these halls, these rooms, these pills, and then he will decide for himself whether he is sane; he will figure out on his own the causes of the abject existence that has so rapidly assembled around him.

The nurses—terse, attentive ladies, many long ago inherited

from New England's defunct Victorian orphanages—are down the hall, opening doors and announcing breakfast. When they knock at the door four down from Frederick's, they release that daily scream, that morning bugle blare of terror, as James Marshall awakes. James Marshall, the one-limbed war hero, awakes to find himself deprived of three appendages, and screams, as he screams nearly every morning, at the horror of his present. As the day grows, there will be many men who scream at similar realizations. In the moments just before the midday sedative dosing, there will nearly be a dreadful cacophonous chorus echoing through these peeling, gilded halls. My grandfather pulls his pack of Pall Malls out of the bedside drawer, lights one, sits upright in his bed. He cannot know how, by the next morning, things will have changed.

Out his window, the high leaves of the summery green sycamores receive the first morning light. From Frederick's place on the bed, these trees, the azure sky, and the intervening cage on the window are all he can see. But beyond are more trees, in admirable variety, each planted and arranged sixty-five years before by the great landscape architect Frederick Law Olmsted for their placating, transcendent beauty. Beyond Olmsted's masterpiece perched atop Madhouse Hill in Belmont, the city of Boston spreads incandescently, as it receives the morning sun. A single edifice, a massive, nearly completed office tower, rises luminously over the convoluted streets, cluttered with their Colonial row houses. Beyond the city, the last sign of human enterprise, the Boston Harbor Lighthouse, is half-invisible in the cling of morning fog. And beyond, the sea is calm and expansive, as placid and precise as Frederick's mind, at least for this moment. Any sign of what will befall Boston that evening lies much farther still, nearly all the way to Bermuda, where the waves suddenly rise, exultant and choppy, buffeted by the periphery of a late summer system. There, fish, whales, sea turtles either attempt to flee westward or else go downward, to protective depths.

. . .

Half an hour later, Frederick is on his feet, enjoying the only nondrugged walk of his day. In July, the miasma that spends half a year in the American South shifts northward to Boston, and often the air is isotonic with the body, every bit as moist and warm, one's clothes soaking from osmosis. But today is perversely beautiful, almost an insult to Frederick that even here, even on this ancient, rusting Madhouse Hill, such irrepressible beauty is possible.

Frederick pulls in air, testing the phlegmy constraints of his smoker's lungs, as he passes through the courtyard outside Ingersoll House. It is here that a sentence suddenly materializes in his mind. The words come in such an unconsidered, instant way, the way Frederick imagines that language must come to great poets, that he repeats the words to himself several times, believing they might be valuable, might be a vital sentence in one of the many literary projects he has told himself he will execute while at Mayflower. Frederick thinks: *The sadness of always being at a distance from things, either above or else beneath.*

There in the courtyard outside Ingersoll, Frederick finds Marshall, who seems already to have forgotten his waking horror. At the flagpole, Marshall carries out his morning ritual. Dressed in his military uniform, as ever, Marshall performs a daily raising of the flag with his one remaining arm. For years, under the permissive administration of Mayflower that will fall this very night, Marshall has been allowed every morning and evening—rain, snow, or sun—to raise and lower his flag.

Frederick waits for Marshall's eyes to meet his own and offers a smile. In his fifties, Marshall is gifted with the rare sort of face in which time and the elements have only sharpened its rugged handsomeness. If looking at a photograph of Marshall from the neck up, one would assume the face was affixed to a commensurate body, muscles nearly ossified by will and trial. A wider perspective, however, reveals the sickening absences: his uniform safety-pinned to itself, folded cleanly around the stumps of both legs and one arm. The precise means by which Marshall lost each appendage are common topics of hushed gossip and speculation among the men of Ingersoll House. What seems certain is that not every limb was lost at war. On his first day at Mayflower, Frederick watched the fingers of Marshall's remaining hand carry out a search and destroy mission across the bald plane of his head, hunting hairs and plucking them away. The general consensus is that only Marshall's left leg was lost to the war. Normandy, or so the story went. The rest, supposedly, has been his own doing. Several fingers of his now missing left hand had been excised with a willful application of glass, or so the rumors went. The arm itself, an escape one night to the train tracks near South Station. No explanation of how Marshall lost his second leg seems plausible to Frederick.

Stay to salute, soldier? Marshall asks Frederick.

Though the sight of Marshall, after three weeks at Mayflower, still stirs Frederick's pity if no longer his revulsion, Frederick does take a kind of pride in this seemingly privileged relationship, that a war hero regards him as a comrade, a fellow soldier. On two or three occasions, Frederick and Marshall have reminisced about their military service, as if they were someplace else entirely, perhaps a saloon tucked in an alleyway of a rain-swept port town.

The tension was just unbearable, Frederick told Marshall of his four months as an ensign aboard the USS *Wonder. And we never even saw any action. But I would be there on the deck all night, just waiting for the world to explode.*

Frederick has never told Marshall the truth of how his time with the Navy ended, nearly identical to how his time with the White Paper Company ended, nearly identical to how his early promise in the private academy he briefly attended as a child ended: with a bottomless desperation, with unmanageable, surging notions, with drastic physical transformations.

Correlation does not imply causation, one of Frederick's Harvard Business School professors would often remind his classes. Just because two things happen at the same time does not necessarily mean one causes the other. Yes, his breakdowns—if they even deserve so certain a word—have tended to come alongside heightened responsibilities, but that does not necessarily mean Frederick cannot be equal to the fortitude his challenges require of him. Sometimes, something within him flares or extinguishes, but it is separate from him, this cycling, a pattern that has its own unknowable logic.

Do do dee do do do do dee do doo, Frederick sings the opening notes to reveille into his fist, mock-blowing on an imaginary horn. Frederick laughs, and usually Marshall laughs at this too. Today, strangely, Marshall does not laugh. Marshall only keeps his gaze upon the flag, as if the notes Frederick sings were more than some enlivening tune, as if they somehow carry a tremendous and mournful truth. Then an orderly comes, as every day, to wheel Marshall toward the cafeteria along the paved pathways.

As Frederick makes his way toward the Depression, that bowl-shaped green in the center of campus that the men must cross on the way to and from the cafeteria, he negotiates through a cluster of cows, standing idly in the shade of an elm. Thirty years before, Frederick has been told, Mayflower had again aligned itself with the popular thinking of mental hospitals of the time. It had been the latest belief among the psychiatric professionals that those interred in mental hospitals required regular work, a daily structuring purpose. And so aristocratic Mayflower, like any state hospital of that era, had become a full-fledged funny farm, the mad Brahmins poorly tending to newly constructed chicken coops, gardens, milk cows. Predictably, the staff soon found itself in charge of both the insane and their livestock, and the project was largely abandoned. Still, the administration has allowed these cows to stay, to wander like holy Hindu bovines, as if in respectful credit to the failed notion, as if not to hurt the feelings of the ancient psychologists who dreamed it up. A few of the oldest orderlies and nurses, recruits from this bygone era, still feed them hay, clean their mess, and seem to take the cows' continued presence as a personal respect.

Passing the Depression's nadir, Frederick is planning. He tells himself that after breakfast he will finally write the letter to Katharine. He has been considering this letter for some time; he has already drafted many sentences in his notebook. Never mind that he is not allowed to send her any letter, just as he is not allowed to phone her, until his psychiatrist grants him those privileges. He will write the letter, and then he will begin to write for himself, something that his vaunted poet ward mate, Robert Lowell, has encouraged him to pursue. He will do these things, even with the Miltown. He will try, as he has tried and failed time and again, to avoid the pills. But even if he must capitulate to his prescriptions, he will do these things.

Frederick is in an asylum for the mentally ill, and he can agree that sometimes he gets confused and acts in ways that surprise even him. But he is lucid now, many call him brilliant, and he is only forty, practically a young man still. He is a youngish man of talent, of passions, enthusiasms, and intelligence. And he is attractive, if not exactly handsome: his hairline is rapidly recoiling from his face, his ears protrude at such angles that he likes to joke that, should he be pushed from a cliff, his ears would perform Bernoulli's principle, and he could simply glide to safety. Frederick tells himself that he is only here temporarily, for the same reason that a number of similarly gifted men are here: too much intellect, too much passion appearing to ordinary men as madness. He will make the most of his time here. He will write, as he wishes he had time to write but never does amid the responsibilities of his life outside the hospital. It's not that Frederick thinks he has wound up at Mayflower for these reasons. Frederick knows better than to believe, as his wife sometimes claims to, that all things happen for a reason. Things happen; it is up to us to invent for them purpose.

2

This is the morning of the day that will change everything, but the men and women of the Mayflower Home cannot yet know this. One, however, will later claim to have sensed a foreboding. At the top of the far side of the Depression, Professor Shlomi

Schultz sits at his mahogany desk in Upshire Hall, the grand old mad mansion. Years before, Upshire was dubbed the Harvard Club, and though it has never exactly been official hospital policy, the four corner rooms on the first floor, each ornate with the trappings of Victorian-era prosperity, each with soothing pastoral views, have been occupied by mad men who have attended the illustrious university, after which the Georgian colonial grandeur of Mayflower is modeled. In keeping with tradition, Professor Schultz is former Harvard faculty, once the P. A. McIyre Professor of Linguistics, before his schizophrenic condition intensified to the point that his colleagues concluded Schultz's work had tilted past visionary, into the realm of the insane.

Initially, when Professor Schultz cryptically claimed to have discovered an unknown language, his colleagues had responded with an amalgam of curiosity, skepticism, jealousy, and worry. When, however, it became clear that this language was derived from sounds that only Schultz heard, they referred him to Mayflower, where he has remained for decades. But Schultz, having lost his family many years ago, does not mind his current position, does not perceive its indignity. For here, far from the demands of students and curricula, deans and symposia, he can focus singularly on his work. And the work couldn't be going better. These days, nearly everything makes a sound, and each sound is composed of a variety of subsounds, all the way down to the screaming clouds of electrons around their nuclei.

Usually, Schultz tries to ignore that static always coming out of the upper atmosphere; he has grown accustomed to its fluctuating whine and muffled babble, just as the men of Ingersoll have grown accustomed to ignoring the television always chattering in the common area. But today there is a new sound, distant but insistent, which he cannot ignore.

3

Is your stomach readied to receive that gruel?

From a distance behind him, Frederick hears that famous voice, with its inescapable gravity. Frederick turns to face Robert Lowell.

Before Lowell, Frederick's few encounters with the famous had invariably left him disappointed. Jerry Lewis at a USO show in Boston, an airplane ride shared with Mickey Mantle, Billy Wilder lecturing at Harvard. It had always been impossible to reconcile that which had so moved him, abstractly and at a distance, with the human-size person before him. But Lowell has proved rather the opposite of Frederick's previous brushes with fame; he is grander in person than even his grand poetry. Lowell's face is carved with a severity simultaneously biblical and Hollywood, not unlike that of Kirk Douglas. Even in Lowell's overt madness, not a word or a gesture seems undetermined; his every movement can still appear guided by some nameless furious brilliance within. When Lowell is delusional, believing himself Christ, Milton, or Shakespeare, it can all seem part of his poetry, his poetry bursting beyond the language that cannot quite contain it, becoming his life itself. Even now, in this simple exchange, Frederick—the generative, the imposing, the brilliant Frederick—feels reduced to his childhood gangliness. Frederick glimpses himself as the sick boy he once was, withering to skeletal on his bed, trying to explain himself to his mother and the doctors, shamed to find himself without words.

Part of Frederick's anxiety around Lowell, Frederick knows, derives from the unpredictable nature of Lowell's attentions, from Lowell's imperviousness to Frederick's charisma. Near Lowell, Frederick is struck with the troubling realization that, set in relief against Lowell's true, recognized genius, his own minor genius is insufficient, perhaps not genius at all. Frederick wants to be taken into Lowell's private machinations, to be the object of Lowell's creative exertions, as he has been only once, on his first day at Mayflower.

Do you see the sign? Lowell had approached Frederick that first morning with his arm extended, pointing to an empty white space near the entrance to Ingersoll.

Sign? Frederick asked.

Lasciate ogne speranza, voi ch'entrate.

Excuse me?

Abandon all hope, ye who enter. Dante's Inferno.

Ah, Frederick said.

Lowell took a step back from the new patient, his eyes traveling Frederick's length, not so much in judgment, but as if to limn Frederick's psychic affliction. Eventually, Lowell stated his conclusion in Latin.

Arma virumque cano.

Frederick scrutinized the man before him for a moment before the recognition came. He had heard of the famous poet's frequent sojourns at Mayflower but had not until this moment, not during all the vertiginous confusion of his admission, considered he would find Lowell here like this, simply another man on the ward. That first day had been one of Lowell's *up days,* his arms flailing in his French sailor's jersey, his eyes unfocused, his pupils occasionally disappearing into his skull, his hair jutting from his scalp in electrified tufts, as if charged by the profound wattage within.

I sing of arms and a man at war, Frederick said. *Virgil.*

Lowell flashed Frederick a sly smile, leaned to his ear, and whispered, *I wrote that.*

Excuse me?

For the following two hours, Lowell had not let Frederick stray far beyond the span of his arms. In his unbrushed breath, Lowell spoke rapid Latin and Italian into Frederick's ears, occasionally muttering to Frederick how grateful he was Frederick had come, how he recognized Frederick's rare form of intelligence, how Frederick was just the sort of man he had been waiting for, to assist in his escape into a place that was his own, where he could begin his true poetry.

Lowell, the other men later told Frederick, has reacted similarly to a number of new patients, their newness their true appeal. Their newness, which implies a chance at revision. This, Frederick senses, is part of Lowell's affliction and also his poetry, forever seeking exit from the chaos he carries through new forms, new friends, new lovers. Lowell can go to sleep fizzled, cracked, too worn to raise a brush to his leonine mane, then wake in a manic awareness, entirely other, believing himself the true author of *Paradise Lost* or *Hamlet* or the *Inferno,* all of which he seems to have memorized in entirety, all of which he believes in need of revision.

Frederick understands this in a way he would be too timid to admit to Lowell. With his eyes spinning in his skull, his manic mannerisms, could Lowell comprehend him anyway? Frederick, too, has taken new women, for no reason, he often realizes in retrospect, other than the newness they promise. There have been a shameful number, but Frederick never lets himself count. Perhaps, if he allowed himself to focus, he could remember what it was, those bourbon-stained nights, that each seemed to offer him. But when Frederick thinks of them now, all those women and the sad, anarchic acts that began at lonesome, emptied bars, he generally remembers them as one, a single smear of exhilaration and failure, a collective otherness, moaning sullenly beneath him, the newness they had promised quickly disintegrating into the old familiar shame. He is sorry for Katharine, of course, but the memory of other women is most shameful not for his betrayal of his vows, but for the betrayal of a singular, knowable life that had once, with Katharine, seemed so possible.

Lowell does not wait for Frederick to respond. He surges ahead toward the dining hall, with its World War I bunker mode of drabness. Frederick follows, and, in the vacuous, scrubbed room, with its anachronistic long oak tables (seemingly borrowed from a nineteenth-century German beer garden), Frederick encounters the scene that never fails to remind him of the Eloi answering the Morlocks' call in *The Time Machine*. Here, men and women, fearful of censure, drugged into compliance, line up for their morning servings. Invariably, some will protest the scene. Some will grow fearful, or suspicious, or simply rebellious. They will hurl food, cry out, smear pudding, beat a fellow patient or an orderly with a spoon. These patients, the others know, have signed their papers for a morning, if not a whole day, in the solitary ward, that squat concrete structure Frederick is grateful never to have entered, from which screams can echo all the way across the Depression. At meals, more than any other time, Frederick thinks of Mayflower's success in rendering people into numbers.

Perhaps others receive this scene similarly. Pushed up to the table at which Frederick sits with his tray of dandelion yellow eggs and dry corned beef hash, Marshall gazes down at his food as if it were an illegible text. Marshall then lifts his head, looking about the cafeteria, as if trying to decipher its meaning. Then he makes that gesture, common as a shrug in Mayflower: with his one arm, he clutches his skull and begins to cry. Later, Frederick will not have the energy for such social efforts. As soon as his stomach metabolizes the pills that wait for him at the end of breakfast, it will be difficult to muster a sentence. But, now, Frederick tries to cajole Marshall into a laugh.

This garbage isn't even food, Frederick says. *It's simply prefecal matter.*

Marshall raises his face, and gives Frederick a look that is not quite sane, something unspeakable caught in his throat.

A half-catatonic named Stanley, sitting at the table's far end, breakfasting on the only sustenance he allows, orange sherbet and ginger ale, barks a sound, like an engine turning, but failing to catch.

Trays are cleared. Pills are announced. The Eloi gather. Frederick, who has sworn to himself at least to try to avoid the dosage, panics at the face of the severe woman in the dispensary, and the large orderly who stands by the window, inspecting gums and mouth to make sure all prescriptions have been ingested. Frederick reminds himself that if he is to have any hope of freedom, then he must appear to obey, and sometimes that means he must actually obey. He capitulates, swallows. Already, it seems, he can feel it. He has already begun to submerge.

I had fallen asleep a boy, a part of the living matrix, and woken up something else, trapped inside the tiny room that was myself.

I told my mother I wasn't feeling well. How else to say it?

I did not eat. Doctors were called. It seemed I might die. But, eventually, I found a way to continue. I ate her thick gravies and fatty beefs. I tried to turn myself back into a normal boy.

But after that the world and I were never the same. Occasional

moments maybe. A bottle of beer in my dorm room with the promise
of a night's revelry building in the hall; the downy weight of a girl's
head on my stomach; a solitary cigarette on the deck of the ship in
an ocean vast and intimate as love. Sometimes the world suddenly
seemed equal to what I required of it. But, otherwise, I was under
the world, a cockroach-man scuttling beneath stones in filth, scram-
bling from the light. Or else I was above the world, as certain and
mighty as a fundamental force, as electricity. The sadness of always
being at a distance from things, above or else beneath.

Frederick scrutinizes the words he has written into his journal. He still is not sure whether this is a part of a letter to
Katharine, or something else. The incipit of a book, maybe. Frederick tries to write more, expecting another sentence to materialize, but none does. The Miltown is a warm, calm front pushing
away the bracing bluster of his mind. Frederick rises from his
bed, paces around the room, in a small fit, trying to will the
medicine out of his awareness. But his words are trapped. Even
his body feels trapped. An invisible molecular net has descended.
And now, again, the ever-present question: how, drugged, left to
long empty days, is one supposed to get better in such a place,
when the omnipresence of the sedatives never admits clarity?

4

Dr. Wallace repeats what Frederick has just told him.
Arma virumque cano, says Dr. Wallace.

Looking upon the old doctor sometimes reminds Frederick of reading the early Sherlock Holmes novels, or seeing Jimmy Cagney's first gangster movies replayed on television: one's first impulse is to laugh out loud at this perfect cultivation of cliché, but then consider the cliché's origin, how the seemingly absurd character before him is in fact a progenitor of an archetype that has only recently, through countless imitations, come to seem absurd. Dr. Wallace possesses all the accoutrements of his illustrious, plush office: from elbow patches to tweed to mustache wax.

I sing of arms and a man at war, Frederick says. *Virgil.*

Quite, the doctor says. *Care to elaborate?*

It's just something Lowell said. I don't know why it just came to me. It doesn't mean anything.

No?

Nope. Just trying to fill the time, like you.

A man at war, the doctor repeats thoughtfully. *Is that how it felt? How what felt?*

Your life with Katharine and your daughters. All the responsibility. All the fighting. Did it feel like you were at war?

Frederick shrugs. In the past, in the first week or two here, he would have argued with Dr. Wallace, or at least managed a pithy, cutting reply. But this combativeness of his, justified though it may be, certainly got him no closer to release. Still, it is not as if he is capitulating now, not exactly. He has merely adjusted to the lethargy of this place, the futility of his words and actions. Frederick, almost antithetical to his character, lets certain things pass now, unremarked upon. Is this ennui, this distance from life, the sanity to which others want to force him? When he feels nothing, will he be released?

Diagonal ghosts, moted afternoon light through the flaking green slats of the venetian blinds, hover lazily behind Wallace.

Such light, it seems now, has come with Wallace every morning to this office in Upshire Hall since the late Victorian era, may hold the apparitions of all those mad Boston Brahmins who have hanged themselves, poisoned themselves, or simply faded on these bucolic grounds.

Frederick, wanting to relinquish this line of conversation, turns his attention to Wallace's mahogany bookcase. On the penultimate shelf are twenty or so copies of the same text, written by the good doctor Wallace. *Fugue: The Remarkable Story of a Man with Fifteen Personalities.* This book, a copy of which Wallace has many times denied Frederick, describes, if not Mayflower's most famous patient, then Mayflower's most famous case study.

Frederick has witnessed this book's subject, Marvin Foulds, few times; typically the famous madman remains in his little cabin in the woods behind Upshire. But on the rare occasions that Marvin does emerge, he immediately draws the focused scrutiny of all those ethereal, delusional men and women, who turn into impromptu paparazzi, glimpsing what they can, gossiping about whatever strange persona Marvin has donned that day. Marvin's myriad selves may range from a French poet to a naval admiral, but like the disparate voices of, say, a Shakespeare play, all seem to Frederick to share the aesthetic mark of a singular creator's sensibilities, each a hyperbolic identity, each engaged in hysterical congress with the Absurd. Frederick has often wondered if Marvin receives a share of the royalties from Wallace's book, or if his payment for being one of the world's most famous psychotics is simply the exalted court jestership he holds within this mad kingdom.

The point is that even if one's daily life may appear quotidian, Wallace says, *one can still wage a silent and extraordinary war.*

Wallace took this office nearly two decades ago, and has ushered Mayflower through a time of quiet and comfort: qualities well appreciated by the board of directors in the aftermath of his predecessor, an ambitious modernizer who—like so many in the history of mental health care—was apparently drawn to the treatment of the mentally ill for deeply personal motives, ending his own life while still holding the office of psychiatrist in chief. The board of Mayflower, seeking to contain the spread of a thanatotic contagion, had moved quickly to install Wallace, whose approach has never been overly dynamic, whose touch is arguably too light, whose greatest failing is a nearly pathological avuncularity. For almost twenty years the hospital has been nearly what the well-heeled residents of Boston like to imagine it to be when they deposit their inconvenient loved ones at its gates: a quiet, idyllic place of rest. The last twelve years, Wallace is proud to proclaim as he nears retirement, have marked the longest period that Mayflower has ever gone without a single suicide.

The balance of Frederick's session passes in the familiar plati-tudes until scheduled time ticks to its end. No great progress, but also no great distress.

All right, Wallace concludes, as he often concludes. *I know it's hard not to get frustrated, week after week. But try to be patient. Try to stay confident. I've seen men like you do quite well in this place. A month or two, and I'm sure you'll be feeling back to your old self. What you need is a good rest. And there is no better place than this.*

A good rest, Frederick echoes.

Precisely, Wallace says. *My prescription is a warm bed, a chat with me three times a week, two hundred fifty cc's of hot cocoa, twice a day, and, of course, your medication.*

Wallace hands Frederick the two tablets in a paper cup and waits for him to swallow.

5

Professor Schultz did not always hear the sounds that he now catalogs in his room at the Harvard Club: his daily work, his life's great labor. As a child, like any, he assumed his parents' tongue was the only way to speak. Perhaps he heard fragments of things, just faint whisperings. Perhaps he turned his head to a sound he thought he had heard, but on second thought realized he had not. In his whole, happy childhood in Bolbirosok, Lithuania (or Poland or Germany, depending on the year, or one's perspective), Schultz perhaps discerned just the faintest rumblings of this hidden language at the edges of his perception. But it was not until his mother's death that, for the first time, Schultz perceived a tongue unlike any other, the sounds that things made to him directly, unobscured by human speech.

When he was a boy, Schultz and his mother had a closeness that other mothers envied and other boys ridiculed. Schultz and his mother had been as two parallel lobes of a single functioning mind, until, one June day, the half that was his mother vanished. That afternoon, on a walk back from the well in the rain, Schultz's mother had carelessly crossed the Milavetz Road, a dirt path primarily used by farmers and their horses. She had crossed the road, oblivious to the motorist from Vilnius, out for a weekend joyride with his girlfriend, exploring the back roads with teenage velocity. It had been as simple and stupid as that: she was struck. She was killed.

The sounds had begun almost immediately, at her funeral, the torn pockets of the grieving crying out with their own *sh-rook,* the rabbi's beard emitting a *ffff.* Schultz had not been worried, not for his sanity, and not for his hearing. Whatever these sounds were, they sutured, at least temporarily, the unbearable gap that had suddenly opened, with his mother's death, between the world and him. The vast distance of his mourning, a vast silence that separated him from others. *Cococo,* the wooden slats of a floor called out to him. *Bleee,* a crow's abandoned feather said. He had not yet begun to comprehend what he heard; he was simply glad for the sounds, the small compensation. Four months later, his father, Moshe, finding no equal compensation, one morning left for work at the bookshop he owned, bypassed the shop, and walked instead to the river, to the tree under which his wife and he had first kissed, and hanged himself from a wide, low branch.

Thereafter, when the people of Bolbirosok tried to speak with the seventeen-year-old orphan, they grew increasingly concerned as Schultz would either not answer them or answer them with words that were not quite words. But how could Schultz be expected to attend to conversation in that restrained language? The world had begun its own conversation with him; daily, more things revealed their sounds. With each step, his pants told him of their motion. Each sympathetic face spoke with something other than its human voice. The hair of Irit Mendelsohn, the girl he had always loved from afar, made a string of vowels, like wind passing through barley.

As fate or chance would have it, over the years that followed, Schultz lost a great many things, more than one might expect any person to bear. Each loss, however, seemed to allow more and more sounds. And it was not until he had lost everything—his parents, his wife, the town of his childhood, his career, his freedom—that he could begin to perceive the true names of all things. He has suffered greatly, he knows, but he also suspects that this suffering was absolutely necessary, that if he still maintained all his human relations, with all those exchanges spinning out in their common words, noise would have obscured the other language he is now able to catalog.

The universe is a text, Irit's father once told him. *An unending text, in which all is written in living words.*

Schultz remains uncertain if the language he perceives is a part of a text authored by some higher mind, or if it is merely the true and natural sound of things; he does not know if it is fate or chance that has brought him this far. But he knows all that has happened to him has been essential for his revelation.

Schultz has focused his morning energy on the specific sounds emitted by each pen in his jar, tuning out, as much as he can, the sound rising from the east. But now he lets himself listen. It is like a single syllable screamed by a baby who is just learning the word for *want. WAWAWAWA,* the storm says.

6

Instead of circumnavigating the Depression's lip, as the senescent and catatonic do, Frederick and his escort, one of the interchangeable old ladies, pass straight through the center, climbing the slope that ascends to Ingersoll. At the far side of the Depression, Frederick asks if they could pause for a cigarette, and the nurse agrees, but only if she can have one too. As Frederick leans over to offer her a light, he is careful to avoid the fresh dollop of cow excrement deposited there, an offering from a sacred bovine.

At the far side of the Depression, Frederick glimpses Marvin Foulds, descending from his cabin. Today, it appears, Marvin has taken perhaps his most outrageous persona, a Carmen Miranda–inspired Latin singer, supposedly named Mango Diablo. Marvin has tied a bedsheet about his slouching fifty-year-old body, tethered coconut shells over his sagging breasts, and now makes his way toward his daily meeting with Wallace by leading an imagined conga line—his fourteen other personae, perhaps? Frederick turns to the nurse, who peers at Mango, scrutinizing without apparent judgment, as if he is a television melodrama set before her.

Frederick whistles, cigarette smoke corkscrewing from his lips.

Geez. Talk about setting the bar, he says. *Next time I go nuts, I'll have to get more creative about it.*

A fascinating case, isn't it? the nurse says evenly.

Mango Diablo disappears into Upshire, and Frederick turns his attention eastward. From that height, he can see beyond the treetops, beyond the squat, complacent buildings of Belmont to the sleepy, tweedy city of Boston. Frederick thinks of when his parents drove him into Boston for the first time. He will never forget his first glimpse of it. At that distance, similar to the distance from Mayflower, the city had appeared before him as metonymy for his entire adult future: a place of human industry and sophistication waiting to receive him. But here, from this canted, elevated angle, it seems a different city.

Frederick looks to the horizon beyond Boston's harbor. The regal day proceeds spectacularly, unaware of the wretched throngs it passes. It was a day much like this one, every bit as obliviously flawless, three weeks before, that ended with this hospitalization. Dr. Wallace often tries to speak with Frederick of what may have led to that night: of his stresses, of his failures, of his frustrations in both marriage and career. Yes, Frederick acknowledges, perhaps they all played some role, all part of that invisible calculus of motive and explanation that we cannot ever entirely deduce. Wallace and the other men of Ingersoll have asked Frederick to recall that night many times, but the truth is that he has little to say about it. The truth is that his actions that night felt no more serious—perhaps even less serious—than those of the hundred nights that had preceded it. That night had culminated, as had so many nights, in an electric two or three hours, in which the bourbon he used to medicate his agitation conflated with the energy his agitation opened.

In the long history of his electric states, Frederick has been seized by many notions; much of what he has thought and done has felt to him—still feels to him, even in sober states—poetic, radiant. Some nights, he would insist Katharine put on a dress, and he would take her dancing. Other nights, he would gather the men from his office for an impromptu poker game, which rapidly transformed into an impromptu concert, with him singing to them all. That night, the one with which his present is so obsessed, was merely another notion that he persists—no matter what anyone says—in finding, in a profound way, hilarious. He had been bored, with all those dull and self-righteous relatives and friends, and he had wanted to scandalize them, entertain the few among them who thrilled to such transgressions. Once, such behavior had thrilled even Katharine, hadn't it?

That night, drunk, he had remembered one of the most popular spectacles he'd performed for his friends in college: without warning, one sophomore evening, he had stripped himself of all clothes and run a lap around fraternity row. Electric and seduced by this memory, Frederick had done it again, or something like it. Out he marched, from the cottage that night, wearing nothing but George Carlyle's raincoat. And then up Providence Road to Route 109, where he opened the coat to each passing car, making of his body a carnal punch line.

He had done it again, assuming it would conclude as it had twenty years before: with hysterical laughter and a few comical expressions of disdain. Perhaps, at worst, the memory of the incident would earn a placement at the top of his regretful, hung-over inventory of misdeeds the next morning. Instead, as the next morning came, Frederick was bound, literally and figuratively, for the Mayflower Home, spending the final hour of the night and the first of the day in the backseat of a New Hampshire state police vehicle. But it was only after Frederick had sobered and arrived at Mayflower that every moment began to feel gravid with consequence. He had been perplexed then, wanted only to accommodate, to downplay, to be amenable. He had simply believed, even when they arrived at the Mayflower Home, even when he signed his own admission papers, that all could be and would be reversed. Frederick could not have imagined an act as inconsequential, as utterly frivolous, as flashing two old ladies on a small country road in New Hampshire would have a resonance measured in years (indeed, in generations). How could he have? A few inches of a raincoat's material held one direction at one moment, it seems, has permanently altered his remaining years on this planet.

A cow walks before Frederick and the nurse, offers a skeptical gaze, and moves on. The nurse tells Frederick she needs to get back to help out with checks.

Frederick knows what awaits him in Ingersoll: another Miltown haze, men's screams, and the smoky, greasy drabness, like a bowling alley in the midafternoon. When he is inside his room, when his mind has adjusted to his place, he will be able to bear it. But still, each time he returns, it is an only slightly dulled reenactment of the morning he was first led into Ingersoll. For there they are now, passing through the ward's front doors, confronted with the same screams that greeted Frederick that first morning. The same catatonics clutching the common room's corners, either silenced by or enraged at their private sounds and visions. The same airless corridor; to open a window a massive undertaking, given the cages, the locks. The same cigarette vapors, clinging to the men like their madness, always visible, harmful, emanating. Once back to his room, the same crush of solitude, loneliness not merely a concept or a feeling, but a palpable physical presence. It is all the same, except for the awareness he possesses now that he did not, somehow, when he was first admitted.

The morning he had signed those forms, Frederick had seen his admission as a simple, if embarrassing, way to avoid police charges. It then seemed a choice between a stint at the local lockup or a few days in the nuthouse. He did not understand—no, not for another week, until Wallace, after Frederick's repeated demands, finally put his questions about Frederick's marriage and his mother on hold to answer him directly. Because the police had brought him there, Frederick had signed a modified version of the voluntary admission form. A modification that meant that his leaving Mayflower would require the approval of the psychiatrist in chief, who presently seemed to have no interest in his speedy exit. Frederick had given his freedom over to something far worse than the judicial system. Here, his psychiatrist was judge and jury, the case on trial, his sanity. And what recourse? Other patients have told Frederick that he could attempt a plea for his release from the board of directors, a patrician-aloof set that mindlessly defers to the judgments of the psychiatrists they have hired. Frustrated with their legal obligation to attend these hearings, the board reportedly accomplishes nothing more than an ongoing demonstration of their annoyance: a nearly flawless record of denied appeals.

Frederick is drowsy again; the Miltown has settled into the crevices of his brain, and he shifts back to his bed, for the afternoon sequel to the morning's Miltown paralysis. For a while, even with twenty milligrams of tranquilizer cycling through him, it is hard to drift to sleep. Every time his eyelids begin to descend, he is jolted back into grinding awareness by another scream.

7

It is night now. The men have had their final meal of the day. In an hour, during the final checks of their shift, the nurses will dispense the nightly dosing, sleeping pills for all, mixed with stronger sedatives for some. Most of the men in Ingersoll register this as merely another night, cannot know the horror that awaits them, a horror that will alter, in significant ways, the texture of their daily lives on the ward. The most observant, however, have noticed that the rain has begun, softly, to tick at the windows, beyond the cages that separate window from room.

But even they cannot know the storm's magnitude or what it will deliver. The storm clouds, like surreptitious Trojans, have slipped in under the cover of night, no one suspicious after the gift of that complacently beautiful day. For the most part, the men are restful now, some even in a rare festive mood, plotting a small improvised party that will soon commence in Lowell's room, marking the occasion of the four bottles of scotch a few visiting students brought him as a gift.

(Cocktails on the men's ward of the mental hospital! This is how it is, in this era that now draws to a close.)

The first bolt of lightning to reach Belmont speaks its name. Stanley peals manic laughter. Lowell says something in a language the others cannot understand. A limb of an oak tree snaps near Upshire Hall, the Harvard Club, where Professor Schultz registers the sound with normal human perception, and also with his strange form of awareness, the sound cracking through both. The gabbing electricity in the clouds above, each raindrop a fading scream, the wind murmuring like Jews reading the Torah, but garbled and at much greater volumes. All of this, nearly deafening, will soon find echo in the normal human register. But this is not what concerns Schultz. The tumult is not what prompts Schultz to relinquish his pen, not what drives him to clutch his ears, forgetting it is not his ears that receive these sounds.

. . .

As every night, James Marshall carefully wheels himself toward the bureau drawer that contains his flag's box, removes the box, sets it on his lap, and then, in deliberate vectors, points himself toward the door. He moves slowly, as he must, excited motion making his wheelchair veer to the walls. He must be deliberate now. Something foreign and unbearable has claimed an essential part of him.

In Lowell's room, the last of Mayflower's patient cocktail parties is at full tilt. The rich brown contents of the four bottles of Glenfiddich 12 splash around in each of the room's fifteen glasses. Marvin Foulds, now in the persona of Guy DeVille, a foppish (perhaps, judging from his behavior around the men, homosexual) French poet, spouts off Rimbaud to Lowell, who corrects his French. A rarity: there are even women at this party, a special privilege before their release. Ruth, a pyromaniac housewife from Wenham, and the beautiful Brenda Logan, whose father patented some crucial alloy used on high-speed airplanes, whose reason for hospitalization seems little more than avid late-adolescent sexuality. Dr. Wallace is not present to witness the irony of Brenda celebrating her pronounced recovery by drinking too much whiskey and placing her hands upon Frederick and Lowell and others as well, in her masterful, just vaguely lascivious way. Other than the occasional glower as Brenda moves her attention among the men of the room—that and Stanley's unintelligible conversation with invisible guests—the spirit is convivial, the cocktails temporarily eclipsing the men's interminable, listless days.

Outside: the bluster, summertime cracking and breaking. The rain is driven horizontally and at such speeds one might not even recognize it as rain, one might perceive only a particularly lashing wind and come in wet and know there must have been rain.

Marshall wheels past the open door of the party. None but a nurse notices him. The nurse, however, only admires his dedication, seeing to the flag's lowering in such hostile weather. She is glad to see he wears his poncho. She does not know that, underneath it, he conceals his folded bedsheet.

When Marshall cracks ajar the front door, it is an invitation for the wind, and the door slams open the rest of the way with a bang that makes the partygoers startle and giggle, would take the door clean from the hinges had it not been reinforced for the security of patients and staff. Marshall reaches the ramp, and descends.

If Marshall had hair, it might be blown into his eyes now, but, schizophrenic, he is aerodynamic as he approaches the pole, rain bouncing around the curvature of his head. Marshall looks up: the flag at the pole's top is nearly invisible in the storm.

Then, with the assistance of his mouth, Marshall pulls on the glove necessary to manipulate the thin, lacerating metal cable. Even though he is one-handed, the hospital must buy Marshall these gloves in pairs, and he has run through a considerable number, the wire having burned straight through and badly cut him several times.

Marshall is untouched by fear as he lowers the flag. Is this the calm of a man who has been blown apart by Nazi ammunition and survived, or only the calm of a man who has claimed that final power? Even in the chilling winds, he does not waver as he reaches his one arm to unhook the flag. Soon it is folded into the box in his lap.

With the dexterity born from years of one-limbed existence, Marshall locates the clip that binds the line's two ends and unfastens it. In the wind, the unbound line comes to sudden life, bucking against the pole like a cobra grasped by its tail. It nearly lashes his cheek but just misses.

James Marshall, the Amputation Artist of Mayflower, has now

settled into the execution of his masterwork, and he is careful to attend to all the details. With his one hand, he manages to pull the line through the loop at the pole's summit and lets it fall next to him. He feeds the slack through the glove of his hand until again he locates, at its end, the two clips to which he has so devotedly fastened and unfastened his flag. He removes the folded bedsheet from beneath his poncho. With simple double knots— he pauses to wonder if he should spend the time on a knot more elaborate, then decides it is enough, it will hold—he ties the four corners of his sheet to the fasteners, two corners to each clip. And then what was a bedsheet and a slack flag line has become something between a kite and a sail.

Does he think now of Normandy? Does he think of the absurdity that he has survived as he has survived, plucking hairs, fingers, whole limbs to keep some poison, some evil he contracted that day from reaching his heart? Or does he think of his parents, his only family, and how they have never been able to look directly at him since that day, looking away for another boy, their boy, whom they lost moments after his boat capsized at Normandy? Or is it mere, pure art? Is it merely an act, symbolizing nothing or maybe a great deal, a gesture of the unconscious, like Pollock's splatters? Marshall gathers the tail end of the line, and when he has enough slack, he wraps it around his neck four times. Already, he has begun to bleed.

Inside Ingersoll, the partygoers are singing songs from Frederick's favorite record, *New Faces of 1952*. "Waltzing in Venice with you, isn't so easy to do . . ." In the corridors, nurses pace beneath their cottony white hairdos. *Checks, checks, checks, checks.* High above the city of Boston, particles of moisture sing through the late summer storm. Just beyond Madhouse Hill in Belmont, a boy deduces an answer to a multiplication problem;

a plump young woman half-tearfully gives up on waiting for last night's date to call; a widow on Beacon Hill sniffs her milk, decides its time has passed. Clocks tick, people sleep, kiss, fight, make love.

In Upshire Hall, Professor Schultz sits at his desk in the room from which he will soon be removed. He has been hearing strange sounds, as always, and he has been attempting to transliterate them. But there is that terrible sound now, something that cannot quite be transformed into letters, at least none that he knows. It is not unlike the ululation of Middle Eastern grief, but much, much deeper, and incomparably more horrible. One by one, this sound obliterates the unique sounds of each of those other things: the singing, the boy with his homework, the spurned young woman, every particle of rain.

The wind makes violent demands upon the sheet; Marshall's wheelchair nearly topples. But now all that keeps the sheet from its airborne ambitions is the grip of Marshall's one hand. It promises to be as swift and as certain as physics, and it is. The wind takes the sheet; Marshall lets go.

IT HAD BEEN HER DECISION HADN'T IT?

1

There is my grandmother, in the summer of 1962, twenty-seven years before she will climb into the attic, resolved to incinerate her husband's words. Katharine sits in precisely the same spot— even the chaise lounge, with the avocado vinyl cushion, the same. The same lake spreads before her. Katharine looks at the lake with eyes that, in her early forties, have only just begun to blue with age.

On the raft tethered fifty yards from the shore, my mother (now only a thirteen-year-old girl named Susie) play-fights with her two younger sisters. It is already August. Today is unseasonably cool, a foreshadowing chill: school will be starting in a month; soon they will return to their house an hour to the north, and prepare for winter. But now, her younger girls, with children's obliviousness to discomfort, bolstered by their desperate desire that the summer continue, swim as if it were fifteen degrees warmer. Upstairs, Katharine's eldest daughter, fourteen-year-old Rebecca, listens to music as she writes of boys or to boys. The day is crisp and blustery. Whitecaps have been heaving themselves across the lake for three days straight.

Already August. Frederick has been gone for more than a month now. Several times, Katharine has had to abandon her unspoken beliefs about when to expect her husband's return. And now, once again, she must reconsider the reset deadline. A month longer? Two? Just a couple weeks ago, Katharine felt certain Frederick would be home by the end of July. Now Katharine knows she must learn to discipline her expectations.

To the left of the porch, two squirrels court manically, sprinting among the trees. A strong gust unleashes a battery of acorns, which thump against the roof. A loon, apparently complacent in the waves a hundred yards from shore, is suddenly seized by a notion and disappears into the water. Katharine thinks of how simple it could be to become something else. Her cousin Joseph strolling contentedly up the path, her girls delirious with the sunshine, the new renter with her scandalously younger boyfriend in the Bristols' place down the beach. Even the squirrels chasing each other in the woods. Why, Katharine wonders, must she be as she is? How did her life become this narrow and burdened? She wonders if anyone else has such thoughts, and wonders about Frederick, whether this notion would make sense to him. *Yes,* she thinks.

Katharine tries to correct herself. *This is the danger of his illness,* Frederick's psychiatrist has warned her. *This is why you have to keep yourself and your daughters away from him, at least for the time being. Frederick is sick, and part of his affliction is to pull you into his confusion.* Frederick's psychiatrist, Dr. Wallace, has sounded much like her father when making these pronouncements, has nearly sickened Katharine by lending her father's notions professional credibility. Her father, however, carries this logic further than Frederick's doctor. Her father told her, just yesterday, that the solution is obvious: simply, his illness should no longer be their burden, financial or otherwise.

This is charity money, her father said. *My charity money! And I don't see where it is getting us.*

They say it takes months sometimes. Sometimes years.

Years? How do you know that place has his best interests in mind? Those people are looking to make a buck, like anyone else.

What other choice do we have?

Look, Katharine, I support you. I support you and the girls. I will never let anything happen to you and the girls. But that husband of yours. You don't need to try to reason with his madness. You need to find a feasible solution.

Katharine felt the need to protest, the moment requiring her to defend the wisdom of Mayflower, of this hospitalization. But suddenly she found herself tremendously exhausted, and couldn't muster a viable counterargument.

What? her father eventually said.

He just needs to come home.

Well, if that's how you feel—I mean, wasn't it your decision to put him in that place?

2

It had been her decision, at least in part, hadn't it? Maybe the idea had first come from the men—her cousins George, Edward, and Herman, the two state police officers—but the final decision had been, in no small part, her own.

And why deny it? There had been a relief to it, the acknowledgment, in front of friends and family, in front of the authorities, of the nameless affliction that, for years, had been the great secret of her marriage. Of course others were familiar with the idiosyncrasies of Frederick's liquored behavior: his conversational and sometimes just nearly physical pugnacity, his sloppy advances on other women, the sophomoric nihilist manifesto that the bourbon and he would often coauthor (*This is all there is, the pain of remembering and drinking to forget*). But, in front of others, Frederick had always seemed able to sheath this darkness within the electric luminescence of his charismas, passions, and erudition, and others seemed to take these behaviors as necessary eccentricities of his brilliance, vaguely dangerous embers his powers sparked off.

Only Katharine, or at least she had felt, knew the depth of that darkness, that in the way joy and sorrow secretly generate each other, this grandiosity, this affability, this brilliance had a grim bride. And the two were so intimate, one a form of the other. Sometimes, one Frederick—drunk, effusive, pyrotechnically articulate—would go into the night, and another—sober, shattered—would return just hours later. There was one Frederick who would berate Katharine for the smallness of her aesthetic ambitions (her collection of Wedgwood tableware, her insistence upon matching outfits for her daughters), one Frederick who demeaned the very way she lived (*clean, shop, chat chat chat, sleep,* he had once summarized her existence), until she felt utterly reduced, less significant than the town drunk (at least he had a kind of celebrity). Hours later, there was another Frederick, maudlin and curled in her arms, pleading with her to teach him the secret of her simple goodness, her simple calm. Electric or fizzled: there were perhaps many Fredericks, but like iron filings to a magnet, they all congregated around one pole or the other.

Perhaps her true weakness, her true shame was that she had done so much to help him hide what he wanted so much to conceal. In the mornings, she would brew pots of coffee to rouse him from hangovers. When his drunken diatribes would tilt to offensive—as when he began to theorize upon a vast Jewish conspiracy in front of the town banker, Samuel Levine—she would clutch his thigh and laugh so that no one could be certain whether he was serious. Once, before a crucial meeting with the board of the White Paper Company, she had to spoon a weeping Frederick in bed, whispering to him of his brilliance. She made of herself an anti-Delilah, reapplying virile powers to his balding head.

The secret had grown as vast and indescribable as his affliction. It was a fathomless depth over which they both had to work, laying tenuous ropes and gangplanks, to try to continue to navigate the world's surface. Sometimes, her secret made her feel she and her husband were frighteningly alone; the solitude of their secret was perhaps its worst aspect. Other times, though, she would wonder if perhaps this was simply the truth of adult life, this unending project of keeping up appearances. Sometimes she would look at her married friends, watch the ways their eyes tracked their spouses with contempt or fear or gratitude, and Katharine would think, *My god! The secret lives everywhere! The true complexities! The unspoken burdens!* Sometimes, she could believe that, not only for Frederick and herself but for everyone, the visible world was a collective fantasy, to which we all consented in the attempt to obscure the ineffable stories of our true afflictions.

Of course Katharine wondered, at times, how she had ever let herself marry him. But then, at certain moments at social gatherings with her husband, Katharine startled with a spark of what Frederick had been able to kindle, when they first met. She has often chastised herself for her decisions, for her rash rush to marriage with this man she did not really know at all. Still, in certain moments, Katharine knew there was no mystery to her decision. Once, after all, Frederick's charms—which could enthrall the entirety of a crowded party—had been ray-beam-focused upon her. Their courtship, before he left for the war, had been two months of his total attentiveness, his limitless charms, his canny metaphors, his poignant humor, his astonishing range of intellect and wit. She had never known a man like him.

There was no mystery to why she had fallen for him; the mystery was why she had continued with him despite all the fearsome evidence, what the better part of her knew almost from the beginning.

She had known, for the first time, only weeks after they met, on that trip Katharine made with Frederick to Chicago, halfway to San Diego and his time at sea with the Navy. On their last night together, the imminence of his departure and of war hung darkly over them. Trying to cheer or else distract themselves, they had gone to a bar near Lincoln Park. In those first months, their dates always smeared into late night drunkenness, but Katharine convinced herself all the liquor was only an element of the celebration of their having found each other.

As Frederick consumed his fourth and then fifth bourbons, Katharine nodded in agreement with his tirade on the absolute madness that a man living his own life should be sent to die for others. She tried to be agreeable for Frederick, as she had already learned she must. That night, however, for the first time, his screed narrowed to her: no longer just theories about universal ignorance but theories about Katharine's own ignorance of what he suffered, what awaited him. On the street outside the bar, they encountered an olive-skinned man speaking in an accent, which drunken Frederick took to be German. Frederick could have beaten the life from the poor man had he not managed to scramble away from Frederick's fists. Katharine told herself then that it was just terror, reasonable in its way. That it was not Frederick, not really.

But then, just months into his service, Frederick's letters began to arrive, without explanation, not from his ship but from a naval hospital in California. Katharine pressed Frederick for an explanation, but she so quickly accepted what now strikes her as his ludicrously vague reply: *It is nothing but exhaustion, dearest,* he wrote her. *And some weight loss. But I'm certain, under your care & love, I will improve in no time.*

In her letters, Katharine asked:

What is the diagnosis?

How much weight loss?

Has this happened to you before?

Frederick did not answer; he merely pleaded with her not to worry. When he sent Katharine a ring through the mail, she agreed to marry him.

But the Frederick who returned home, the Frederick she married, was also, she had told herself, not really Frederick. This other Frederick, hollowed with starvation, who would often weep in their bed at night, and sometimes in the mornings as well. This other Frederick, who failed to charm, failed to understand, failed even to cross a room without stumbling. This other Frederick, who navigated the world with a left hand's crude and fumbling attempt to imitate the right hand's dexterity. Well, Katharine thought, she herself had never known war. But she could comprehend, as women's magazines constantly instructed soldiers' wives to comprehend, that the traumas of war could be transformative. This was not really Frederick, this emaciated man convulsing with grief in the sheets. But through love and care, as Frederick had written her, she could restore the Real.

And for a time, at least, it seemed she had succeeded. Or at least there had been the evidence of success: there was Harvard Business School, then his career. And, occasionally, it had so perfectly resembled a perfect life. They had many moments of great happiness. Even after all his betrayals and failures that followed, there were many moments when it seemed they had succeeded, just barely, high-wiring their family on the ropes they stretched over her knowledge, his abyss.

But, that night, just over a month ago, the ropes finally snapped.

Frederick's behavior at the beginning of that July evening was a mere extension, a slight deepening, of his alcoholic charisma, his nightly discovery of a radiant otherworld, refracted and luminous, through the browned light of his bourbon glass.

The regular crew had congregated, as they did nightly, in the new cabin Edith and George Carlyle had built up in the forest, to allow the adults time and space away from the children. As ever, Perry Como, Sammy Davis Jr., Frank Sinatra crooned from the record player. These evenings were often wonderful times—laughing, chatting, sometimes even dancing—in the piney newness of that cabin, while their happy, healthy, numerous children slept safely in the next house. Despite her constant fretting, despite her inability to keep from contemplating possible bad outcomes, Katharine often found herself able to enjoy these evenings. She sometimes even had the thought that it had been precisely this, this prosperity and mirth, for which so many men had fought and died not twenty years before. Katharine had lost her best friend and cousin Bud to the Battle of the Bulge, her brother, Roger, was still addled with shell shock, but at least here, in this brown house with these people, the world seemed restored in exactly the way the war's end had promised.

But, of course, people always complicate things; paradise on earth is never tenable, or even tolerable. Frederick began to complicate things. Frederick—in whom alcohol opened an insatiable appetite for conflict, a desire for the niceties of normal social transactions suddenly to break apart into high drama— would find ways to pick fights between married pairs. His litany of questions about the specifics of Edward's mortgage on the island he had just purchased would chafe at his wife, Martha, who would eventually cry out her suppressed resentment of the entire acquisition. Frederick would suss out a small rift between Lieutenant General Pointer and his wife, Marjory, in their political beliefs about the Vietnam situation, and he would plunge his brutal fingers into the schism.

Oh, General Pointer would then say to his wife, *now we're finally saying how we feel. Swell! I've got a few things to say myself.*

Late that night, the night Frederick was taken to the hospital, had been like a hundred other nights, tensions snapping as Frederick settled into his fourth bourbon. Katharine sometimes wondered if others could mistake his boorishness, his lewdness for simple drunkenness or even topped-over charm. Perhaps to recognize when the other Frederick was in command required a wife's intimacy.

Or maybe not. Katharine would later learn that earlier that week, down at the docks, the men—Herman, George, Edward, and Pointer—had held a long conversation about the ways Frederick preyed upon them, drove them to confrontation.

Do you think we should worry about his drinking? George had put forth.

Well, I for one am damn worried. Damn worried, Pointer had said.

Herman had proposed a theory: *It's not the drinking, per se. The drinking is only a symptom. There is something dark in him. The man needs help. Don't forget, he's had breakdowns before. When he was just a boy, and also when he was in the Navy.*

The men had nodded.

The men all thought of this conversation when, that night, Frederick's humor reduced, as it often would, to baser elements. By the fifth bourbon, gone were the displays of his erudition and wit. Now he was making jokes about fighting and fucking, jokes Frederick always seemed to have in a never-ending abundance: did he read these somewhere or, when the bourbon fuel was poured into his mental machinery, did his mind simply begin to manufacture them? As Frederick ascended, in rapidity of speech, rapidity of motion, the other guests slowed, muted. George, always the peacemaker, tried to acknowledge Frederick's edgy humor, to laugh, but also to pat the other guests sympathetically on the knee. Several times, George slapped Frederick on the back, as if in a shared laugh, but then tried to usher him back to the couch.

Hey, John Winthrop, Frederick said to George. *Tell the Puritans to lighten up.*

The faces before Frederick had no intention of lightening.

Dour, dour, dour, Frederick said, brushing off George's hand with a shudder of his scapula, and then turning away down the hall.

As soon as Frederick was out of the room, Katharine tried to clear the befouled air her husband had left. *I am so sorry,* she said. *He's behaving terribly. We should go.*

Martha turned to Katharine, to accept her apology. But before Martha could speak, George interjected.

Oh, for heaven's sake, Katharine, he isn't your child. You must stop apologizing for him. The man needs help, not excuses.

Maybe, Katharine said, not knowing—how could she have then?—how this admission would haunt her.

It's the damned bourbon, Katharine said. *If he could only lay off the damned bourbon.*

Enter stage left: Frederick in the change of costume that marked the opening of the evening's final act, one that would close with him in a mental hospital, away from Katharine, away from his daughters, for months and months. Frederick, robed in George Carlyle's raincoat. He entered the room primly upright, his lips pursed, in mockery of what he perceived to be the puritanical self-righteousness of the others.

Should anyone care to join me, Frederick said, *I'm going out to do the Lord's work.*

Is that my coat?

Frederick pulled the coat open, just a fraction of an inch, to reveal a vertical sample of six and a half feet of his naked self.

For God's sake, Frederick!

Leave him be.

It's the middle of the woods. Where could he go?

With remarkable swiftness, they would find out. Frederick proceeded to climb Providence Road to Route 109, where vacationing Bostonians piloted chrome and steel behemoths between lakeside retreats. At the intersection of Providence Road and Route 109, Frederick greeted each passing car with a display of either his genitals or his bare ass.

After only ten minutes of Frederick's performance, an ancient Ford happened to approach Providence Road. On their way back from a potluck dinner in town, the two widows watched their headlights illuminate the familiar trunks of birch and pine trees, the handcrafted road signs, the scurrying wildlife. And then the twin beams lit up Frederick, his manhood springing from the folds of a raincoat like an aquatic mammal rising for air. As soon as they arrived home, the widows phoned the police, and within minutes the naked drunkard was safely in their custody.

It had been so simple.

George and Herman suggested the idea to Katharine, presented her with a simple solution, *best for everyone,* they said. *It's either this or jail, I'm sure we can convince the police. This is what needs to happen, and it has needed to happen for some time.*

Katharine nodded.

Just explain, the men told her. *Explain that he has been having these issues for a long while. Explain that he needs help. Finally, Katharine, he will get the help he needs. Something good will come of this. George says Mayflower is the best place in the country, for people like Frederick.*

Still, Katharine cannot know why, exactly, she agreed. Had she actually thought George and Herman were right? Had their semiprofessional judgments—George a Dartmouth-educated family physician, Herman a Harvard-educated lawyer—been enough to sway her? Or, more darkly, had she not truly agreed but, in her fury at Frederick, wanted a kind of revenge? Or had it merely been the appeal of a respite, time away from her implacable husband?

When the police brought Frederick back to the cottage, Katharine and the men of the party convinced them easily. After the police consented, with the condition that they see to his admission to Mayflower themselves, Katharine explained to Frederick what he must do.

She had then spoken to the other Frederick, the one their friends and relatives didn't know: sober, shattered, and scared. She had explained to him that this was best for everyone.

They'll take you to see some doctors, she'd said, *and then all this will go away.*

Frederick had then nodded as a child nods. Brilliant, grandiose Frederick was reduced to her judgment, like a child.

He had trusted her.

3

In the following weeks, as the notion of his short stay began to disintegrate into the inscrutable opinions of Mayflower's doctors, all of those party guests tried to reassure Katharine that still this had been the best decision. *There is a reason they want to keep him there so long,* they told her. They had seen what Frederick had put her through, they said. *The man needs help.*

Even if these were encouragements made only from the obligations of friendship and family, Katharine tried to believe them: his hospital is the best in the country, maybe in the world; the opinions of the men and women there are the opinions of professionals, who have studied, diagnosed, and treated mental illness for decades. They must be right.

4

They must be right, Katharine thinks now, as she observes the afternoon from the chaise. *They are right,* she thinks, perhaps even says out loud. *He is sick.*

With the spastic logic of a flock of birds, Katharine's three younger daughters all suddenly run for the house, as one. From her room upstairs, Rebecca calls them children, as an accusation.

Perhaps Katharine could be many things, and perhaps things could have happened in many other ways. But history has happened; Katharine must now be what she claims to be. For her daughters' sake, if for no one else's. She must hold apart their fights, make them lunch, quell their angers, reassure them in their fears. She must make them believe entirely in her singularity. She can do this, it is this that will keep her sanity and redeem her, the needs of her children.

Katharine asks her daughters what they want and pulls from the cabinet and fridge the array of jars, meats, cheeses, and fruits required. Since Frederick first went to the hospital, she has tried to accommodate, as best she can, each girl's requests for simple pleasures: records, movies, books, food. When her relatives criticize Katharine for these indulgences, she offers justifications, which always begin with the sympathy-absorbent clause *Since Frederick has been gone.*

Since Frederick has been gone, Katharine says, *I have trouble saying no. Since Frederick has been gone, I always feel a need to make things up to them somehow.* She justifies, to others, her indulging her children as a compensation, but there is a vindicating pleasure in it as well. Yes, Katharine questions her decision. Yes, she sometimes panics with a guilt that is as plain as hunger. But still there is an undeniable gratification in her response to all that has befallen her. Still she is proud of her survival, of her family, which still thrives, still finds pleasure, in this summer without Frederick. And when he comes home—when? By the end of this month, early September at the very latest—they will be stronger, she will be stronger for what she has learned herself capable of.

You're making me a fluffernutter, right? my mother asks my grandmother.

Katharine displays the jar of whipped marshmallows. Susie, aware of how happy her happiness seems to make her mother, performs a celebratory jig at the prospect of fluffernutter. They all must make an effort, Susie knows. They must work to fix what her father has broken.

Katharine laughs and pats her daughter's hair. There are still moments of happiness, when Katharine's responsibilities and her needs are suddenly in perfect alignment. Perhaps she is even a hero, in her own dinky way. Katharine is married to a sick man, whose illness nearly spread to her, but she has kept it away. He is sick, still, and, still, she is well. Yes. She plunges the knife into the jar.

THE

VAST UNKNOWABLE

1

The wind buffets the treetops, fall's first pronouncement denuding the higher limbs. Between tree trunks, the dying grass is clipped close to the earth, the first time anyone in Belmont remembers seeing the grounds of Mayflower properly mowed. Bulldozers plow old sheds, smooth earth to make way for new parking lots. The cows of Mayflower, no longer roaming Madhouse Hill, are presently mooing in a truck bound southward on Interstate 95, oblivious to their near future as hamburgers. Two months have passed, and now it is September 1962.

In the woods behind Upshire, the newly emptied cabins, buildings that were, until weeks before, the residences of the wealthiest mad, are being prepared to house programs unknown before on the campus: preprofessional training, occupational therapy. In their modest homes in Belmont and Newton, freshly laid-off orderlies and nurses—those kindly, terse old ladies—have been severed from their close proximity to madness and now drive their families to something similar, unable to stop serving lunch at the designated hours, unable to stop themselves from scrutinizing the schedules of others' bowel movements.

The patients, many of them grown up and old in their private dwellings, are now forced, like university freshmen, to share rooms: a result of the new administration's emphasis on the importance of the social milieu. And so, lining the ward halls are confrontations and conspiracies, the discordant madnesses of the forced roommates often erupting in violence or, on rare occasions, aligning to engender friendship, but often birthing more madness.

High upon the far side of the Depression, the new conference rooms in Upshire Hall are cleared of their former Harvard Club inhabitants. In the place that was just weeks ago Professor Schultz's quarters is now a linoleum-lined room, still sour-scented with construction chemicals, in which young men and women, aspiring orderlies, are taking the newly devised entrance exam. Down the hall, men in painters' masks lay linoleum over rotten oak, apply baby blue paint over Victorian paisley paper. At the end of the corridor, in a room largely unchanged, sits the new psychiatrist in chief, the purveyor of all this modernization, Dr. Albert Canon.

A file is on Canon's desk. An old patient, Stanley Fuller, for whom Canon's subordinate, the meek Dr. Higgins, has suggested a course of shock therapy. Canon, as usual, will recommend other treatments.

Canon rehearses the speech that he will later enjoy making with a belabored sigh to Dr. Higgins. *I know they seem beyond language sometimes,* Canon will say of Mayflower's catatonics. *But good old-fashioned words can be miraculous things.*

Canon, overly caffeinated to the far side of focus, lays the file upon the green cloth ledger and turns to his window to watch Robert Lowell stroll across the Depression, accompanied by one of the new orderlies he has recruited from Boston University. They look so similar, all these Irish boys with their crew haircuts, that even Canon sometimes has trouble differentiating them.

For the last three decades, Albert Canon has made a close study of the history of success and failure in psychiatric institutions, research that culminated in his publication of the field's essential text, *The Mental Asylum*. Canon has drawn many conclusions from his data, but none so important as the necessity of uniformity, the absolute imperative that the orderlies, nurses, doctors, and administration act as one. To this end, Canon has gathered a mostly new staff, hired by himself and thus loyal to him. Mostly, he has recruited and continues to train freshly graduated alumni from B.U., boys in need of money, eager to please, seduced by the dark allure of a job in a mental hospital, untainted by the independence of opinion that Canon has observed, time and again, older orderlies and nurses often exhibit.

Following the horrific suicide of the war hero James Marshall, both the board of directors and Canon's predecessor—that docile dinosaur Wallace—decided that finally it was time for change, a systemic and dramatic modernization, an assurance that the Mayflower Home would retain its vaunted, preeminent repute. Canon was phoned at his office at Harvard on a Monday; by the following Friday, he had presented the majority of Mayflower's staff with appreciative letters, which also communicated the end of their employment. A great blow, he knows, to all those families, and yet, for the sake of his patients, it would be only the first of many exorcisms, revisions, demolitions, and clearings.

Out the window, Robert Lowell, struggling against the autumnal tumult, seems to take the wind as a personal affront, a call to arms. He battles against the wind, feet and arms swinging.

Resentment of more powerful forces, Canon will later write in Lowell's file, *the denied love of a parent?*

Like an MTA train making its scheduled stops, every six minutes, Canon's thoughts arrive, again, to memories of last night's sex. It seems to Canon that his particularly exemplary performance can be credited to the recent surge of wellness that has come with this reformation. It comes back to him in aspects: an insertion, the way her breasts bulged when leaning back. The desk! Come to think of it, his tailbone has felt tender all day. Canon smiles. The buttoned leather chair groans beneath him.

Canon has been hired to revitalize the nation's premier mental hospital. It is the greatest psychiatric hospital in the country, maybe in the world, and now he is its leader. He will oversee the mental health of great but troubled minds, his mind guiding theirs, a tremendous honor bestowed upon him through the transitive property, like defeating in arm wrestling someone who has defeated a great many others. The sun shifts; the papers before him are luminous. The intercom buzzes, reminds him of his eleven o'clock with the new class of orderlies. Canon stands, straightens himself in the mirror, exhales, and turns to the corridor. Dr. Albert Canon, newly ordained chief of Mayflower, walks the halls of his mansion. Birnam Wood has come to high Dunsinane Hill. Things are different now.

2

Two hundred yards away in Ingersoll House my grandfather lies propped up in his bed. The light angles through the caged windows to illuminate the journal in which he wants to write. But Frederick still feels the breakfast's tranquilizer in his hand, as if the tranquilizer has oppositely magnetized pen from paper.

He pulls at what remains of his hairline. Hour by hour, moment by moment, he feels himself breaking the promise he perpetually makes to himself: to transform his incarceration into a creative exercise, to take each meaninglessly passing moment and find the art within it.

The shame we have brought we have brought. The injury we have caused, we have caused, Lowell once told him. *Why not try to turn that history to art? Why not say what happened?*

At this moment, the bedside clock ticks with its grumpy persistence, the fluorescent tubes above buzz, his left foot itches between the toes, a squirrel makes some devious sounds on the opposite side of the wall. How to find a story in this, the moments, which just continue to pass? How to make all of these meaningless facts add up to something meaningful?

Frederick stretches his six feet, six inches, shifts on the bed, his pajamas sticking to him with their unpleasant dampness, a result of how warm they now insist upon keeping it at night. At the far corner of the room, just beyond the foot of the second bed— empty, until Canon—his new roommate experiences none of Frederick's writerly frustration. As he sits curled over his steel-legged desk, Professor Schultz's concentration is unremitting, his output ceaseless. Whereas the sound of a pigeon cooing at the windowsill can throw Frederick into an entirely other mode of consideration, Schultz, apparently, does not mind any distraction. He responds to Frederick's occasional questions, or the inquiries and demands of the staff, and then returns, immediately, to writing. Even the change in location, from his ornate room in the Harvard Club to his present Spartan dwelling, seems to impose no discernible stress upon Schultz, no distraction to his attention.

When Dr. Higgins informed the Ingersoll men that most would now be forced to have roommates, Frederick had risen in a fit of indignation, had almost talked the other men into something close to mutiny. But when Schultz first came to the door, escorted by two of the new orderlies, Frederick's animosity instantly dissolved in the professor's affability.

Shlomi Schultz, he said, extending a hand. *Might I say what a marvelous skull you have.*

Frederick laughed then, and so did Schultz.

You should see Jones, 'fifty-six, on the correlation of the frontal region with intelligence, Schultz continued, his Yiddish childhood giving each syllable a phlegmy consistency. *That slight, might I say, bulge, not to mention the wide plane of your brow, yes? I can see you are a man who understands things. It will be a pleasure to share this office.*

Frederick knew better, from his months in Mayflower, than to correct the professor (*office?*). Instead, Frederick shook his new roommate's hand and left the room for Schultz to make himself comfortable.

Frederick couldn't help but feel a bit flattered that the doctors had decided Professor Schultz and he would be fitting roommates, these two men of fierce intelligence. For the first few days, Frederick had devised and rehearsed clever observations, pithy witticisms about the ineptitude of the staff, the logical fallacies of the new protocols, with which he later tried to charm Schultz.

But Schultz has hardly said a word to Frederick. He has responded to simple questions of whether he is hungry (always in the negative), and he has congenially replied to Frederick's rehearsed insights by meeting his eyes, nodding amenably, and saying, *Quite right, yes, yes.* But then Schultz has immediately turned back to his work, his focus neither manic nor fitful, just simple, pure concentration.

And the work itself? Frederick has yet to decipher its purpose. Some days, Schultz has piled on his desk a selection of books from the hospital's library. Books with no obvious similarities: *Wuthering Heights,* a guide to cribbage, *The Yearling.* Schultz opens these books seemingly at random, leans down close to them as if he were investigating the ink rather than the words, mutters to himself, and hurriedly scribbles a note in his journal. Other days, Schultz sits in his chair, closes his eyes, tilts his face to the ceiling, as if transfixed by a private, internal concert, and then—struck by some notion—immediately jots it down.

His curiosity an irresistible force, Frederick is not above peeking at Schultz's notebooks. However, other than for mandatory reasons—meals, group therapy, requisite bathroom breaks—Schultz either sits with his notebooks or else carries them under his arm. The few glimpses Frederick has just barely managed have only deepened the mystery. The words he has seen look familiar, but are not quite English. Or at least not recognizably English. Is it a shorthand? Is it Yiddish? Schultz was a linguistics scholar; is this some obscure language he simply prefers? Or is Schultz's work simple nonsense? True madness?

Madness: Frederick has never, in fact, seen his roommate asleep or in any advanced state of undress. There have been times at night when the scratching of the professor's pen on journal ceases and he crawls into bed, but Frederick can then still hear Schultz mumbling, the static of his garble not quite tuned to human frequencies. When the moonlight slips between the gaps in the cage over their high single window and illuminates Schultz's face dimly, Frederick tries not to startle to find Schultz's eyes open and alert.

Before Canon, lunch was optional. Before Canon, evacuating bowels and bladder was a private matter, undocumented, unless for a specific medical reason. But now this intake and output is closely scrutinized. Any deviation from clean, healthy transference at either end can earn one stricter oversight, force-feeding, a world of misery, delivered by one of the interchangeable boys with crew haircuts. The boys with crew cuts have been objects of the patients' antipathy, rage, and compensating humor since they arrived and immediately began berating patients for failing to meet their demands with militant avidity. Two weeks after their appearance, Lowell offhandedly referred to these new boys as the Crew Crew. All laughed; the name has stuck.

A Crew Crew boy enters the room, and tells Frederick and Schultz it is time for lunch. Frederick stands to make his apathetic, compliant march to the cafeteria. Schultz, focused as ever upon his work, fails to hear the orderly's announcement, and so the kid goes to Schultz, nudges him, and repeats himself. Schultz turns, smiles warmly.

So kind of you, Schultz says, *but I'm not hungry.*

Lunch isn't optional.

No, lunch is sandwiches, nu? Haha!

Come on, Professor.

Schultz nods, as if the Crew Crew boy were a loved one reminding him that a disciplined mind requires nourishment; Schultz nods as if to say, *yes, well, of course you are right.*

The change of air, from room to hall, irritates Frederick. The way the Crew Crew boy cleans his ear with his pinkie finger irritates Frederick. The other patients lining up in the hall irritate Frederick, especially the new fat old one, Bobbie, who forever scratches his genitals when faced with others, as if he has invented a new crotch-oriented salute. At least today he has come from his room with gray slacks covering what he scratches—just two days ago, Bobbie darted from his room, like a toddler escapee from Mother's bath, bleating *yee-ha*s as he mounted a common room chair like a horse, his mass Jell-Oing as he bucked up and down. Some moments, like the present, Frederick is irritated by nearly every aspect of the totalitarian stupidity of this place.

Ingersoll, like the rest of Mayflower, has been given fresh linoleum and paint. But, in the hallway, Frederick stands before the only door Canon's renovation has neglected, a cracking wooden slab with no knob and a rusting lock, nearly fuzzy with oxidation. The furnace? An electrical closet? Frederick can't know what is behind it, but it almost seems as if this is the point. It almost seems Canon has left it here deliberately, this one un-openable, ancient door, as if to say: *this is where the past belongs.*

As they cross the Depression toward the cafeteria, Frederick is confronted with the image that irritates him most: the convergence of so many others, from their own wards, with the sluggish phalanx of Ingersoll men. Frederick watches his feet walk.

When they reach the cafeteria, the line to receive the lunch's six compartments of scooped food is notably extended from its previous length: a result of Canon's great pride, a ballooning admission to the homes for troubled young women and young men.

One of the few legitimate pleasures, at least at first, of the Coming of Canon has been the opportunity it has afforded the Ingersoll men to at last glimpse Marvin Foulds as Marvin Foulds, stripped of costumes. What was once a right has now become a privilege, and Canon has taken a radical approach to Marvin's condition, forcing him to wear hospital gowns until he can put aside his other selves and speak with his own true voice.

Pills always come at the end of lunch, not a patient or milligram is missed, but Marvin, as they sit at the table, frets for when the time of his sedation will come. Marvin asks the others whether they should already begin lining up. Frederick pities him. Mango Diablo, the Admiral, Guy DeVille: these people were tangible to Marvin, friends, family. When Canon denied his access to costumes and makeup, Canon murdered Marvin's closest relations. Or perhaps that is not precisely the reason for Marvin's present abject state. Perhaps, once he was put into hospital gowns, once denied his other selves, Marvin's posture shifted inward, his gaze darkened, his hair began to spring in the frizzy curls to which it naturally tends, as Marvin became someone else, a madman character, a mental patient named Marvin Foulds.

Lunch passes with a few perfunctory words, and then there are pills, and the Crew Crew's checking of sublingual and gingival hiding places. And then time, once again, has begun to slow.

3

Frederick is privately impressed by the swiftness and precision with which the new protocols have been enacted. It has been only two months since Canon took office, and already there is a lockstep efficiency in Mayflower.

It helps that, for the most part, the patients have been uncommonly compliant. In the wake of Marshall's suicide, the men of Ingersoll were, in truth, grateful for the promise of new order, grateful that the powers that be had recognized the magnitude of what Marshall's death had opened. It wasn't merely that the men mourned their lost friend—and they had, the depressives darkening for days, the manics ascending, the ravers escalating their angry babble. No, the greater terror was what Marshall's death suggested. Amid their imprisonment—in the walls of Mayflower, but also in their own skulls—here was a gelid, exhilarating promise of liberation. Amid the cacophony of internal chaos, the promise of silence. Amid confinement, the possibility of release. Amid an abject, pitiable existence, the possibility of transformation. In the history of mental hospitals, suicide attempts rarely occur in the singular; the notion of suicide, once devised, can catch as simply as a yawn. Thoughts blackened with fearsome new considerations. Even Frederick had become delirious with that dark concoction of dread and exhilaration. And so, when Wallace announced his expedited retirement and his successor—the famous scholar Albert Canon—the drama of the change, the possibility of a compensation for that horror, was a welcomed rebuttal to Thanatos.

In the temporary confusion that came with the passing of power, with the release of much of the old staff, the meticulousness of patient privileges was briefly relinquished. For the first time since his admission, Frederick had been permitted to speak with Katharine.

Of course he had rehearsed it. Often, an hour of thought would coalesce into a simple sentence that he would transcribe into his notebook for later use when finally he was able to speak to his wife. Frederick knew well how arguments with Katharine, born in coherence and certainty, could quickly drift into a desultory and bitter dumbness, both of them trying to transform the truer fight—one of disappointment, of fading love, of failed expectations, of thwarted need—into rational, accusatory statements of the small thing that was the argument's ostensible object, more often than not financial. Frederick knew how these fights could sometimes render him mute, feeling absolutely the rightness of his position but lacking language to describe it. And so he worked diligently to prepare his case. He had even rehearsed various forms of argumentation: the Socratic, for example, in which he had devised a carefully worded litany of questions that could only lead their recipient, like a bowling ball down a bumpered lane, to a singular conclusion: he did not belong at Mayflower and, for her part in placing him there, Katharine had failed him. Other times, he would scribble off something as saccharine and desperate as the letters he had written to Katharine after they first met, when he was off at sea: a form of appeal that he thought perhaps persuaded her more than any other.

Soon after the news of Wallace's retirement, Frederick easily talked the cavalier, about-to-be-unemployed night nurse into one-time phone privileges. Before he dialed, Frederick sat on the wooden bench in the antique phone both—gone now, with most of the other late Victorian bric-a-brac—and consulted his notes, memorizing what he could, tagging particularly cogent language for later reference. And then he dialed.

Katharine.

Frederick.

And then there was her voice, instantly muting his argument and his certainty.

I need to come home.

These were not words as most words were words. This was an

utterance produced in some fundamental place, bypassing the usual gates of language.

Frederick.

It was a strange argument, if that's even what it could be called, one that alternated forms of discourse. It was also punctuated with pregnant pauses, Katharine beginning sentences then stopping herself. While Frederick had been composing volumes on what to say, Katharine, apparently, had been practicing what not to say, knowing well her husband's ability to burrow into conversational fissures, to force apart, through logic or sentiment, any weakness she demonstrated, leaving her outwardly complaisant and inwardly furious. This time she would not allow that victory. Katharine reminded herself that she was the sane one. *Manic-depressives can present a persuasive logic,* Dr. Wallace had told her, *which is why it's best not to speak to him until we feel he is better.* No one had yet told Katharine that her husband was better.

I've already spoken with Dr. Wallace, Katharine said. *He doesn't think you are ready.*

What else can I say?

Silence.

What else can I say? I don't belong here.

These people are professionals, Katharine said. *Don't you think they might know better than you?*

Might know what better?

Whether or not you are well?

Is that what you think? You think that I'm crazy?

I didn't say crazy. But you know that things have been a little—

Goddamn it, Katharine. Now you too? It's the world that's gone crazy. The whole world that has gone goddamned nutso!

Frederick knows well Katharine's sensitivity to anger. An accommodating woman, Katharine can be inordinately overwhelmed by any display of aggression. Such anger is so far beyond the range of what she is capable, it can make her feel that she must have done wrong, must be in the wrong. But, after nearly twenty years of marriage, Katharine also knows that Frederick knows this. Katharine then remembered—in a way she likely would not if Frederick were there, in the room with her—that this was merely one of his tactics. She was proud of what she said next, remained proud of it for days.

This is what I'm talking about. Most people don't need to resort to rage just because someone disagrees with them. That is what children do.

Children? Frederick yelled, or at least whispered with the intensity of a yell, careful not to alert the matronly orderly, who had already, during Frederick's last tirade, given him a skeptical glance.

Frederick's anger was not then a tactic, as it often had been in the past. Often, as he berates, he feels paradoxically calmed. In those moments, as he assaults with hurricane fury, his mind is as calm and resolved as a storm's eye. But just then, as he spoke to Katharine, his rage projected both outward and inward. He was shaking now, had to press the phone to his cheek to keep the receiver at his ear. *Whether or not you are well.*

Many times, both privately and in conversations with the other men of Ingersoll, Frederick has repeated that common madman's refrain: *it is the world that is crazy.* Perhaps. And yet, why deny it now? There was something else. Something that, at certain moments, suddenly opened and unleashed terror. Within him, in some space he tries never to perceive, there is something vast and nameless, something he knows he can never quite comprehend. Perhaps the world is crazy; perhaps this vast, unnameable chaos he perceives is the truth. Perhaps others feel it as well, the true unreckonable entropy of things, and those who are called mad only receive it more acutely.

The vast unknowable something: it is a consumptive, obliterating fathomlessness, but also a place of radiance, of astonishment, and of eternal complexity. And it is what Frederick senses is to blame for all of his failures. Into the vacuum of itself, it has drawn everything that once seemed so simple and complicated it irreversibly. Occasionally, in moments like this, he glimpses it in its stunning largeness, its incontrovertible demands. But Frederick knows he must not look at it, must not contemplate it, for it is beyond words and beyond reckoning. To keep himself from it, Frederick has done all the terrible things he has done: yelled, fought, starved himself to nothing, taken other women, drunk himself to stupor, night after night. Conversely, all the good that he has ever felt has, in some way, borne a relation to it. All he has accomplished in his career, the birth of his daughters, the people he has tried to love: all have seemed to promise respite, something good and knowable to obstruct the vast dark thing.

He wanted, then, to say this to Katharine. He wanted to find a way to say that it was only once, only with her that he sensed something else, the promise of something as vastly good, as vastly knowable as the terror of the unknowable thing. Something that might, at last, throw light into that darkness. But now, the dark something had consumed that promise too.

Katharine, Frederick eventually said, *I don't think this place could ever give me*— and then his voice faltered.

Give you what?

Frederick did not know exactly how to describe it. What exactly he requires is perhaps as unnameable as the thing itself. Maybe the word *clarification* is closest, but it seems entirely insufficient, a laughably shabby symbol of that measureless need, the little word—*clarity*—like a battered church advertisement on a country road, falsely promising redemption. And, anyway, exactly what clarification did he think anyone could provide? Did he really believe that others progressed through life as singular characters in some story they knew would reach meaningful conclusion?

Maybe. Certainly, a few individuals he had known seemed to possess this gift of confidence. George Carlyle, the eldest of his daughters, his mother: he did not understand how, at all times, these people remained so entirely themselves. Frederick, at any moment, could be one or more of many things: malevolent, loving, brilliant, drunk, visionary. The opening of potential selves like first kisses that soon fail to deliver what they seemed to promise.

I want to make love to you, he said, the last word coming with a chuckle.

More silence. Non sequiturs, particularly of a lascivious nature, had always been a part of the charm he cultivated. Until recently, Katharine had been excited at these random proclamations of desire, perhaps even saw his spontaneity as evidence of brilliance. Had this hospitalization changed all that? Instead of brilliance and vitality, did she now see only symptoms of the illness the doctors had convinced her that he possessed? Or was she simply angry?

Susie wants to say hi.

And then his daughters took their turns with the phone, each effusive, ebullient, gabbing. Each voice lanced Frederick with a new wound. They all echoed back his sentiments of missing them, loving them, but this sadness was different than with

Katharine, not a sadness of schism and misapprehension, but a sadness of lost time. When each picked up the phone, he instantly entered their lives in medias res, as they narrated the triumphs and frustrations of the last hours, as if he had simply come home from work and sat down at the table for dinner.

Mary Catherine kissed Brad on the mouth Mrs. Garrett won't let us have snacks anymore my armpits smell like chicken soup, but Mum thinks I'm too young for deodorant Mum won't make lasagna but she makes everybody else's favorites Ooo ooo Daddy Daddy I have to show you the turtle I drew my tummy hurts can you tell Mum that I can't go to school Brad thinks it's weird that my dad is in a nuthouse but then I tell him that his dad is a drunk and sleeping with his secretary when are you coming home?

Time, stories, information passing like all unaccounted moments, like the squirrel in his business, the light tube's glowing gases, the careless lazy sunlight. Everything beyond continues in its immeasurable vastness; Frederick is still confined here, in a mental hospital.

4

It is one o'clock now. Outside, the clouds keep drifting, the grass continues to blanch and die, the squirrels persist in their scurrying rodent dramas. Inside, in the common room of Ingersoll House at the Mayflower Home, time has been partitioned into schedules. The next sixty minutes will be given to a group therapy session, every man required to attend. Canon, naturally, will helm the session himself.

The assembly of Ingersoll men before Canon can be parsed like a family sitting nightly at the table: power, alliances, needs suggested by where men place themselves. Bobbie sits at the very front by himself, raising hand from crotch, if ever Canon asks who would like to speak. Arranged in a circle around and just behind Bobbie are the marginally mad, seven or eight men, including Schultz, Marvin, Frederick, and sometimes, as today, Lowell. The others, the catatonics and the ravers and the geriatrics, the men who ornament the halls with their frozen bodies and provide the howling ambience one expects in a madhouse, stand and sit at the periphery in their Greek choral way. Canon's progress with these catatonics has been, as Canon himself admits in his notes, sluggish. Many of them simply sit where they are placed, no more or less a part of the meeting than they are on the third moon of Neptune.

All right, Canon says. *Last time, we were talking about Stanley's mother, and her abusive tendencies.*

Among the catatonics, Stanley stands apart in his strange form of silence. Sixty-year-old Harvard alum Stanley, without explanation, rises every morning to attend fastidiously to his appearance: pomading his hair, donning an elaborate crimson and gold fedora, scenting his palms, carefully folding a handkerchief into the pocket of his blazer. And after all these morning exertions, he remains nearly motionless and silent for the balance of his day. Last session, Canon alone had discussed an absent man's biography, while Stanley stared pensively into the middistance, haunted by some private phantasmagoria—who knows what? Perhaps an army of multicolor hedgehogs bent on his destruction.

Okay, then, Canon says, finding Stanley as unreceptive as the session before. *Why don't we move along to you, Professor Schultz?*

Schultz looks up from his journal with a receptive smile.

One topic, Professor, we have yet to raise with the group I know will be a sensitive one. But I think it's essential we all help you address it. So we can work on finally getting you back to Harvard, where I know you are still missed.

Yes, yes, agrees Schultz.

Lowell and Frederick narrow their eyes at each other. Both are already a little furious at Canon, with the anticipation of this intrusion, his airing of Schultz's concealed history. Also, both are curious.

That topic, Professor, is your family.

My family? Schultz says.

His family? Frederick thinks.

Already, Schultz has begun to metamorphose. Kindly, tranquil Schultz suddenly clutches himself. He binds his arms to his face, his tweed sleeves absorbing—what? Tears? Fury? Fear?

It is the past, Professor Schultz. Remember that. It cannot hurt you more than it already has. Now listen, your family is gone but—

At once, Schultz completes his transformation. In all the weeks Frederick has known him, the lines of Schultz's body—his clavicles, his twin femurs, his elbows, the crook of his neck—have pointed inward, toward a spot near his heart. Schultz has been obsessed by his work, and has built of it a strange mind-grotto, a place in which he dwells. But now, with Canon's mere reference to Schultz's vanished family, Schultz suddenly inverts: arms, legs, chin flung outward; a posture of remarkable grandeur, which, in conjunction with the bizarre utterances that he then speaks, evokes, unmistakably, a wizard.

Acalama Maakala danud faluuk! Schultz rages.

Bitoola Kistera! he continues, before happening to fall into his chair. He instantly slackens with such abandon, like a marionette clipped from its strings, that he would have fallen right to the floor, had the chair not happened to intervene.

Or maybe not a wizard so much as a Pentecostal. Receiving holy fire from the heavens in a fit of babble, a temporary articulation in some nonsense language.

Soon, however, Schultz resumes a variation of his perpetual mutter.

You are truly an A-grade asshole, Frederick, resolute, tells Canon. *It's too bad for Germany that they didn't have you in the forties. But I'm sure you'll meet all those fellas someday.*

This, Frederick often thinks, is one of his true gifts. In moments of rage, where others falter, where voices waver and words fail, the right words often come to him.

Oh, Mr. Merrill, if you feel like participating—

Oh, let's, Frederick says.

Ohhhhh let's. Ohhhh let's, echoes one of the catatonics in a baritone, like the bass section of a barbershop quartet.

What I'd like to discuss is what brought you to us in the first place.

Absolutely, Frederick replies. *A New Hampshire squad car, driven by an officer who looked as if he was not quite finished with high school, perhaps prepubescent.*

Some of the half-mad laugh, flattering and emboldening to Frederick that Lowell is among them. For a passing moment, perhaps indistinguishable from a cough, Canon also appears to laugh. But likely this is only a display to keep the group within his emotive grasp, to let them know that he understands this attempt at humor, but that there are more important things at stake than a good laugh.

I know that you use humor to mask your anxiety. It's a very common defense mechanism. But what I'd like you to speak about are the events leading up to this incident in New Hampshire. The concerns of your friends and your family. Why, for example, your wife thought this was the best place for you.

You goddamned— Frederick begins. *And who are you? You're a feebleminded paper pusher who has tricked—*

Marvin has passed the first half of the meeting in a dejected silence, but the rage of Frederick's protest appears to unlatch something within him. Marvin cries out, such a shock to hear his voice with any measure of passion that it has the effect of a gun fired into the air above a mob.

I want my clothes! Marvin screams. *I want my clothes! I want my old house! Now! Now! Now!*

We'll get to your concerns when it is your turn, Canon says, concealing his fluster poorly.

Now! Now! Now! Now!

Nownownownownow, the baritone catatonic repeats.

Canon has observed, many times in his studies, the importance of not engaging with the passions of patients, the importance of maintaining a calm, even tone. Though few, if any, could discern his words under the noise, Canon says, *Mr. Foulds, if you can't be civil, you won't be able to continue this session with us, which, as you know, will result in further loss of privileges.*

I said now! I want my clothes now! Marvin yells, lifting his hospital gown over his head and displaying his considerable manhood to the group.

Canon gestures to the eager Crew Crew, who quickly descend to extract Marvin by the armpits. Marvin won't be seen again until late that night. When he will return to Ingersoll from solitary, he will be restored to his silence, appearing in a fresh hospital gown.

But what will not ambition and revenge / Descend to? Who aspires must down as low / As high he soar'd. Lowell fills the following silence with Milton.

Oh, Professor Lowell, could you contextualize the quote for us?

Who overcomes / By force, hath overcome but half his foe.

THE

STRONGER

WILL

1

The final Friday of the summer of 1962. On Monday, at the end of the holiday weekend, the Merrills will return to Graveton for the start of the school year. After Frederick's stay at Mayflower vaulted all of Katharine's previous imagined deadlines, this weekend, which so recently seemed so impossibly far, had been the date she had told her family to expect his return. It had a kind of logic, at least to Katharine: she and the girls would spend the summer at Echo Cottage, Frederick would spend the summer at Mayflower, but of course they would reconvene for the fall. It would almost be as if they had only taken separate vacations. Back in Graveton, in the autumn, things would be as they had been before, but also, Katharine tried to assure herself, better. Frederick would return with them to Graveton, and he would be better. But now it is the Friday before Labor Day, and her husband is still gone.

One in the afternoon, and the day over Lake Winnipesaukee is faultless again, placid enough to delight the few remaining mosquitoes, warm enough to allow sleeping without blankets. Katharine sits in the living room recliner, considering the day's perfection through the cinematically proportioned window overlooking the lake. Her daughters, preparing for the fall in their own way, have set out with a summer's accumulation of their excessive allowance—a part of Katharine's reparations for the loss of their father—to stock up on chocolates and taffies at the Hansel and Gretel Candy Shoppe on the far side of Barvel Bay.

It has been over two months since Frederick opened the rain-coat on Route 109, and when last Katharine spoke with her husband's psychiatrist, he seemed to suggest the work had just begun. *Your husband has finally gotten the rest he so badly needed,* Frederick's new doctor, Canon, told her. *But we have yet to address the major psychic underpinnings of his condition.*

Katharine wants, as ever, to be amenable. She wants to believe, with the faith of Frederick's doctors, that the time and will of those professionals can repair Frederick, as if her husband's mind were simply some faulty intricate machinery, which only the best technicians can render operative. Still, Canon's prognosis, his schematic approach to Frederick's chaos, often strikes Katharine as absurd.

And yet, when finally Frederick phoned her from the hospital, Katharine for once had not accommodated, not placated. She had made a decision to remain firm, to echo her relatives' faith in Mayflower without attenuating that confidence with her skepticism. She had resolved to remain firm, and that is how she had remained. Her sustained conviction in their short conversation was perhaps a small victory, but suggestive of greater powers. She had made a decision, and—at least for a moment—she had changed.

In the dimmed daylight of the living room at Echo Cottage, Katharine thinks of the impossibility of the immediate future. Here, they are still plainly blessed for this house, their prosperous history that has gifted them all this, but in a few weeks, she will be a single mother of four in a sleeted town on the far side of

Mount Washington. She thinks of Nero, fiddling away, with his back to the fires. She rises from the chair.

Katharine must talk with someone else, someone who can consider her uncertainty. All of Katharine's relatives only reiterate their blind faith in Frederick's doctors, doctors who diffuse into jargon whenever Katharine pins them to a single cogent question. She must talk to someone else, someone other than her daughters, to whom she knows she has to parrot the doctors' institutional-vague certainty.

The morning after the night that Frederick exposed himself on Route 109, Katharine woke the girls early. Her eyelids had burned with exhaustion then, her voice had thickened from a dozen anxious cigarettes, and her body had turned clumsy, as if she had spent hours hefting suitcases. But when she gathered the girls around the warped plank table on the eating porch, she produced a piece of psycho-script that perfectly resembled what Frederick's doctors would later tell her. Like Frederick's doctors, Katharine then spoke in a tone of infallibly official judgment, easily slipping into some bearded armchair character Freud scripted a half century ago, a costume to disguise herself from uncertainty. But maybe there is a reason that such language comes so easily to both Katharine and the psychiatrists? Perhaps it is simply the obvious truth?

Assembled on the eating porch that morning, the girls, pajamaed and groggy, mustered the kind of attention her daughters usually delight in refusing her. Katharine tried to offer the performance they clearly needed.

You know that Daddy has had a very difficult year. I'm sure you know that he has not been himself. All his yelling, and all the late nights. We should have done something sooner. The truth is that he is just ex-

hausted, and so we've decided the best thing for him is to take a nice long rest. There is a place your uncle George recommended. It's called May-flower, and it's near Boston. It won't be long, but Daddy can rest there—

Surprisingly, the girls asked few questions. They seemed eager to accept the nebulous reasons Katharine provided to explain why their family had imploded while they slept. Maybe Katharine's performance had successfully softened the news, or maybe the news was not the shock Katharine had thought it would be. Maybe her girls had for years silently carried a feeling about their father that this news clarified, and promised to mend.

The girls had believed her then, but now it has been more than two months since that morning, and still Katharine must act as certain as she first claimed. She must; she knows that she alone is the bridge that conveys the adult world to her daughters, and her daughters to the adult world. And she must convey them perfectly, even if she perceives invisible foundational fissuring, the pilings shifting and snapping beneath her. Most adult failures, Katharine believes, can be attributed to the failure of that conveyance, adults marooned at the age at which their parents failed them.

When Katharine was only four, for example, her doctor diagnosed her with a heart murmur, and for a time the doctors believed she wouldn't live to eighteen. No longer worried for their daughter's adulthood, Katharine's parents concerned themselves only with fulfilling her wants, making her siblings toughen in the way children ought to, while Katharine received only her family's gifts and attention. Her heart's syncopation eventually self-corrected, but her childhood has remained her childhood. And now she must imitate an adult, she who grew up never having to do a thing for herself. Conversely, Frederick has told Katharine how his own parents, fracturing under the pressures of the Great Depression, made clear to Frederick, at twelve, that his boyhood was nearing its end, that the family's future solvency would depend, in no small part, on him. As Katharine has, in ways that shame her, remained that needy sick girl, so has her husband remained petty, boisterous, subject to his megrims, possessing the emotional constitution of a twelve-year-old.

And so, what if Katharine allows herself to fail her daughters now? Jillian is only five; she could remain forever impetuous, always expecting others to receive and grant her demands. Louise's common eight-year-old experiments with deception could proliferate into pathology. Susie, at thirteen, could never shake her yearling awkwardness, her aversion to others' eyes, her uncertainty of the worth of her opinions. Rebecca's fourteen-year-old irony could deepen, she could remain forever disaffected and defiant (Katharine cannot let herself think too clearly of what Rebecca might allow those boys she sees).

Doctors and relatives act so certain, and that is how Katharine must act as well. But if she could just clearly explain what has happened to someone not involved, perhaps she could understand it herself. *Teaching,* her math teacher once told her, *is the best way to learn.* Katharine lifts the phone and looks up the number in her address book.

She tells herself *Yes* once, then *No* three times, and then she dials the number anyway. Just after it begins to ring, the voice is in her ear.

Hello?

Hi, Tat. It's Katharine.

Katharine?

Why has she called Tat? Tat is hardly a friend. She is only the closest to what Katharine might call a friend in Graveton. Does she really want to unburden herself to an acquaintance? But maybe Katharine's purpose is not only to seek commiseration. It is, more honestly, something else: a chance at explaining herself and the abject state in which her family has concluded the summer to someone in Graveton before she returns there, and the news becomes evident.

Yeah, Katharine says, then adds, *Merrill?*

Katharine Merrill? Is that you?

Tat affects the perfect tone so effortlessly. Her voice is just right, an enthusiasm that transmits only delight, making Katharine feel extraordinary while simultaneously forgiving her for not at all being the friend Tat would like her to be. Often, when Katharine agrees to attend Tat's bridge nights, she panics at the last moment and grasps for the handiest excuse. But Katharine envies Tat and her friends. Together, as middle-aged women, they are in continuity with what they have always been. Just the girls, still laughing together at their stories. They laugh about their children as they once laughed about boys at school, teachers, lackluster report cards. These women raise children without becoming fundamentally different from the women they were before they had families. Katharine, by contrast, was once one thing, a young woman hungry for society, and then she became something entirely different, an anxious mother, the wife of a difficult man. No wonder she panics at Tat's invitation; the ladies' intimacy always displays to Katharine her failure.

How are you, Tat?

Katharine tries to imbue her greeting with Tat's enthusiasm but succeeds only in amplifying her volume, as if she were speaking to a very old woman.

Couldn't be better. Back from Paris, refueled for the fall.

Paris?

It was Ron's big birthday present. And what a gift! That whole city. My god, I feel like I spent the last three weeks inside a Fabergé egg.

Katharine has phoned this mere acquaintance, this cheery woman whose friendship Katharine always fails, and what should she say now? Should she counter Tat's Paris with her own desperate story? Katharine sees plainly: within her extended family camp along this stretch of Barvel Bay, the Merrills have sympathy, and Katharine is nearly heroic for taking the action she finally took; beyond Barvel Bay, they are simply a failed family. Katharine thinks about abandoning the call's purpose. She could cheerily respond with a story of a pleasant summer spent by the lake, a vague plan for cocktails soon. But she has come this far already. And why not say what happened? She might as well say it, and at least practice the way she has thought to tell her story.

It's been a rough summer for me.

Oh? Please say it's nothing serious.

Katharine tries to think of an artful way to begin, but then other words escape.

Promise you won't tell anyone? she says, like a child.

Of course, Katharine.

Katharine is surprised by the instantaneous empathy with which Tat accepts the secret, as if it weren't at all unusual that an acquaintance should call and swear her to confidentiality. But, of course, Tat is so skillful in the ways Katharine never could be. Of course people must tell Tat their secrets all the time.

It's Frederick, Katharine begins, and then stumbles through an awkward, rosier version of the story. She does not mention the police, or the nudity. She focuses her staggering narrative upon the bourbon and Frederick's restlessness. But when Katharine says the name Mayflower, she lapses into a momentary silence, knowing all that *Mayflower* says about chaos and delusion, madness and genius, screams and straitjackets.

Well, Tat says, *he couldn't be in a better place.*

They think he just needs a rest, and some time to sort things out.

And what do you think?

I think— Katharine begins, and pauses. She then tries to respond as another version of herself, more like Tat, a person who can receive misfortune and transform it to theater, for the entertainment of others. *I think that husband of mine could use a strong slap in the face.*

Katharine decides her tone is almost perfect, Ethel calling Lucy to complain. *I think someone needs to tell that man to pull himself together!*

Tat does not laugh as Katharine expected.

Have you ever told him that? Tat says.

And now Katharine wants again what she wanted just before she dialed. She wants to be seen; she wants to lay it all out for Tat; she wants to open her skull so Tat can observe the infinity loop of considerations and reconsiderations cycling within her. Katharine is suddenly nauseated and giddy with gratitude for Tat's empathy.

Oh, of course, Katharine says. *Yes, well, not as often as I should have, I suppose.*

The memory, from near the beginning of her marriage, comes to Katharine again now, as it nearly always does when she thinks of her failure to confront her husband with his plain wrongs. There is an opening here, to let this memory outside of herself. For once to admit to it, and perhaps slightly disperse its needled pressure. But Katharine does not say anything.

Well, at least you've spoken your mind. Good. Tat unfastens the suspended silence, then skillfully changes the topic to the latest happenings at church, another invitation to bridge, and finally excuses herself from the conversation with such tact that Katharine does not realize, until well after they have hung up, that it was Tat, not Katharine, who ended it.

Katharine crosses back to the living room window, looks out over Barvel Bay, a postcard of itself. The memory, opened in the short conversation, casts its images: Frederick kissing that woman in the water, Katharine's sickness in the woods, the latched suitcase.

2

They had been married just two and a half years then, and had known each other for only three. In a different time—in, say, 1962—they might have only just married after three years together. But the war was still on when they met; annihilation, at any moment, seemed entirely possible. Everything seemed precious; it seemed you must take what love you found immediately and wholly. When Frederick returned early from the war and they married, their courtship had been little more than a correspondence during Frederick's military service, and that of only a few months. But they married, and after only two and a half years, there was that first failing.

Frederick was still in business school then and, with money tight, they spent their summer under her parents' dole at Echo Cottage. They had little other choice, but the arrangement worried Katharine from the start. She already knew well Frederick's absolute intolerance for confinements. When they went out for dinner, he would routinely leave the table four or five times over to make a phone call, to use the restroom, or for no given reason at all. In the winters, he would violently tug at his sweaters until they were shapeless. He seemed never able to remain in their Cambridge apartment for more than two hours at a stretch. And living under the generosity of Katharine's parents that summer, Frederick behaved just as she had feared.

Often, Frederick would vanish from Echo Cottage for entire days. At first, the outcomes of these trips were innocuous, even delightfully eccentric; though Katharine's father denies it now, Frederick then could charm even him. Frederick would return with a report on the conditions at the top of Mount Chocorua, or he would reveal a day spent repainting the water shed in the woods.

Late one June evening, Katharine spotted a lone figure oaring some lopsided vessel toward Echo Cottage from Nineteen Mile Bay. The lake was a perfect purple mirror, disturbed only by the paddling silhouette. For twenty minutes they debated whether it was he, until the sight was unmistakable: Frederick, helming a rusted dinghy he had discovered, its waterlogged hull little more than a refashioned bathtub, its mast bent impotently to one side.

For the following two or three weeks, Frederick was wholly engrossed by his dinghy. Katharine, checking in on her husband, could find him woodworking out back, hammering on the dock, or else engaged in whatever semblance of sailing that boat was capable of. For those weeks, he stopped complaining to Katharine about the knowing glances of her mother, the silent, judging Waspery of her father. Often, Frederick would sail up to the shore and ask Katharine and her parents to help him test his vessel's *lakeworthiness*. Each time, despite Frederick's most recent repairs, the four would make it no farther than one or two hundred yards before the water rose precipitously in the hull/tub, and they all began to cackle with laughter, half-submerged. One day, near the end of the month, the mast snapped in two and Frederick let the boat drown.

Once again, Frederick began to vanish for the entirety of days. But Katharine was not suspicious, not then. Daily, she expected him to return from some Sawyeresque adventure, with some new boyish booty. Instead, he would return long after sunset, speaking in glib ways of trips to the diner, the library.

Frederick's psychiatrists like to speak of Freudian trauma, a scene that imprints itself onto the subconscious, some haunting iconography from toddlerhood. But the image that most haunts Katharine, the one that only delusions can censor from her memory, etched its indelible vision one afternoon of that summer in her early adulthood.

That afternoon, Katharine and her mother took a walk together along the shoreline. It was a Saturday; the bay was dense with splashing weekenders. Katharine did not see Frederick when they passed, but her mother did. *Is that Frederick?* her mother asked.

As she looked onto the scene, Katharine's first apprehension was not betrayal. At first, it seemed the mistake was her own. There was Frederick, bare-chested in the water, embracing that woman, the renter from Abanaki Cottage. Frederick, kissing that woman's cheeks as her boy floated beside them. The scene looked simply natural: a sound familial triangle, mother and father and child. It seemed as if this were simply Frederick's reality, and Katharine and her family were some alternate, fictive dimension. It was the plainness, the unabashed openness that was so horrific. Frederick was neither hiding nor flaunting. Frederick, guiltless and free, was simply kissing that woman. Katharine's mother guided her by the elbow, away, and later helped Katharine pack Frederick's suitcase. Together, in shared fury, they rehearsed a speech, ornamented it with baroque reprimands, his plain failure from personal, ethical, even religious vantages. Both knew neither could ever invent such a speech in the moment of confrontation; that moment stupefied both.

When Frederick returned home that night, he climbed the stairs, crept down the hall, opened the bedroom door, and found Katharine sitting on the bench of the vanity, suitcase latched and upright before her. Unsurprisingly, she forgot her script, entirely.

Katharine could only say *leave*. She said it, then said it again, then kept repeating it until Frederick stopped her by saying her name once.

Then Frederick looked at her, looked at the floor, then back at her, cycling through the logic of the moment. Potential counterarguments, pleas, excuses cycled so visibly through him, she could nearly see the considered words scrolling behind his eyes. But in the end he said nothing, and for a moment it seemed to Katharine that it could be that easy. You make a decision and become something else. Years before, she replied to his proposal by mail with a letter containing nothing but the word *yes*. One *yes* had transformed her from who she had been into his wife. *Leave,* she could say, and the unknowable future could open freshly to her.

But Frederick did not leave. His expression slackened as he fell to the bed. He curled into himself, as if shame had some contracting effect upon his tendons. Katharine had known his lies, his manipulations, his restlessness, but she had never before known this, not exactly. She had never before looked at her husband and thought so entirely of the word *pathetic*.

I must be deranged, Frederick said. *I must be sick. I need you to make me better.*

It was Katharine, not Frederick, who left then. Katharine walked out the front door of Echo Cottage and made her way toward the docks. As she tried to steady herself, tried to remember some of the soliloquy she and her mother had scripted so that she could return to the bedroom and expel him, the pine needle floor of the walking path suddenly betrayed her, began to pitch and shift. Before Katharine could consider the vertigo, the sensation condensed to a rising in her belly, and then she was vomiting between the trees. This was how Katharine first knew her cycle was not merely late. She spent a half hour sitting with her sickness in the forest, and by the time she stood, she had already begun to understand it as a directive.

After all, except for her memory of what Frederick had done, everything was in place. With Rebecca swelling inside her, they returned to Cambridge and Frederick began to come home at the expected hours. Even Katharine's mother, writer of her rage, seemed eager to forget. Eventually, Katharine allowed herself to make excuses. A year or two after his affair, and the furies it stoked, she convinced herself that this first failing was merely an obstacle that would, finally, prove the endurance and transcendence of their union. After all, they once again had wonderful moments together. Eventually, she again laughed so simply at Frederick's punning, his impromptu living room tangos, his antic reenactments of Abbott and Costello routines. This was a time before Frederick's charm and his humor seemed tinged with his darkness, long before Katharine began to consider her husband's charisma and comedy as symptoms. Katharine read recently that often when soldiers run into battle, they laugh wildly. Perhaps Frederick's continued power over her could be attributed to a similar effect.

But what else was she to do? Maybe, by forgiving and pretending to forget, she has imprisoned herself; maybe, if not for her sickness in the woods that night, she might have delivered the speech she had wanted to deliver. Frederick might have left for good; she might have made a better life.

3

Katharine, looking out onto the lake, lets her thoughts drift to a glancing inspection of the upper branches for any early traces of autumn. After five or ten minutes spent considering nothing but this scenery, the tainted past and ruined future seem impossible against this day.

There have been good moments. Yes, not only good moments but entire good years. And isn't it possible for those memories to expand and buffer the others? A single kiss the night she met Frederick, a happy afternoon in his sinking dinghy, this moment, the scene before her fecund and perfect. Simple happiness exists, and you must gather it around yourself. With enough will you can choose to believe in a better life, until the better life becomes yours. Katharine thinks about calling Tat again and trying to explain that to her. That she is not weak, that she is not merely a woman who has let herself be swayed by more forceful wills. The stronger will is her own, a choice to believe in the best of things. Katharine wonders: would Tat see this as a gift for transcendence, or a gift for delusion?

And what will others think?

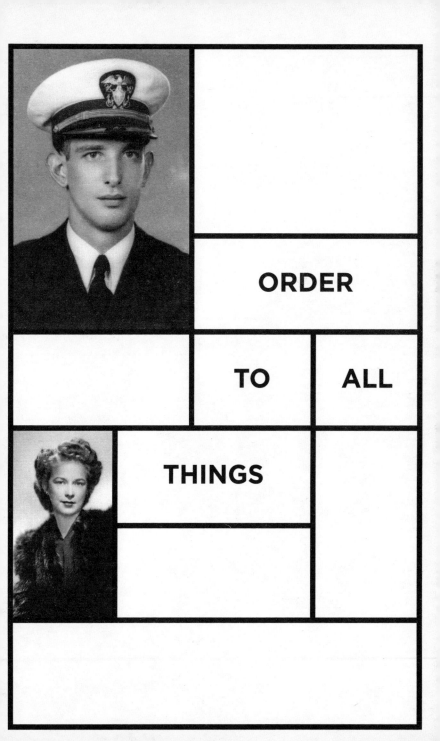

ORDER

TO   ALL

THINGS

1

They all laughed then, Albert Canon thinks, exactly in those words. It is early evening now, and Canon strides the Depression, emptied and silent.

They all laughed then. For the last weeks, Canon finds himself thinking these words again and again, feeling their talismanic shape, hoping to engender the story they imply. In fact, no one had laughed.

Yes, when he had set out on his research decades before, finding ways to observe and empirically measure the functioning of mental hospitals, some of his colleagues had expressed skepticism, had wondered whether the inherent chaos of a mental hospital milieu could ever be dissected with data, wondered if the governance of psychiatric institutions was more a craft, earned over a lifetime of refining finely tuned instincts. But, in truth, the same skeptics had also expressed gratitude for Canon's findings. Still, in his office in the basement of Memorial Hall at Harvard, Canon, the academic, had always felt besieged by the practitioners, had felt they possessed the same misplaced brand of rugged smugness as labor unionists, claiming a superiority of knowledge of how things should be run at the highest level simply because they had been down there, for a lifetime, digging ditches with their hands.

The truth, Canon knows, is that the complexities of daily

work in a mental hospital can easily become a fog of war. Like the military's high commanders, the psychiatrist in chief must maintain some clinical distance, the perspicuity of an empiricist. Just today, for example, Dr. Higgins flew into a panic at the staff's inability to calm Marvin after his outburst in the group session, then, yet again, suggested an extreme course of electroconvulsive therapy.

Electroconvulsive therapy! Marvin needs a lucid mind to address the profoundly advanced defense mechanisms of his major psychotic disorder. The last thing he needs is one hundred fifty volts scrambling his consciousness. But Canon tries to remind himself that no one is blameless; we are all only human. This awareness, in fact, is at the very heart of the research he has conducted and the conclusion he has drawn and now enacts. We all must recognize our own human failings before the patients do; we maintain uniformity and control by recognizing the ways we are different, the things over which we feel we have no power. Canon, for example, knows that he too is flawed. At this very moment, for example, Canon is walking the hallways of Upshire, dim in the twilight, to meet his mistress.

Just a few more times, Canon thinks.

Does Canon ever feel guilty? Not guilt, exactly. No, that is what has surprised him most about his first affair. What he feels, when slipping into bed with his wife, is instead a kind of repulsion. Not that he is repulsed by his mistress, or his wife, or by himself, exactly. Canon, who has dedicated the twenty years of his professional career to probing the psychodynamic motives behind behavior, tries not to think of this, this obscure repulsion. But he resolves now to end it soon, the affair and the sensation that is always waiting for him just beyond climax, as inevitable as his postcoital slackening. He is in control, he tells himself. This,

Canon often thinks, is his one true gift: his ability always to distinguish truth from delusion and then to plant truth inside of delusion, thus causing delusion to implode.

Not pausing as he often pauses—now certain in resolve—Canon pushes open the office door. Soon, he will end it. It will be bittersweet, he thinks, like a soldier leaving behind a foreign love affair to embark on another war campaign; nothing, not even a woman, will veer or dissuade him from the pull of his duty.

At first, however, he thinks she has not come. As he sits alone in the empty room, something akin to the familiar repulsion rises within him, something birthed by repulsion but redder, a feeling nearly identical to when Jeff Wittgenstein, his doctoral classmate at Yale, was made associate professor just five years after graduation while Canon had remained a lowly lecturer. She hasn't come. She has decided first.

There is always a power balance to these things. Someone is always in control. And it is always he. But she hasn't come. The affair is over. Canon wants desperately not to be there in his office, with his failure, his powerlessness. He wants to be in bed with his wife, or even watching television with his children, but he knows that every motion from this moment to that will be cumbersome with his self-recrimination. She hasn't come. He was going to end it soon anyway. Just a few more times, and he could have set things right; the affair would have ended, delivering the wistful fulfillment he has imagined.

In the dim light, Canon glimpses himself in the antique gilded mirror hung near the bookshelf. In the last five years or so, he has adopted a new strategy with mirrors, approaching them only at close proximity, then casting his gaze only upon details: the part of his hair, the grain of his beard, the spaces between his teeth, which seem to hold artifacts of food more than do others'. He has learned to observe himself in detail because if he considers himself in his entirety he can feel nearly like one of those rare Cotard's sufferers, baffled by the stranger who faces him in mirrors.

Within, Canon's ambitions and energies seem only to grow. Go ahead and fault him, but he sees the world as young men see it: its deficiencies, its hypocrisies, its need for innovation, and he wants to be the one to make the required changes. On the outside, however, age has bloated and warped his features. Each pore of his cheeks is now stretched like a marker dot on an inflated balloon; his jowls are beginning to dangle like fleshy ornamentation from what was once the attractive angular aspect of his jaw. Looking at himself now, in the half-light of his office, Canon deflates with an approximation of his postejaculatory repulsion.

Like what you see?

Canon startles. As he pivots, his belly swings with centrifugal motion. There she is, sitting on the analytic divan. Canon cannot help smiling, delighting in the slow adjustment of his eyes to the dark, she revealed slowly, as in a vaudevillian fan dance.

I thought you didn't come.

I shouldn't have.

No, probably not.

Canon is near her now, but not too near, one of the cheeks of his annually widening ass balanced on the divan's corner. He touches her shoulder, shoves the meat of his fingers into the nearly imperceptible texture of her hair. His decision, he tries to remember, his determination. *She is here and you will have her, but soon you will end it.* The curvature of her back on his palm, his mouth craving with a hunger stronger than hunger.

What good is his determination? For a moment afterward, as

ever, he will mentally perform his ritualistic recitation of this wrongness and how it must stop soon, but his determination will be as false as ever. After all, these things are stronger than reason and determination. *Stronger than logic.* And there, again, is that repulsion.

2

The television's volume is now permanently set to somewhere between deafening and stupefying. Even with the door shut to one's room down the hall, one has no choice but to listen. To Frederick, the television's volume is another cause for wild irritation. And yet, sometimes alone in his room, when confronted by two equally retardant forms of Ingersoll noise—the television and the screams—he is grateful to be able to focus on the TV's babbling narratives. And sometimes, such as this evening, Frederick places himself with the catatonics on the couch, simply to receive it.

A local news special on the new tower downtown recites statistics over footage taken from airplanes. Frederick gives the television the lazy half-attention it wants until he perceives a hovering presence behind him. He turns to find his roommate, seemingly drawn from his room by the television's sound. Schultz, for one of the few times Frederick has observed, distracted from his work. Lowell, sitting in the corner with a copy of Sylvia Plath's *The Colossus,* also recognizes the rarity of the moment.

An architecture aficionado, Professor? Lowell asks.

For this tower, we all should be, Schultz says.

Schultz's wonder for the tower puzzles Frederick. Sure, the new tower is an impressive architectural feat. Impressive, like their new psychiatrist in chief, in its arrogance, in its steely confidence of its soaring newness, history be damned. But to Frederick, as he suspects it must be to a great number of New Englanders, it is also a great disrespect of glass and steel to the city of decorative curlicues and Colonial ornamentation that has taken four hundred years of development, and continues to reward one strolling its streets with strange surprises, architectural oddities both miniature and major. The tower, in the new International Style, rises over the town houses, cobblestones, and esplanades like an ascending middle finger, courtesy of the new postwar America. It is the insane vision of academics, dreaming of conceptual cities that bear almost no relation to the cities in which people actually live. Frederick does not see how Schultz could love it.

Making it, by a large margin, the tallest building in New England— the television says.

Schultz watches, his pen temporarily still over the journal he clutches. Then the segment ends, shifts to weather, and again Schultz's fountain tip skates with its normal velocity as he ambles back to his room, several times nearly colliding with the wall.

. . .

The afternoon rather suddenly gives way to night—fall is here, unmistakably now—and the trees out the window become moody charcoal sketches of themselves; the Colonial grandeur of the other halls reduces to a constellation of tungsten lamps, burning dimly. The lunchtime dosing of Miltown has begun to dissipate, and it feels to Frederick that something in him has suddenly come uncoiled. In his journal, Frederick manages two paragraphs before he feels himself tripping over language, accelerating in nervous energy. He writes:

All I wanted was to convince you and the girls, that something was possible. That hard work and love and reason would be enough to make of our lives something that nothing could ever take from us entirely. I tried to be as you pleaded with me to be, as parents must be. Consistent. I tried never to betray my faltering.

I remember one night, in Graveton, I had been drinking. You had told the girls I was at work, but the truth was that some darkness had opened again, as it always opens. And so I had tried to fill the chasm in my common, cowardly way, with bourbon. I don't know when I came home, but I know it was not a normal hour. I had crashed the car, and I was bloody from it. It did not seem relevant to me. In fact maybe I wanted the pain, eclipsing what it did. But then it was Susie who came to the door. She pulled it open, and the father she had known had vanished. In Daddy's place was a monstrous thing. It was the first time I knew, entirely, that I had failed. She looked at me and I knew she saw I was not myself, that there was no myself.

The two Crew Crew boys end their shift, switching off with a comically indolent boy—still a part-time philosophy student at Boston University, *The Meaning of Meaning* nearly always clutched in his left hand—and young Rita Weld, the only member of the staff to whom Frederick feels any human form of relation. Why deny it? It helps that she's beautiful. Maybe not beautiful in a common way, not a photographical beauty, but one that yields and alters to the object of her engagement, her expressions mirroring with youthful empathy feelings you have become so accustomed to carrying around privately, unspeakably, that you had forgotten they might be known by others.

Well, hello there, Rita greets Frederick. *You're looking energetic.*

Frederick realizes that he has been pacing, again and again, the few steps between the corridor walls.

Just feeling a little nervous, he surprises himself to admit. *I don't know what it is. Something about the night.*

Unlike the cool, doltish Crew Crew boys, who seem to have taken the job for the simple sake of employment and the power their positions carry, Rita, Frederick suspects, has come to Mayflower for that other reason. She is that other breed of mental health worker, much more common among the old administration, quite common, Frederick remembers from friendships with aspiring psychiatrists when he was in graduate school, to the profession at large. Rita, he thinks, has come here for this proximity to madness. Maybe to learn something from madness but also, and more important, to learn how to keep herself from it. This, he thinks, is why she is the best nurse here, and also why she will not last.

Lucky for you, Rita says and lays a hand on his shoulder, as if that is simply how the staff touch patients, *soon, you'll get to swallow the knockout pill.*

3

The Morlock call, the slop line, a silent and repellent dinner. And then the pills, with their unrefusable soporific demands.

An hour later, my grandfather has returned to his bed. He looks down at the length of his pitiful self. His pajama pants are hospital-issued; his socks poof awkwardly at the toes. A pathetic, moribund sight. A priest ought to be coming by any moment now to administer last rites. These are not the legs, not the feet, of a man in the middle of his life, at the peak of his responsibilities. These are the legs of an invalid.

Out the window, crows call faintly. Above the trees in screaming parabolas, bats arc through the twilight, angry for lack of flies. Condensation pearls on the window, foreshadowing the blinding fog that will claim Boston tomorrow, a prefiguration of winter.

Behind each thing is a demand for his attention, each thing pregnant with dark implications. Faced with the dark implications of everything, down to droplets of condensation, Frederick must think of something else.

He looks to Professor Schultz, muttering to himself, as ever. Frederick has deliberated for days now, even jotted down potential approaches in his notebook, carefully worded questions about linguistics and semiotics with which he might cajole his roommate into revealing something of his possibly deranged, possibly brilliant project, which might, in turn, reveal something of him. But now Frederick forgets his notes and just asks Schultz outright.

Shlomi, Frederick says, *can I ask you what it is you're working on?*

Oh, just experimentation, mostly.

Frederick can see Schultz means this as an earnest reply, and wonders whether Schultz would be so forthright if not for Frederick's intervention on his behalf in group that day. Frederick, proud of his little rebellion against Canon, likes to think that, before that afternoon, Schultz would have remained even more cryptic, flapping his hands and saying, *Oh, work, work.*

Experimentation for what exactly?

Ah, right, well— Schultz says, turning to Frederick. Frederick scrutinizes Schultz's face for traces of his earlier despair. Perhaps it is there. Perhaps, but Frederick cannot find it behind his roommate's sprightly, almost juvenile enthusiasm. Maybe Canon is onto something, at least when it comes to Schultz and his denials.

Soon I will be ready to make a formal explanation for everything, yes? Schultz says. *For now, I can say it is a combined pursuit of linguistics and anthropology. A sort of verbal excavation, yes?*

And then Schultz turns back to his journal. Like an exhausted toddler placed horizontally and falling immediately unconscious, he instantly resumes his work.

Frederick thinks of Schultz's outburst in the group session. He thinks of Schultz standing there, like a strange conjurer, and wonders if truly he does conjure visions, wonders if now, in his scribblings and murmurs, Schultz is conjuring still. Maybe, Frederick thinks, it's his family. Maybe they should all leave Schultz be, in this, this asylum he has found, one that looks like madness to others but allows him to impose another world, spoken in strange tongues, onto this unbearable one of time's passage, chaos, irreversible loss.

Frederick closes his eyes and tries willfully to push the Miltown and the sleep medicine out of his awareness, and to pretend that the second pillow, between his elbows and curled knees, is his wife. For a moment, it seems he is nearly successful, and a wistful bliss tugs at his periphery.

4

There was some irony, Schultz recognized—or, rather, *had* recognized, back when such thoughts still interested him—that he managed to ascend into the rarefied airs of academe, and yet he never truly graduated from Bolbirosok's humble yeshiva. Schultz had been only months from graduating when his father made of himself a gruesome fruit, dangling from the riverbank tree. Thereafter, Schultz's private language grew louder by the day, muting the common words of his schoolwork. But Schultz had for so long excelled so far beyond his classmates that he had accumulated a certain academic currency at his yeshiva, sufficient, his empathic rabbi concluded, to purchase his early graduation. Schultz's rebbe falsified the balance of Schultz's grades, and when Schultz was recognized with the highest honors at the graduation ceremony, his classmates had to discipline themselves, with willful recollections of the horrors that had befallen him, in order to hold aside their jealousy and bitterness.

For the year that followed graduation, however, Schultz inspired no further envy. He sequestered himself in the little office in the rear of the bookshop. The shop was Schultz's now, but only nominally. It was, more truly, now the domain of his father's once part-time assistant, the aging widow Abrams, who had come out of her semiretirement to see to the store and to its babbling heir. Rarely traveling beyond the distance between his desk and bed, young Schultz required little physically from Abrams. But she did all she could, making him the meals he would half or one-third eat, changing his linens far more often than they needed changing. There seemed, to the widow, an inverse relationship between the physical and the emotional burdens Schultz imposed. Worried for Schultz's welfare, she wished she had more to do for him with her hands. But Schultz required nearly nothing, had whittled his existence to a lean simplicity that exceeded monastic. While his former classmates caroused and drank and generally caused the sort of mischief of which the older generation is half-proud, the whole of young Schultz's existence was now confined to the eighteen square meters of the shop's back office, from which the widow could sometimes hear him speak in his nonsense language. His own private universe, bound in a stockroom.

At least he still reads, Abrams would reply when others inquired after Schultz's well-being. And yet, the truth was what she witnessed rarely resembled reading. It is true that Schultz would sit before books, but he was often stooped over them so closely his eyelashes must have touched the pages. Sometimes, Schultz would hold the side of his head just over a book, as if reading with his ear rather than his eyes. And most disturbing of all: Schultz dissected the books with the blade of a letter opener and then tacked the excised pages to the walls of his room. When Abrams opened the door, the pages would rustle in waves, like the scales of some mythical, ineffable beast. It seemed Schultz was assembling a living thing, a room-creature that might, one morning, spring suddenly to life and devour them both.

Abrams solicited her fellow Bolbirosokers for help, and they tried their earnest best. The Mohel, Isaiah Kogen, of the generation that still believed in things such as the Evil Eye, performed a heartfelt round of rituals. Marion Levine, matriarch of Bolbirosok's wealthiest family, concluded that the boy just needed some familial company, and several times brought Schultz along on her family's outings. But as the teenage Levine children drank purloined wine, narrated their invented sexual escapades, and chased one another in the forest, Schultz only sat like Buddha upon a picnic blanket, muttering at whatever happened to be set before him. The Levine children begged their mother to cease her insistence upon the eerie boy's company, and she soon capitulated. Of course Abrams brought Schultz to the town physician, but Dr. Dreyfuss's efforts proved as unhelpful as any. Schultz, in his febrile enthusiasms, had always had a slightly elevated basal temperature, which Dr. Dreyfuss interpreted as a fever that refused to cease. The doctor had seen fever dreams provoke similar babble in others, and so he concluded, in his pseudoscientific way, that Schultz's body had misinterpreted his grief as a foreign thing, an infection that must be fought against. Dreyfuss tried various measures to suppress Schultz's fever—cold compresses, long immersions in the Bobir River, radical quantities of aspirin—all of which temporarily succeeded in bringing down Schultz's temperature, but still his babble persisted. Schultz neither objected nor consented to these efforts; these external events were irrelevant, eclipsed by what engaged him within.

Dr. Dreyfuss, at least, was humble enough to recognize his failure. Dreyfuss summoned a young psychiatrist from Vilnius, who conducted with Schultz whatever semblance of an interview two men speaking in incompatible languages can have. After, it took some time for the physician to clearly delineate for Abrams the difference between the Evil Eye and schizophrenia.

Most Bolbirosokers, however, accepted Schultz's condition as tragic, but natural in its way. Many were old enough to remember how the famine, in the last century, had displayed grief's remarkable variety. Irretrievable loss, they knew, rendered some sullen, some perverse, some ecstatic, some psychotic. Grief was the floodwater that carved to a ravine whatever inherent strangeness creeked through a mind. Most accepted Schultz's muttering as strange grieving, and said the boy needed only time.

Only Reb Menachem Mendelsohn, the peculiar Torah scholar, considered a grander explanation for Schultz's strange obsessions and utterances. Intrigued by the young man's behavior, Reb Mendelsohn went by the bookshop one afternoon. His daughter Irit, always curious about her complex and sullen classmate, came along for the visit and pretended to peruse the bookshelves as she stole furtive glances into the paper-shingled back room, where her father sat on the floor and attempted to converse with the boy.

Reb Mendelsohn asked Schultz many questions, which Schultz could not hear. To Reb Mendelsohn, Schultz occasionally seemed to attempt a reply, but the boy was not even aware he was speaking. Reb Mendelsohn, however, shuddered at the sounds that came from the boy's lips. What was it, Mendelsohn had to wonder, that made him tremble? Was it simple pity for this grief-stricken boy, as cut off from words as an animal? Or was it the sounds themselves? What the boy muttered was obvious nonsense, and yet each noise seemed to resonate in some chamber deep within Mendelsohn's own skull, like when the congregation chanted the Shema at Shul.

Can you try to tell me what you mean? Do you hear voices? Can you hear me? Mendelsohn asked. Schultz looked at Mendelsohn, and then, seemingly at random, mighty syllables suddenly burst forth, as if from laryngeal church bells hung in Schultz's throat. At the end of his interview, Mendelsohn invited Schultz to his house as soon as he was feeling a little better. Schultz managed what seemed a shrug.

Then Reb Mendelsohn braced himself by the knees, stood,

and turned from Schultz's paper-flesh room. Schultz stood behind him and watched a warped vision of Reb Mendelsohn
leave through the sagging, uneven glass of the stockroom window. The bookshop's main room, as ever, chimed with its
cleeeeeep name.

And then Schultz saw her. She belonged to his past, to that
other territory he had left, populated by people who no longer
resembled him. That other territory: he knew, abstractly, that he
was from there, but he felt now that he had already spent a lifetime as an expatriate in his other place. But the sight of Irit, the
girl he had loved once, was a door thrown open to some internal attic. In there, he was surprised to discover, the intricacies of
his past were still stored. In this moment, it seemed possible to
Schultz to return.

Schultz did not then need any word from the truer language
that spoke only to him. There was only one word now, sufficient
for what he felt. And it was only an ordinary word.

Irit, Schultz called, and she turned to him.

5

Halfway down Madhouse Hill, Canon pilots his Ford Edsel
along the winding path that leads from his grand hospital to the
squat postwar prefabs of middle-class Belmont. This moment in
his evening is much like the first molecules of Miltown to reach
his patients' awareness: with stunning swiftness, the exhilaration
of the day is undone. No chief of Mayflower now; he is just a

man in a suit commuting home from work. At the far side of Belmont, where the land begins to rise again—he has been told that when the trees are bare in the winter he will be able to see his asylum—Canon will arrive at his new house. The home will be lit with the dim lamps his wife insists upon—Tiffany, they are lovely to look at, but transmit saloon light. His wife will make a display of her carelessness at his return, hardly nodding at him from her novel or from a telephone conversation. He will make a display of kindness, cheerily asking how he might help with dinner. She will flash him an angry glare. Both will know he makes these displays only to demonstrate supposed goodness; if she does not know, exactly, she must sense something of the affair by now, mustn't she? The children will show little interest in Canon beyond his ability to fulfill their wants: did he bring any treats? Can they watch TV if they finish homework? Can they stay up until ten? In his high office on the high hill, Canon is, at all times, deliberate and decisive. All problems are identified, named, considered, and acted upon for swift resolution. In his home, intentions will remain unspoken, motives mystifying, and discussions always, always agitating.

The dim Tiffany light, the wifely glare, the children arguing over nothing. In anticipation of all this, Canon performs the mental act of transcendence he has nearly perfected since taking the office at Mayflower. As when he lies far from his wife in the bed they hardly share, as when his wife instructs him to watch (*endure*) *The Mickey Mouse Club* with his children, Canon resolves to be silently productive, considering potential problems presented in the day, and how he might resolve them. He thinks of how Truman in the boys' ward was able to resume his self-mutilation with a cafeteria knife, and he decides to consider cardboard flatware. He thinks of the unending headache of the rusting Victorian pipes in Upshire and wonders if it might make more financial sense to gut the whole system and rebuild with proper plumbing.

Canon thinks of my grandfather. Canon knows that, for the scope of what he will accomplish at Mayflower to be acknowledged, he himself must be responsible for amassing the empirical evidence. He has been looking, since his arrival, for a small group of patients—four, five at the most—to serve as case studies in the paper he will, by the end of the first year of his tenure, present in *The New England Journal of Medicine*. Though nearly all the patients meet regularly with the lower echelon of psychiatrists assigned to each ward (the ward chief, Higgins, in the men's case), Canon will conduct personally the one-on-one therapy of these chosen few. Canon resolves, now, to take Frederick Merrill into this selective group, and he is immediately struck by the ingenuity of his decision: Frederick Merrill—perhaps manic-depressive, as Wallace diagnosed, but perhaps more accurately on the borderline between neurotic and psychotic—will make a fascinating subject of empirical scrutiny, in his ambiguous affliction. Canon also senses that the proposal will appeal to the narcissism that he has gleaned to be a prime symptom of Merrill's disorder, will disarm the antisocial behavior that this narcissism generates, rendering a more positive milieu for the others.

The social milieu, Canon's mantra. The social milieu is the true scene of therapy. This is what his predecessors and colleagues fail to see clearly; it is this awareness that will grant Canon a lasting place in the history of psychotherapy. Psychiatrists can spend only so much time with patients. Ultimately, a patient's success depends upon his fellow patients, upon a healing, productive social atmosphere. But that atmosphere does not come about by chance. It is the great labor of the psychiatrist in chief to control, shape, even to manipulate every detail of patients' lives, until he has cultivated the salutary environment. Canon knows the orderlies and nurses can think him obsessive. But every detail must be considered. With tremendous will, close scrutiny, deliberate decisions, and unflagging enforcement, the mad can be rendered sane. They can devise a comprehensive, elaborate equation, with a single solution.

Canon is now at a traffic light, five blocks from the base of the hill. In the rearview, he can just discern the lamps of Upshire. There are so many details, each to be considered and decided upon. There are almost not enough hours in the day. And so, Canon resolves: as his wife ignores him, maligns him on the phone with her friends, as his children ask only for more, more, more, Canon, in his mind, will move from room to room, patient to patient, seeking flaws and rectifying. It requires immense focus and will, but Canon will try to bring order to all things.

EVERYONE

KNOWS

1

The church, the plain white space of it, Puritan sparse. The minister, Hank James, coordinated to the building's austere theme with his white and balding head, and also with his sermon, in which he tells of desert wanderings in his arid language. Before the minister, in fours and fives and sixes, mothers and fathers with their progeny, all in their plain suits and dresses. Near the front of the church, two rows from the pulpit, the family that will one day be my own: my grandmother Katharine; my aunts, Rebecca, Louise, Jillian; and my mother, Susie. My grandfather is absent.

When Katharine lifts her head for a split second during another recitation of the Lord's Prayer, she catches, from across the aisle, what she takes to be a scrutinizing glance from Donna Littleton, Tat's best friend. Katharine assumes Donna's gaze is no accident. Tat, sitting with her own family alongside Donna's, notices Donna's gaze and seems to assume the same. In a hardly masked panic, Tat tries to redirect her friend's attention to something in the program in her hands.

It is the first Sunday of October. The congregants of Graveton Congregational Church rise and sit, chant and bow their heads, in various patterns until it is time for the moment Katharine dreads, when the choir sings them off to the foyer for the tea and pastries that the church supplies every year on First of Fall Sunday, a time for reconvening and chatting about the summer that has passed.

So it has come now, this moment of accounting. Suspicions and rumors will be confirmed. The father of their family is absent, and now everyone knows it. All other fathers are here; all other families have resurfaced from the summer, prosperous and intact for the season of work to come. It is October now, Frederick has been gone three months, and Katharine has stopped allowing herself to consider what date she expects him home.

Katharine and her daughters walk down the center aisle, shuffling among the other families in their new autumn outfits. No new outfits for the Merrills, given the cost of Mayflower, the loss of Frederick's income. Now work has resumed, and there are (or so it seems to Katharine) the curious and judging looks, and the rumors.

Katharine sees now that she simply cannot continue in her cheery assessments. There is no knowing when Frederick will return; clearly, his time at Mayflower is something more than *a rest*. Still, Katharine cannot yet say those words, the ones that the pamphlets for Mayflower carefully elude, in the way advertisements for funeral homes elude the word *death*. Katharine cannot yet say *psychosis, manic depression, madness.* So she has begun to seek other words for it. What is between exhaustion and insanity? Katharine has settled on *nervous breakdown,* which she told only Tat when she bumped into her at the grocery. *I guess you could call it a nervous breakdown,* she explained, trying to clarify her earlier call, and then once more swore Tat to confidentiality. But clearly Tat has broken that promise. For there the Merrills are, in the foyer now, Susie displaying cookies to Katharine, as Minister James approaches directly, bypassing the rest of his flock. The girls, curious about the minister's attention, assemble around Katharine.

Why! Hello there! Minister James greets them. *And how are we this morning?*

Beatific, Rebecca says, proud of the erudite irony she has just this year begun to affect.

James smiles and casts his gaze over the girls, simultaneously judgmental and benevolent. Perhaps like a father's gaze, but that of a father different from theirs. *Excited for the new school year?*

Thrilled, Susie says.

And how are you? James asks Katharine. *I hear you've had a— trying?—summer.*

Katharine shrugs and considers words for what has happened. But she simply cannot think of it, nothing that will convey what she wants to convey and still pass as graceful here, in the foyer of this church with all these friends and neighbors and daughters around her. And so, she instead offers only a wistful grin as she begins to search for other innocuous objects to set the conversation upon—worries about Susie's math grades? Dread of the coming winter? Some kind thought about the minister's sermon?

Eventually Susie pipes, *My dad is just getting some rest.*

James smiles. *Precisely what he needs, I'm sure.*

Susie firms her lips in a proud grin, as she returns her mother's gaze with a look of obstinate solidarity. But then there is something surprising in her mother's face, some shame her mother tucks in between her eyebrows that collapses Susie's smile.

Katharine thinks: her daughters know much more than she admits to herself. Her daughters are only playing the parts they know they are expected to play in the story Katharine tries to contrive, a fiction of a life and a family better than the one they have. Katharine has failed in keeping the truth and her girls apart.

There, again, is her father's face, his haughty vindication. Years ago, after one Christmas when a drunken Frederick had just barely managed to stay vertical long enough to get from the living room to the car, her father had warned her, *children understand more than you think.*

But of course they understood. Of course her girls had understood each time that there had been a knock at the front door long after midnight, and they had answered it to find their father in the doorway, slurring his maudlin or spiteful words, occasionally bruised or even bleeding. They understood each time their father swaggered home in the middle of dinner, sweet-smelling of bourbon, in the company of an unannounced dinner guest— either one of his equally drunken friends or else a strange woman. The girls understood the grim fact of their father's affliction when, drunk and volatile, he would mutter to some tormenting, abstract presence, and then berate whichever of them came close to him. Not just berate, but verbally abuse, condemning his own daughters as ignorant. And, more than by anything Frederick had done, the girls had learned the truth about their father by what he had failed to do: his long absences, his business trips that stretched for weeks, his endless nights out, his weekends away, his apparent intolerance of home. Susie's defiant grin informs Katharine that the girls have been acceding to their mother's cheerier simplifications only for their mother's sake.

Katharine has spent years concealing what her husband wanted to hide, but the girls have understood anyway. She has tried to obfuscate, when clearly she ought to have confronted. And yet, for all the years of their marriage, only twice has she dared it. Once the night when she and her mother adorned her rage with lofty language and packed his bag. And then again, one night just last spring. This time, there had been no scripted monologue. Irrepressible words had simply expelled themselves.

One Tuesday night, last May, Frederick had yet to return from a weekend *business trip* to Pittsburgh. At two in the morning, with the girls asleep in their rooms and Katharine in bed bitterly enumerating her husband's failings, the fender of Frederick's Oldsmobile glanced off the curb out front as he sloppily turned his car up the drive. Katharine did not go to greet him at the door; she did not try to hush his ascent to bed, for the girls' sake. Frederick careened up the stairs, came into the lit bedroom, and nodded once at Katharine with a sad acceptance, as if, on his way home, he had not been certain he would find this reality still existent, his family he had failed again. When he climbed into bed, turned off the lamp, and rolled to his side, Katharine could smell another woman's smell. And then it had come forth: years of silent accounting and recriminations finding words, inwardly shot rage ricocheted suddenly outward.

How? she said. *How? How can you lie to me again and again and again? And so stupidly? Do you think I am stupid? Do you think I don't know? How could you lie so stupidly? How could you let yourself be so pathetic? I know, Frederick. I know. I know. I know. I know their names. I know all about them.*

And then Katharine, for the first time, named They Who Shall Not Be Named, the nefarious Hamans of their marriage. *Sheila from the bank. Peggy Maxwell. Irene Mills. Shall I continue?*

As Katharine counted his betrayals, Frederick lay there perfectly still, curled into himself and his apparent disregard for Katharine's tirade. He was drunk; likely, he was asleep. And so Katharine did what she would never dare, she put her hand into the lion's mouth, touching a drunk Frederick with something other than gentleness. With all her strength, she turned him to her, expecting his rage, wondering if, for the first time, he might strike her. There could even be a paradoxical kind of victory in that, his cruelty finally manifested into something showable, her private misery finally welting publicly.

But, instead, he was lucid and composed. No grand theater of Frederick's suffering this time, no spectacle of denial.

I love you very much, Katharine. But this is not what you are. You choose not to see things. Not to see those women, just as you haven't seen me for a very, very long time. You see only what you want to see. You with your rose-colored glasses. There is something bad in me, I know it. But you want never to see it. Why do you think I need them?

How? was all Katharine could muster in reply. *How could you love me so little?*

I love you tremendously.

I can't live this way anymore, Katharine said, and meant it.

Frederick left to sleep in the guest room, but later he returned and shook Katharine awake. He flipped on the bedside lamp, and she saw that his eyes had lost their lucidity, now moving with a bird's ratcheting, mechanical movement.

What? Katharine said. *What is it?*

You are right, Frederick said, *I'm going to tell her to leave.*

Tell who to leave?

The woman downstairs. I don't want anyone else. I only want you. I'm going to tell her that.

There's a woman downstairs? Katharine asked. But already she knew there was, of course, no other woman in the house. Only a few times had Frederick's febrile energy, warped with bourbon, carried him to such notions, and Katharine did not try to correct him. She thought then of the simple word she tries so hard now not to admit. There was no word for it but *madness*.

Frederick staggered dreamily into the darkened downstairs. He lit room after room, seeking to expel some imagined presence. After he had checked each room twice, he finally turned to Katharine, not in apprehension of his delusion, nor in confusion, but in delight.

She's gone! he said.

She is?

Gone for good, he added and clenched his eyes, measuring what this meant. *It's just us now. From now on. I promise.*

This is how entirely Katharine has let herself believe in false things: she thought this resolution, even if derived from delusion, might be authentic.

That night, Frederick was at his worst, drunk and manic. But he was also right. That night, Frederick believed in a person who was not there, but then, in her own way, so did Katharine.

It seems to Katharine now that she has spent all of this time loving and grasping not for the real Frederick but for just another Frederick, a trickster spirit who takes occasional possession of her husband's body, just long enough for a few sweet or needy moments, a loving week or two, just enough to keep Katharine's faith in his existence.

At least now, Katharine thinks, there is this clarity. With her husband gone, there is no false Frederick to distract her, no incarnating trickster rearranging the past with his affection and need.

2

The minister nods. *If you ever want to talk.*

Maybe James wants to help, but Katharine also sees now that he is only an ordinary person, hungry for gossip, for the proximity to the vague celebrity that disaster has lent her. Katharine sees the minister not at all as she sees him from her pew—an ethereal wisdom manifested in a face seemingly painted by John Singer Sargent—but just a person breathing his rotten breath, with a thousand oblong indentations for pores, with overly long, carnivorous teeth. She sees Tat, across the room with Donna, eyeing Katharine the way Tat might eye a dinner plate that arrives before her friends' orders, a hunger she must pretend to ignore. Katharine suddenly wants, very much, to be away from this church and these people.

She nods a good-bye to Minister James, makes no parting gesture to Tat, and tells her girls it's time to go. Even with cake still to be eaten, and their church friends they have not seen all summer, the girls leave without objection.

Outside, they climb into the family's Ford Country Squire. In the hushed interior, with its used smell, all are silent as Katharine navigates the roads home.

My mother and her sisters watch their town pass by, back-to-school specials painted onto store windows, fall already infecting the upper tree branches.

Your father had a nervous breakdown, Katharine surprises herself by saying. *If anyone asks, you can say that's what happened.*

In the front passenger seat, Susie turns to her mother.

He just needs a rest, Susie corrects her.

I hope that's true. But we can't lie to ourselves anymore. He's had a nervous breakdown.

There is a darkness through which Katharine has willed herself to sleep, a darkness she has glimpsed only at its peripheries, when it was altered and nearly visible in rosy diffractions. She has looked away from that darkness, in which her husband has raged and wept and fought and fucked. Katharine sees now: we can persist to see with our rosy vision, but still the night comes, concealing what it conceals. And there is no rosy way to see that blackness.

Katharine is a mother of four, with a husband in a mental hospital. The winter is coming, and the money is running out. Her marriage has failed, everyone knows it, and she has no real friends. Her relatives have turned against her husband first, and now they are turning on her too. She can no longer be anything other than what everyone plainly sees her to be.

And yet. Katharine thinks now of her secret. She thinks of another conversation she had last week, which she has not told anyone about. She thinks of everything this conversation might promise, ruin, or fix. Destruction and creation, each holding the other's secret, one secretly a form of the other.

HORRORLAND

1

The rain falls steadily now, for the fifth straight day. The Boston fall—prone to both heat waves and freak snowstorms—seems to have paused to allow a moment of pure autumn: the cool rain, the subdued expressions of the redbrick buildings, the foliage more vivid in the pallid light.

Whether attributable to the lull in the weather or the grateful calm that has followed the completion of Canon's most dramatic changes, the majority of Mayflower's patients seem to have accepted one of the chief's highest aims: a respite from chaos, order, calm. It has been almost three months since Canon's ascendancy, and now in the cafeteria, most food is simply transferred from tray to mouth, rarely going airborne. In the metal-mirrored ward lavatories, it has been weeks since a patient has assaulted an orderly with foul ammunition.

Bobbie, whose torment seems to manifest in the form of a devilish internal doppelgänger, no longer violently rebukes his double, now only pleads with him softly, *Please please stop tickling me down there it itches so terribly.* It even seems the catatonics have dialed down their endless utterances of staccato English.

Over the last weeks, Schultz has aligned his daily exertions with the new rigid schedule, complacently handing himself over to meals and therapy, neither anxious for nor distracted from his work, which continues at the same velocity as ever.

Lowell has had two weeks straight of *down days,* his attendance at meals and group therapy requiring no small effort by the Crew Crew, as the great poet pleads with them to be left to his horizontal despair and recites his work: *I myself am Hell; / nobody's here.*

Even Marvin, on whom the patients and staff of Mayflower—indeed the psychiatric community at large—have been able to depend for a grand theater of psychosis, appears entirely to have taken up his seemingly final role, Marvin Foulds the Depressive. Marvin's face has lost the theatricality that had animated it, and now he simply lets himself be ushered from appointment to appointment. No longer any of his strange personae, he often seems no one at all.

. . .

In the grim afternoon quiet of Upshire Hall, my grandfather nears the end of his thrice-weekly one-on-one with Canon. Though Frederick immediately agreed to Canon's offer to make him one of Mayflower's case studies, he remained guarded and largely uncooperative for the first two or three weeks. It wasn't until Canon, stalemated in the fourth week of therapy, began to delineate what Frederick needed to do to leave that Frederick began to yield, and Canon learned how to render his rigid, angry patient malleable.

Usually, Canon tries not to discuss the prospect of leaving with patients. He wants them to see their goal not as a return to their old life, but as recovery. Recovery from the affliction that brought them to this place the high accomplishment, freedom a lovely subsidiary benefit. But with Frederick, Canon learned he needed to modify his rule, dangling freedom as the carrot on a stick. It helped that, in Frederick Merrill's case, Canon's power in this regard is near absolute; Canon unsubtly reaffirmed to his patient that only his professional judgment would set him free, that Frederick must achieve what Canon wants for him before Frederick can achieve what it is that he wants for himself. Surreptitiously, within this crude behaviorist scheme, the psychiatrist will heal his patient.

Nothing else in there you'd like to share? Canon asks, gesturing to the journal he makes Frederick bring to him each session, the record of Frederick's thoughts between meetings that Canon repeatedly requests to read, without success.

Mostly, it's just nonsense, Frederick says with a shrug. *Trying to find the right way to say things.*

Canon shrugs too.

You know, Canon says now, as the session wraps up, as he says at the end of nearly every session, *I think we are really starting to get somewhere.*

Frederick watches the soft rain mystify the window's view of the Depression, then turns to Canon.

Ballpark estimate, Frederick says, trying to muster an ingratiating laugh.

All depends on you, of course. But it looks to me like you'll be home by Christmas.

Frederick nods. He tells himself that next time in both group therapy and in one-on-one he must try harder, not for legitimate breakthrough but to emulate the language of the sort of breakthrough Canon would accept. Frederick knows Canon has offered him no new insight. He has merely repeated Wallace's glib insights, has merely piled onto Frederick the uninspired secondhand notions all those psychiatrists are shoveling in their trench-digging universities. Silently, and in his journals, Frederick continues to know Canon is deluded, though perhaps he applies language less severe than before—*moronic ideologue* downgraded to *foolish pedant*.

These sessions with Canon, now that he has managed to subdue his animosity in the service of his liberation, are not entirely unpleasant. It is something of a challenge, like a brainteaser, trying to limn Canon's questions and responses for precisely the optimal reply. The subtextual goal, freedom, singular but rarely spoken; each word measured for its success or failure in obtaining what Frederick desires. It is not unlike seducing a reluctant young woman.

Okay, you're free to go back to your room. Progress, Mr. Merrill. Real progress.

Frederick nods again.

2

As the Crew Crew kid escorts him across the Depression, Frederick tries to formulate the exact language of his breakthrough, the paragraph that will explain, in Canon's view, the entirety of Frederick's existential dilemma. *What I need,* Frederick will say, *is to understand that I am always trying to replace the love and approval my mother never gave me with other forms of love and approval. My affairs have been an obvious manifestation of this, as has been my difficulty when things at work do not go as well as I hope. I must, over time, with the love of my family, come to understand my value does not depend upon others. I love myself! Sunshine and rainbows!*

Frederick understands well this line of half-logic and the conclusions to which it aspires. He even finds fragments of truth in the argument, from time to time. But he still privately mocks its naïveté, its almost sweetly simple view of the human condition. There is a chaos within himself, Frederick acknowledges. But a mental hospital is not now, nor will it ever be, the place he belongs. Maybe somewhere just at the periphery of his awareness, that place terrible with beauty he sometimes reaches in his excitement, when ideas come so quickly, Frederick might find a way to account for himself. There he might find words for everything, a way to explain to Katharine, his girls, to himself why some days the world seems to him simple, tangible, even compliant to his will, while at other times the sadness of average things—a pain in his stomach, Katharine's failure to coddle him, no dessert in the freezer, clocks persisting in their counting of seconds—makes him consider his end. And why everything that has seemed to promise transformation—his career, patent ideas, countless first chapters and stray lines of poetry, and, more than any, the way Katharine and he were together when they first began—could never, in the end, be enough. Almost none of this, his true affliction, has to do with the cozy Freudian theater of his early childhood with his mother. But Frederick knows that, if he tried to explain to Canon how his true tumult was incompatible with those simple Freudian scenarios, Canon would understand it as simple resistance to therapy, a major setback.

The only one to whom Frederick acknowledges these thoughts is the night assistant Rita, of whom all the men of Ingersoll are fond, with whom Frederick has developed a particular closeness. It has grown, Frederick believes, not as nurse and patient, not as counselor and counselee, but as real friendship.

Rita and Frederick now invariably find a half an hour or more to talk during her nightly shift. And often it is she who talks, telling Frederick what the rest of the staff would not dare tell patients: intimate descriptions of her education and family, a full account of world news, not the filtered version they receive through the common room TV. Rita even shares with Frederick the details of her failed attempts to date and love boys. And in exchange, Frederick has begun, in the last two weeks or so, to speak his mind as simply as possible, without the dissemblance he must use with Canon, even with the other men on Ingersoll.

I don't know, he told her just last night. *Sometimes, everything seems fine. Everything seems normal, which isn't normal at all. And then, all of a sudden, something switches. It could be the smallest thing. I could drink too much and yell at one of the girls. Or maybe Katharine gets fed up with me and makes me sleep in the guest room. Or maybe nothing at all happens. Maybe there isn't any reason at all. Anyway, all of a sudden, it's like a trapdoor. A hidden door. Like Alice into Wonderland, you know? But the opposite of Wonderland. Horrorland.*

And though Frederick knows Canon brought Rita with him from Harvard, Frederick never suspects that these conversations are what some of the other (likely jealous) men of Ingersoll suggest they are: Rita's surreptitious ruse to collect that madhouse currency—his true thoughts, his internal life—to sell to Canon in exchange for respect, or promotion. Frederick simply trusts her. It is friendship, perhaps generated like many—or so Frederick likes to think—from an unspoken romantic dynamic.

The puzzle of trying to satisfy Canon, the possibility of release, and the conversations with Rita: that is all that has made each day of the last weeks bearable.

Frederick and the Crew Crew kid have passed the first doors

of Ingersoll when a panic seizes Frederick. He feels his pockets, reflexively, but knows it is not in his pockets. He has left his journal.

Frederick's journal: written with his skepticism, his disavowals of Canon's notions, his outright contempt, and—worst of all—his true confusion, of which he speaks only to Rita. If Canon reads it, Frederick knows, it will mean the undoing of the last weeks of effort. It will require months, if not years, for Frederick to convince Canon that he does not believe the words he has written there.

Shit, Frederick says to the Crew Crew boy. *Shit. I need to go back.*

Excuse me?

I left something at Canon's office.

Left something?

My journal. I need it back. I need to go back.

You can get it tomorrow.

No, I need it now.

Tough luck, pal. Tomorrow.

At moments of dramatic necessity, where others falter, the right words often come to Frederick. As simply as a cogent argument suddenly constructs itself in a teary-eyed, whiskey-soaked dispute with Katharine, a simple lie now assembles itself in the void of necessity the moment opens.

Dr. Canon told me I have to list my dreams each morning, and then compare them with the morning before. If I can't do that tomorrow morning, I'll have to explain to him why I couldn't. Why I wasn't allowed to get my journal back.

The older generation of orderlies and nurses would certainly have seen through this obvious lie, would have denied Frederick a return to Canon's office, if not out of deference to the psychiatrist in chief then simply to remind Frederick that it was they, not he, who held authority. But the Crew Crew boy, relatively unschooled in the deceptions of patients, now has a dilemma: protocol, Canon's holy scripture, must be violated one way or the other. Either Canon's patient will make an unscheduled return or the patient will be unable to complete the work Canon has assigned him. The Crew Crew boy knows, from a dozen staff meetings, the importance to Canon of Frederick's position in the selective lot of Canon's case studies, and so he imagines greater punishment for the violation of the latter order than for the former. The Crew Crew boy tells Frederick that he is a pain in the ass and checks his watch.

All right, he says. *But you are the one who's going to have to go in there and ask him for it.*

3

Frederick has found the door to Canon's office unlatched, but there is darkness within. The Crew Crew kid is waiting in reception, hoping to avoid the confrontation with Canon he senses would follow, which he senses likely will come anyway. Frederick thinks that he is too late, that Canon has already gone home, journal in hand, to spend the evening reading. Frederick already begins to try to comprehend the horror of it, to measure the immeasurable repercussions. But it is, like what its entries fail to describe, impossible to fathom all at once.

Frederick knocks lightly at the door, pushes it open the rest of the way. A step into the room, the floor gives way, depths open. At first he thinks, instinctively, *Burglars!* Two bodies flung into frantic motion at the far corner of the room, skittering in the illegible darkness. Frederick expects a blow or a bullet to come, his flesh tingles to receive the first strike, until one of the bodies speaks with Canon's voice.

Get out. Get out of here? Canon's voice says, more a question than a command.

Sorry, sorry, Frederick says instinctively, but he does not turn to the door, not immediately. The need to recover his journal is just as urgent as the need to flee. He does not consciously make the decision; his body simply walks the five creaking steps toward the chair in which he chooses to spend his sessions—the divan seems laughably cliché—and he grasps for the journal, which, he is blissful to find, still remains on the side table.

Get out. Now a command.

Frederick has little time to consider as he obeys, scrambling to the light cast from reception. Still, he is able to think: *his wife? A lover?* Both seem impossible. Frederick is on the door's other side now, but he turns to pull it shut. And it is there, in the last backward glance, aided by the Sahara-bright fluorescents Canon had installed in the corridor, that Frederick sees her face, rising from behind Canon's bare back. Her face, which reflects the incredulousness of Frederick's. Suddenly, a trapdoor can swing open. Rita.

4

Fire. The white and blue and red of fire. Nothing, now, other than fire. No avid squirrels, no ticking clocks, no history, no Katharine, no daughters, no failure, no aspirations or accomplishments. No demands from history or future; no confusion of the present. Only the obliterating conflagration. For the moment, there is no Frederick.

Electroconvulsive therapy: the last vestige of the post-Victorian half-science of the kind Canon has been so proud to eliminate. Or nearly eliminate. Talk therapy and the social milieu are paramount, but Canon is able to remind himself that a scientist must not let his own preferred approach suppress undeniable data, and the truth is electroshock can yield good numbers. It is hard to know why, precisely, and it is Canon's belief that it has to do not with an electrical realignment but with trauma. A synthesized, electric version of one's childhood trauma, which shocks into the consciousness that which has remained deeply subconscious. Not to be used, except in the most severe cases. Only three times has he instructed Higgins, now the only one at the hospital proficient with this primitive device: once a boy in North Webster, once a schizotypal woman in South House who wouldn't stop bruising herself, and now Frederick Merrill.

After Canon and Rita had scrambled back to their clothes, to their offices, Canon had acted on impulse, without deeper consideration. The important thing, he knew, was containment. As soon as he had collected himself enough to speak, Canon made the call.

Frederick had been back in his room in Ingersoll for less than fifteen minutes when Higgins arrived. The orderly who had escorted Frederick did not know what his patient had seen, but he gleaned from the tremor in Frederick's gait that something grave had occurred. The boy had already begun to practice the speech to his parents and his girlfriend, explaining why he had lost his first real job.

Higgins, a nervous man who seems never to know quite what to do with his hands, is always grateful for any direct task ordered by Canon. And so Higgins had come, emboldened with delegated purpose, to the worried orderly, and had greatly relieved the boy to inform him Canon had called for an emergency course of ECT, in response to the *deeply disturbing behavior* Frederick had displayed in their session.

The orderly, with the help of the other Crew Crew boy just finishing his shift, pulled Frederick down the corridor just as had the orderlies they had seen in movies, by the elbows to subdue his fight. Frederick, however, had no fight. He wanted, at that moment, only to capitulate, to promise, to be left to silence. When they reached the room, with all its restraints and devices shaped to interface with the human form in those dreadful, inhuman ways, Frederick voided his bladder.

· · ·

The shock has stopped, carrying memory away with it. When Frederick wakes from the sedatives, an hour later, he feels that something has entered him and scooped him out with brute force, replacing what was him with a fluctuating, mindless static. The internal dislocation overwhelms the external. The questions at first are more of who than where. It is only after Canon enters the door to the little white room, admitting the fluorescents from the hallway, that Frederick begins to remember himself, and then to understand his place.

He is a patient at a mental hospital called Mayflower. He is in the concrete building that holds the most problematic, those who must be separated from the rest. This is his psychiatrist, Canon, who has done something. What? Something that is related to the part of him that has been scooped away, a part of him that is perhaps benign or perhaps malignant, but absolutely crucial.

How are you feeling? Canon asks.

I don't feel— Frederick begins, but can't complete the sentence: words, too, seem to have been replaced with this dull fizzling of calming electricity. But, then, perhaps this answer is accurate.

There is nothing more to this room than a mattress on the floor and the padding on the walls, and so an orderly follows behind Canon with a chair in which the doctor sits. Frederick, lying on the mattress, does not quite know how to receive Canon perched over him. The doctor's face seems to ask a question Frederick does not know how to answer. Canon's expression seems an accusation to which Frederick does not know how to respond. Frederick covers his eyes with his forearm, turns to the wall.

Do you remember, Canon begins, and begins again. *Do you remember what happened to you?*

What happened to me, Frederick echoes.

You've been given electroconvulsive therapy. It's normal not to remember.

Electro—

It's a radical approach, only for the most extreme cases.

Frederick turns back to the doctor. No, it is not an accusation, that strange new aspect of Canon's face, nor is it a question exactly. It is, rather, something Frederick has not seen before. In the expectancy of Canon's eyes, the fitful stroking of goatee, the sucking of bottom lip, it is uncertainty.

Rita. Frederick remembers now, his muddled awareness clarifying into the memory of her face, caught in the fluorescent hallway light.

Again and again, Frederick will later scrutinize this conversation, will spend days dwelling within it, feeling out its possible alternatives, what he might have said that might have yielded better ends. Uncertainty: was there some way he could have used it against Canon? If Frederick had threatened instead of cowered, could he have blackmailed his way to freedom? But, no. His instincts in this moment, Frederick will later conclude, were immaculately adroit. He had been the only witness, after all; who would believe him?

I remember now, Frederick says.

You remember— Canon begins. *You know why I had no choice but this terrible electroshock treatment?*

Yes.

Neither says anything. The moment is pulled flat and taut with opposing tensions, like the surface of a trampoline.

Yes, Frederick repeats. *I understand.*

Canon scrutinizes Frederick for a long moment. And then, quite suddenly, the architecture of Canon's face gives way, requiring his hands for buttress.

Things are much more complicated than you think, Canon says. *Just because people work here does not mean they don't have problems of their own.*

Frederick wants to rise from his mattress and beat Canon until Canon joins Frederick in his senselessness. He wants to embrace Canon and say, *Yes, see? We are all flawed. I no more than you. Yes, I have also strayed as you have strayed. Yes, see? We are all subject to forces we cannot entirely explain.* He wants to rage at Canon for the long months Frederick has already lost to Canon's delusions.

But Frederick knows Canon cannot allow revelations of his own. No. All Frederick can do to restore his progress to freedom is to restore Canon to his simple story of doctor and patient, which Canon insists upon. And so, Frederick will later congratulate himself for what he says next, will later feel it was a significant accomplishment, given his state, drugged and shocked and thrown into solitary. Having lost Rita.

We were making progress, Frederick manages through the buzz of his emptied mind. *But I think we can make even more.*

Well. I'm glad that we agree.

5

Canon has fired one of his new employees for the first time: the orderly who, against protocol, allowed Frederick to come back to his office, a convenient excuse to dismiss the only other (half) witness. But still, Canon tells himself, that kid broke the rules, and in a place like this, rules are everything.

In *The Mental Asylum,* his near-canonical textbook, Canon writes at length of how strong leadership demands earnest contemplation of the worst possible outcomes. And so Canon now thinks, *He will tell.* Despite what he says, he will tell. Will people believe him? Likely, even the other men on Ingersoll will not. They will hear his story, spread his gossip, but everyone will know how Frederick enjoys undermining Canon. Still, even the rumor could be damaging, even an accusation like that could grant entropy traction, and then—as Canon has observed time and again in other institutions—chaos could spread with its own mad determination.

Canon returns to the office, which is still shameful with the memory of Frederick in the doorway, looking upon Canon with Rita. *He will tell,* Canon thinks. Or maybe not. And, anyway, no one here would believe him. Not entirely believe him, at least. The only people he could convince are well beyond the walls of Mayflower. In the two conversations Canon has had with Mrs. Merrill, he senses that she remains nearly as doubtful as her husband of Frederick's need for hospitalization.

One of the sturdiest precepts in guiding delusional patients to reason is never to allow the delusion to be considered seriously by another. Any notion, given enough time and disregard, withers.

It is for the sake of the hospital, for all Canon hopes for his patients, but also for Merrill's sake. His therapy, Canon now thinks, is not going as well as he has believed. In truth, he still senses a placating disingenuousness in Merrill's confessions, senses that perhaps Frederick Merrill does not yet truly believe in this, the only way back to sanity, his family, his life.

Canon, the Freudian, the talker, has shot electricity through his patient. But is it not true that, when therapy is stalemated, as theirs has clearly become, the research suggests that electroconvulsive therapy can be profoundly helpful? Yes. There is still much work to be done. Merrill must continue here, until his delusions have withered.

And then there is Rita. The administrative maneuver is simple and obvious: he will transfer her to South Webster, a women's hall. It was strange of him, perhaps a lapse of proper judgment, to allow her to remain the only woman assigned to Ingersoll. That is where she had wanted to be, Ingersoll housing her literary hero, Robert Lowell, and once the math genius John Nash as well. But Canon can no longer accommodate her fascination with poetry and genius; he has far greater concerns.

She did not look back, Canon thinks. When she fled Canon's office, she did not turn back to read Canon's face. Was this finality? She did not look back. She only, like Eve cast from the Garden, covered herself, worried with her own shame.

6

Two more rounds of ECT, another night in solitary. All a smeared perception of vague pain, the ECT performing a kind consideration, obliterating the memory of nearly all of it. It is two days later and, to his gratitude, Frederick has been restored to Ingersoll.

Whatever Canon's intentions, an unintended consequence: the jolt has proved clarifying. Whereas, just days before, Frederick had calmed into the psychic fog that often precedes the boundless dark plains of his depression, he is energetic once more. His body is exhausted from the discomforts, from the dosages and the anxiety, but back in his room, he perceives his heightened sensitivities returning. An evening bird coos out the window; the breeze of the ceiling fan touches his flesh; his roommate scribbles his strange notions. The soft cries of Marvin Foulds, four doors down, are no ignorable madhouse ambience now; the cries transfer through the night, enter Frederick as agony. He is returning to his energy, but now it is tainted. It is like the lights in Times Square: electric and luminous, but also smeared and tarnished. The filthy streaks more prominent by contrast.

Frederick is grateful for the familiar chemical veil of the evening's postprandial dosage settling over his awareness, is happy to surrender the lights and the tarnish, both growing more vivid. He is grateful that after his mind has been flushed with one hundred fifty volts, after he has spent forty-two hours in solitude, after he has spent two days considering that his time at Mayflower has again become interminable, that there in the Miltown and the darkness is his Katharine's face, saying something to him.

What? he tries to ask. *What's that?* She is muffled, but he knows what she has to say is urgent.

Louder, he says. *It's too noisy in here. I said it's too loud! It's too loud!*

7

Schultz's roommate has turned off the lights. Again, Schultz finds himself not tired, not in the slightest. How could he be? He is so close now.

. . .

When Schultz was eighteen, the world had begun to quiet again. Or else, at least, he had learned how to coexist with both human language and the other, truer language. The people of Bolbirosok smiled at his attempts at conversation, limited though they might have been. The other language continued to call to Schultz, but he knew that, if he wanted ever to capture the affection of Irit Mendelsohn, he couldn't come to her muttering in some unknown tongue. For love, he would have to speak as she spoke.

This was still Bolbirosok as it once was; there were rules in place for such things. Schultz knew that the only way to Irit was through her father. And so, young Schultz, in the summer before he would leave for the University of Vilnius, accepted Reb Menachem Mendelsohn's invitation, with the pretense of curiosity about his strange mode of Torah studies. More truly, he wanted only the proximity to Irit that an audience with Reb Mendelsohn would afford. To this end, Schultz found great success, for Irit was her father's daughter, their fascinations shared. Each time he visited the Mendelsohn house, he was led to the study, where father and daughter sat, marking Torah scrolls with red pens.

The Torah we have is not the True Torah, Reb Mendelsohn told Schultz. *The True Torah has been lost to us, but it is concealed within this text we are given. The True Torah would be illegible to us, written in the language that was lost at the fall of Babel. And it is up to us, the Chosen People, to resurrect it.*

Reb Mendelsohn and Irit showed Schultz how the two of them sought strange numerical connections between Hebrew characters, how they tried rolling around the Hebrew words in their mouths, seeking a revelation of the true lost language. *The*

True Torah, Reb Mendelsohn said, *is not just a text, or at least not as you would think of a text. The True Torah is the universe, or rather, the mold from which the universe was formed. The language of the True Torah is the opposite of how we think of language. Instead of words attached inadequately to the things they try and fail to describe, the things themselves—you, me, Irit, this house, Bolbirosok, this entire world—try and fail to grasp at this lost, true language. The division and incompleteness we feel is all things yearning for the words that made us, but are now lost to us. When this language is resurrected it will be* tikkun olam, *the universe will be healed.*

When Reb Mendelsohn and Irit told him these things, Schultz and the Mendelsohns feigned a purely intellectual curiosity; none discussed the subtext for the invitation, the language that spoke only to Schultz. They let that truth remain, like the true and lost language, just behind the words they actually spoke.

The parallels between Schultz's strange form of awareness and the language Mendelsohn described might be uncanny, but even to this day, even now as Schultz sits at his desk in the Mayflower Home, he does not know if the sounds that he discerns have any godly derivation, or whether they are simply a hidden truth of the physical universe, like Newton's laws of motion, or Einstein's relativity. He cannot know, but Schultz hopes that, once the full language is in place, once his work is complete, this truth will be obvious to him.

Still, Schultz sometimes now wishes that he had told Reb Mendelsohn the full truth about his private noises; likely the great scholar would have understood. Perhaps he would even have been proud to have his daughter become the wife of a man who was thus gifted. But at least Reb Mendelsohn had known another, more commonplace pride: that, after all their conversations about texts and language, Schultz had set off for the university, wanting only to study linguistics. A study that would lead him, in postgraduate years, to a thesis that would revolutionize the scholarly pursuit of linguistics. With Irit as his wife in Vilnius and, later, in Cambridge, Schultz performed research that upended standard linguistic practices, research that sought out that which is essential and common to all languages, that which all languages, and thus all human minds, require. Research that, Schultz now realizes, had merely been the groundwork to prepare the field, the world, for his true study. His study of the fundamental language, the one true language, to which all lesser languages, every tongue of the world, aspire and fail to reach.

It may be the fundamental language, but learning it is like learning any other. Once one builds a decent vocabulary and grasps the basic principles—the derivations, the conjugations, the syntax, and the grammar—sentences can start to come to the lips when they must. Just the other week in group therapy, for example, in an unexpected moment of passion, words came to Schultz and conveyed what they sought to convey. The words served their purpose fully, at least for a moment. For a moment, there was a part of her name, a part of her face, and she— Well, he cannot yet even allow himself to think it. What is important is not his personal needs. For example, Schultz knows people think him mad. He knows he is in a home for the mad, but those perceptions will soon enough be irrelevant when people realize the true scope of his work.

But Schultz does not delight in the importance assigned to him. He is merely an instrument, a sort of human radio tower. Simply, it took a man like Schultz, a man informed by the long tradition of his people's linguistic scholarship, a man who has lost everything and thus expects, like a true bodhisattva, absolutely nothing, to receive this truth.

. . .

All around him, each of the bricks of which Ingersoll House is constructed sighs in a low register, dully performing its task. Outside, each of the particles of the atmosphere—O_2, H_2O, CO_2—is a faint, unique soprano, each singing a sound like the English sound *ah,* which is further dividable into subparticles, some contributing to the *a,* some the *h,* all the way down to the vibrating wavelengths, at the base of everything, modulated into different notes, but all, as the Vedic mystics gleaned long before there was such a thing as a Jew, constituted of the sound *Om.* Beyond are planets and stars, galaxies birthing, galaxies dying. Schultz receives them all, coming so quickly in the diverse chorus he has no time to differentiate and transcribe them. They all come together to make a sound identical to the tiniest wavelength, *om,* but at mighty volume. *Om!*

Schultz turns from his journal, tilts his head toward the shut door, the sonic texture of night in this hospital. Somewhere, not so far away, a cigarette lighter speaks a sprightly *galooop.* A lighter that was carelessly dropped as a fired orderly (*kanoowa*) sucked an angry cigarette (*carooo*) in the main corridor of Ingersoll (*booloo*).

There is a hand, *drrrr,* as it lights the lighter with a cheery song in E-flat. *Eeee.* The hand holds the flame, *drrr-eee,* as it moves in a deliberate inward arc, toward the hospital gown, *drr-eee-who.* As it harmonizes with the flame's song, the hospital gown cries, *who-eeeee.* And then the sound of the body, a shriek cried out amid the low hum of night, rushing down the hall in flames, a guttural *cheeee* sound, gaining volume.

The sounds of the other men, startling awake. And the voice, which speaks that dreadful name, the inverse, the cancellation of *om*. It is a terrible voice, the familiar voice that is death, yet Schultz tries to remind himself that the death-voice may be a destroyer but it is also a creator. Birth and death: complex things, each neither entirely just birth nor entirely just death, each always holding the other. The death-voice is speaking, and so Schultz senses that the change is coming, that soon his project will reach its completion.

8

It isn't until well after they put out the fire—one of the night-shift orderlies rushing in with blankets—that the men can calm enough to comprehend what has happened. In the dissipating smoke that still lingers after the ambulance has left, the men of Ingersoll agree that it was no accident. The fact of what has happened is as astonishing as it is obvious: Marvin Foulds, the celebrated creator of Mango Diablo, the Admiral, Guy DeVille, and so many others, has invented yet another identity, has put on a new costume and a new persona, when his old wardrobe was denied him. Out of a forced hospital gown and a dropped lighter, he has made a costume of fire. Out of the ashes of the hospital that Mayflower had just recently been, the lost hospital that had done so much to foster his creative development, Marvin has risen in his most daring persona yet. The Phoenix. The avenger. Marvin may have had a short run in this particular role, the costume may have been extinguished within moments of its creation, but the men have seen the Phoenix, just as Schultz has heard its name. In the ammoniated linoleum halls of Canon's Mayflower, a sound, a notion, the principle of entropy performed. The Phoenix may be extinguished, but what had birthed it will only continue to spread, as fire.

THAT WAS

KATHARINE

1

It is Columbus Day, 1962, and my grandmother is back at Echo Cottage, pulling the horsehair mattresses from the upstairs sleeping porch to the front bedroom, to protect them from the winter. This weekend will be their last at Echo for the year, and Katharine has a list of such chores to complete. In past years, they have hired a woman from town to help with these tasks, but with Frederick at Mayflower, her family's savings have dwindled to alarming balances, and so she must do all this by herself. Katharine moves quickly to check off her list, rushing to return to her daughters and her cousins, out sailing the whitecapped lake on the *Pea-quod,* the aging family boat, a relic of a more prosperous time.

Between the screen windows of the sleeping porch and the vast wind-furred plain of the lake is a curtain of autumn, a riotous pointillism of leaves. It is a cliché, Katharine knows, to talk of how autumn is her favorite season, and yet, this weekend, she often finds herself spontaneously rhapsodizing about the fall. It is perhaps also a cliché to speak of a figurative autumn, how things become most beautiful just before they end. Still, Katharine cannot help but think that the atmosphere along Barvel Bay, this weekend, is like that too: a temporary revival of summer revelry, heightened and giddy in the autumn chill, the knowledge this will be the last time at Winnipesaukee for a long while.

A temporary revival, an autumnal blush to distract from the daylight's dimming. Almost daily now, she and her father fight about money. Her relatives, all those men who were so confident in Mayflower on that night now nearly four months ago, who that night pledged their allegiance to Katharine and to Frederick's therapy, seem to have swayed to the perspective of Katharine's father. Just this morning, Lieutenant General Pointer and George Carlyle came to the porch, where Katharine and her father argued the possibility of Frederick's transfer to a cheaper hospital, and the two men gently bolstered her father's thesis.

Frederick seems no closer to a return; her father seems only days away from refusing all payment; her daughters have begun frequently to ask, in more worried tones, when their father will return. A lovely weekend now, but it won't hold.

As she removes and folds sheets, Katharine thinks of another figurative autumn. She thinks of that one night in Boston, a year after she and her great teenage love, Lars Jensen, had split up. That night, with no letter or telephone call to prepare her for his visit, Lars presented himself at her door. It was the last time they would be together, but in the other sense of the word *together,* it was also the first. Futureless, that night, they allowed themselves new freedoms.

But, as it has turned out, they were not then futureless together, not entirely.

Katharine has a secret. Four weeks ago, in mid-September, Lars Jensen phoned her. Lars Jensen, to whom she had given all of herself, just once. One day, while the girls were at school, the phone had rung, and she had lifted it to hear the voice of a man so distant from this life she has made, he had come nearly to seem abstract, only a character from a film she had once seen.

Had Lars, now living two hours away in Exeter, somehow

learned of her situation? Lars called just as she had become truly desperate, as she no longer could imagine an escape from her present circumstance, as she had begun to comprehend that they were now one of those failed families about whom gossip filled every Graveton living room. He called her, and she talked. He asked for nothing, and listened. She told herself, many times during that two-hour conversation, not to give away too much. And yet, she told him everything: her foiled ambitions, her fears for her daughters, her financial despair. She even told him about Frederick, everything about Frederick. In return, Lars offered little of his own story. *Things aren't working out with Anna,* he said glibly, *but at least work is keeping me stable, and that couldn't be going better.*

But, behind his few words, was he offering what Katharine believed he was offering? Lars was now one of Exeter's three town lawyers, with modest wealth and modest aspirations. Set against Frederick's grand ambitions and vertiginous risings and fallings, Lars's stable little life seemed to Katharine something out of a storybook, how a child might imagine adulthood, before adulthood comes with its revelation of the inevitability of dissatisfaction. Would it be possible, she wondered abstractly—but not seriously, not really—for her simply to make a decision, and then move her family into that fable life?

After their initial conversation, she made excuses for herself whenever he called, citing errands to be run, food on the stove, imminent plans with her girlfriends. But then, one afternoon when her daughters were at school, she simply let herself talk once more, beginning a surreptitious communication that has come at nearly regular intervals—once or twice a week—for the last four weeks.

Katharine knows that she mustn't allow herself more fantasies. And she must be her own now, not Frederick's and certainly not Lars's. But why, then, has she continued this clandestine conversation? Maybe, Katharine thinks, she continues with these secret conversations not because of the appeal of Lars but because of the appeal of the secret itself. Katharine has for so long held back the truth of Frederick, from friends and family, or at least she has tried so hard to hold it back, to gather that darkness to her, force it inside of her, and then emit only rosy light. But now Katharine has a secret of her own. It is a small thing, perhaps ultimately insignificant, but it holds a power that is hers.

Katharine has made a life of accommodating, but now it is time for others to accommodate her. Katharine knows that, in Exeter, Lars daily waits for her next call. How is it possible that this somehow makes her feel guilty, some unspoken obligation she feels to this man who likely is trying to seduce her away from her husband? Katharine tells herself: *he can wait.*

2

Katharine is in her closet now, slipping the contents of a fresh package of mothballs into the pockets of her jackets. When she has finished, she pauses in the wooden space of her bedroom, considering what chore she will do next. Standing there, Katharine eyes the sterling silver trifold frame, an anniversary gift from Frederick, that rests upon her dresser. She has passed by these pictures hundreds of times, as just another object. But now, closing the cottage for the winter, a prefigurative wintry longing for Echo Cottage and its objects compels her to lift the frame and examine the photographs that her husband chose to display in commemoration of the first fifteen years of their marriage.

The left panel holds the picture of Frederick from his naval academy, dressed in uniform, his gaze romantic and lucid, an image that seemed, in a terrible way when he first gave it to her, to belong to an already dead sailor. The panel to the right displays the photo of the girls they had taken last year, all in three-quarters profile, lined up by age and so also by height, a staircase to adulthood: giggling Jillian, blushing Louise, timid Susie, imperious Rebecca. And between the photos of her husband and her children is the picture of Katharine that Frederick loves most. Katharine, dressed in her pilose black fur coat in Boston, during that brief gap between her childhood and Frederick. Katharine can easily forget that there was that time. That woman, for those years in Boston; once that was she. The image can seem vain and self-aggrandizing now, this photograph of Katharine dressed in fur, made up and lit for a future belonging to Ingrid Bergman, when she has only become another anxious housewife, puttering about in her chores.

But that was Katharine. She was, very briefly, neither cheery daughter nor placating mother. She was a desirable young woman named Katharine Mead, who lived in a city, and traveled to other cities, advising department stores on fashion. She was courted, constantly. At dances and at pubs and even at restaurants, men presented themselves to her. It had seemed to her then that she was just coming into an immense power. Marriage, career, and family, when it came: it would all be hers, to make of it whatever she liked. But Katharine sees clearly now that she misunderstood. She mistook the power of her marriageability for a much greater power. That time, it has turned out, was in fact her time of greatest power. An ellipsis in her transformation from placated to placater. The photograph may seem vain now, but Katharine reminds herself this is not a picture of her, but a picture of another Katharine, one who never quite came to be. Katharine decides to take the photograph with her back to Graveton.

Katharine turns the trifold onto its face, then unfastens the copper clasps that hold the backing in place. She removes the wooden slat and is momentarily stunned. It is like when she once happened upon Bea Davis, a girlfriend from her childhood in Concord, now a young woman walking the streets of Boston among the crowds. Or it is like the moment she lifted just another ringing phone to hear the voice of Lars Jensen. A reminder that time, which can seem only to disperse and erase, also holds its continuities. For there, on the back of the picture, is her husband's handwriting. A note dated June 4, 1944, which she has never seen before.

This, then, had been the picture of Katharine that Frederick had taken with him to sea. Two days before D-Day, as Frederick waited on his ship for the orders to battle to come, he had written:

*[The only true friend, the only trustworthy companion, and the only real
woman I have ever known. If all the world were like you darling wars
would cease and this separation would be unnecessary. I love you above all
else sweetheart, always.*

June 4, 1944]

But he had never shown this to her. Why? Maybe he never
really intended it to be read; maybe it was just something he
scrawled in a panic that night, a letter to be returned to her in
the event of his death.

Frederick had been a young man in love then, as she had been
a young woman in love. Across great distances, they had loved
and mourned notions of each other. Frederick had fantasized to
a fantasy of Katharine about another world, in which their separation was not necessary. They could not then have known that
to love each other in the way they imagined required that distance. On his night-shift watch, in the ocean of a world about to
explode, what else did he have but this romantic, false vision?
What choice but to believe in it?

Katharine lowers the image of herself to her thigh and looks
at the picture that stands next to the triptych on the dresser, a
framed photograph of their wedding day. Still dressed in his uniform, arm in arm with his bride beneath a canopy of swords his
fellow soldiers have drawn, Frederick is nearly skeletal from the
strange anorexic condition that he was never quite able to explain to her. But from the caverns of his eye sockets, Frederick's
gaze glistens, as he looks out at—what? The photographer, of
course, but also—it being their wedding day—the future, which
seemed so certain that day, their history safely sealed away beyond what they would build with their unstinting will and de-

liberate consideration. In the pilgrim tradition of New England, together they would settle in the new land of their new lives; together they would create a life, in the way he imagined that artists create their art, coming from them and thus clarifying them.

Frederick had returned early from his battleship and attempted to realize an only slightly compromised version of his fantasy, an entire world spun around Katharine, but still there was war.

Katharine lifts the photo of herself, and looks at it again. On the front is the image of a glamoured young woman, unclaimed and certain that her greatest powers were still in her future. On the other side is what Frederick had once written to his idea of Katharine, who would realize his utopian vision. Katharine replaces the picture in its spot between her husband and her children. She makes a promise to herself. She will wait until one week from today, and, if she still can't bear it, she will call Lars and agree to see him. And then Katharine goes downstairs to empty the cabinets of their perishables.

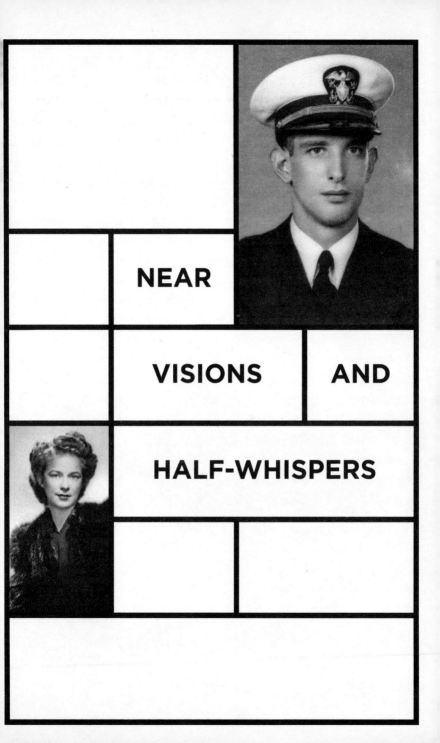

NEAR

VISIONS AND

HALF-WHISPERS

1

In his room at the Mayflower Home, my grandfather writes:

BOOK IDEA: A children's story, featuring a lovable Christian bear, punningly named "Gladly, the Cross-Eyed Bear," who will teach children moral lessons. Merchandising possibilities endless.

PATENT IDEA: Develop and perfect means by which fibrous paper product waste may be rendered into blankets. Perhaps consider seeking independent investment, as those fools at White Paper will likely be incapable of recognizing the lucrative possibilities.

ESSAY IDEA: A CASE STUDY IN HOW GENIUS IS RARELY RECOGNIZED IN ITS TIME, OR: THE BRASS OF THE WHITE PAPER COMPANY CAN GO FUCK THEMSELVES ON A RUSTY FENCE POST.

In the early evening outside, the trees absorb the autumn in effusive tones. High above the slate roofs and the aesthetic arbosphere of Madhouse Hill, Canada geese disgustedly honk in southward Vs, as if pointing out the direction in which the sane should flee the coming winter. In the city that spreads from Belmont to the sea, chimney sweeps stroll from house to house, their eyes peering luminously through their charcoal dustings, their pockets stuffed with the annual glut. In the northern suburbs, store-window artists obsess over the depictions of bountiful cornucopias and chubby turkeys they paint onto the facades of grocery stores. Cycling among all, carrying bits of one scene to the next, is the constant presence of the autumnal wind. The wind emptying treetops, whipping the surface of Boston Harbor into an angry script, rattling the grated windows of Ingersoll House.

And there is my grandfather, in whom this gale seems unimpeded by the walls that separate him from the outdoors. A thought whips through him, then another and another, each enlivening, thrilling, but few finding time to settle. His mind, like his daughters in their front yard two hundred miles to the north, trying to grasp at the rush of red maple leaves racing by.

TO REMEMBER: the next time that lethargy comes, that someday I will again feel this way.

A QUESTION FOR KATHARINE (SAVE FOR NEXT ARGUMENT): Would not the world and I suffer immeasurable loss for my capitulation to "sanity"?

TO CONSIDER: Why my ascension to this state coincides with everything that has happened. Canon and Rita. The ECT. Marvin. Does this energy in some way require that darkness?

A CAREER ALTERNATIVE: Given my education, military background, and cleverness with puzzles, certainly the Central Intelligence Agency could use a man like me. How does one apply? A résumé delivered via Morse code, with a flashlight pointed at the director's office?

Perhaps Frederick is right; perhaps the grim events of the last few days, like leaden storm clouds, have generated this electricity. But this heightening is also undoubtedly an effect of the Miltown that Frederick has, this evening, managed to evade. In any one of the previous ninety-six days of the Canon administration, the thought of escaping any dosage would have been certifiable delusion. But the wind that has blown forth since the night Marvin made of his gown a fiery costume seems to have rushed through the halls of Mayflower in subtler forms, tousling the staff and its protocols. The last few days have reminded all who have been here long enough to remember of the vaguely anarchic gap between the Wallace and Canon administrations.

Despite the denials of the staff, by noon of the day after Marvin's self-immolation, the news had spread beyond Ingersoll House, prompting the defiant, ceaseless questions of the women of South Webster, the teenagers of North Webster and South House. The men of Ingersoll speculated it was even possible that the local news would describe the outcome of Marvin's incendiary sprint, but no television is to be tuned to a news report in the wake of any catastrophe, local or worldwide, to avoid needlessly upsetting the patients. However, whether or not word of Mayflower's famous patient setting himself aflame has yet spread beyond campus, at the top of Madhouse Hill, it is the only news.

Tell us where he is!

Who? the Crew Crew reply.

Fucking Marvin, you dingbat! Marvin Foulds. Marvin!

The Crew Crew boys deny any knowledge, refuse any question, as they witness a name metamorphose into a rallying cry.

A mental hospital, Canon had told his new orderlies and nurses in their courses of orientation, *is a live wire. Staff unity is the grounding. Think of psychosis as a great charge, at all times running, even if the cables appear still. If we do not act as one, the cable snaps free and shoots that electricity everywhere.*

And then, Canon had always said with the theatrical flourish he had learned to affect over a career of touring academic conventions, *there's fire.*

And then there's fire, he had said, exactly in those words, not knowing their prophecy.

Poor, overwhelmed, scholarly Canon. Well-intentioned, ambitious Canon, only months after his ascension to the high office, already providing another case study to support his hypothesis. For it was Canon himself, the great unifier, who did not report to work the morning after Marvin's fiery act. His wife simply phoned the hospital, cited her husband's illness, and accepted no more of the staff's feverish calls. Could Canon, the staff (and soon the patients) wondered, possibly have been broken so simply?

Whatever Canon's reasons, in his absence, the psychotic current surged indeed.

· · ·

Frederick writes, *AN OBSERVATION: So often a thing makes more of itself. Love begets love, and cruelty engenders more cruelty. Chaos, once opened, births chaos.*

· · ·

Just after the patients sat down to dinner this evening, a proper food fight broke out among the girls of South House, cottage cheese splattering over suicide scars, green beans tangling in the mess of schizophrenic hair, chocolate-covered borderlines. The Crew Crew, of course, intervened. They intervened, but—perhaps just faintly—they too seemed, for the first time, receptive to the revelry of rebellion. They intervened, but slowly. The Crew Crew broke the girls apart, but did not bother to stifle their own laughter. More than once, they stood back and watched an anorexic take a pudding to the face.

Later, in the calm that followed this gastronomical conflagration, the men and women lined up, as every night, for the evening's medication, some literally itching with anticipation, some, like Frederick, attempting the normal evasions.

Frederick Merrill, the dispensary nurse said in her stenographer voice. To the nurse, the exchange appeared unremarkable: Frederick extending his hand, the nurse extending the little paper cup containing the tablets, Frederick turning to the two Crew Crew boys responsible for ensuring that each patient swallowed, as instructed.

C'mon, fellas. How about one night off? I just need to get my head straight.

What are you whining about? one of the boys said. *You know how much those blue ones go for on the street?*

The street, Frederick thought. These boys, he knew, had gone straight from their prefabricated suburban comforts to their fraternity houses. *What street would that be?* he wanted to ask. *Shady Elm?* But then Frederick relinquished his unspoken contempt as he sensed an opening. And why not try?

Frederick did not make the offer, at least not in words. If spoken, he knew they would refuse it. He simply pressed the cup's lip in with his thumb and raised the cup to his mouth, the pills catching on the indentation. Then he crumpled the cup, handed it back to the Crew Crew boys, who inspected Frederick's empty mouth. As Frederick walked away, he could hear the beginning of the Crew Crew's protest that did not materialize. In the end, the boys played it sly, as did their new man on the inside.

OBVIOUS: Much more likely than supposed illness, or even the trauma of Marvin's near (successful?) suicide, it is anxiety for Rita that keeps Canon at home.

IMPOSSIBLE: Could Rita actually lust after that flabby blowhard? Could she love Canon? But then why else would she touch him?

PATENT IDEA: Identify and isolate whatever scent certain hoary men must exude to attract young women such as Rita. Bottle and sell in department stores. (Or maybe not—undoubtedly would make me wealthy, but would likely unleash worldwide anarchy.)

As he dashes off his thoughts, my grandfather, for the first time in months, receives the warm radiance of himself. The truer form of himself, both much older and much younger than the middle-aged Frederick in his pajamas, who so often just dawdles there, thoughtlessly obstructing the true Frederick's way into the world. The truer Frederick now speaks from someplace outside the ordinary Frederick's familiar self-silencing iteration of burdensome effort answered with burdensome scrutiny. Before he knows it, Frederick is even performing that rare act, attempting to converse with his roommate.

I feel a bit like you tonight, Frederick says. *I feel like I can finally focus.*

It's the trick you pull with the pills, Schultz replies.

How do you know?

This is the only explanation, Schultz says. *I see it in your eyes, yes? Simple as the color.*

Ha, I suppose— Frederick begins. *But those pills never seem to have any effect on you.*

Of course not, Schultz replies with a grin. *A Jew knows how to conceal.*

Really? But how?

Just before the war, toothpaste we couldn't so easily get. Oy, to tell you the pain in my gums.

Schultz then performs a vaguely revolting trick. He widens his mouth, as if to make way for the passage of a mighty vowel, and shoves his fingers into his palate, freeing the false teeth Frederick never knew he had.

When hinally we come to America, all my top teesh shey pull, Schultz says, the words muddled without the sonic contribution of upper teeth. *Harhfard buysh me denturesh hhit for a king.*

Here Schultz smiles broadly. Frederick now considers that this aspect of his face—his linear, eggshell teeth—is perhaps what lends him a half-credibility denied the other schizophrenics. Toothless, Schultz seems a madman indeed.

Only, shere wash one flaw. Or, better to shay, one idioshyncrashy. Usually I wait until you leaf or shleep to remofe it, but now we are broshersh is shecretsh, nu?

Now Schultz flips his false teeth, revealing a small cavity within, just perfectly cradling two pills. Schultz taps the dentures, and the pills tumble into his palm. He looks at them quizzically.

Wish theesh pillsh, never can I hhocus. And to hhocus, hish ish she mosht important shing of all.

But what do you do with them all?

Ah, much eashier shish wash in she old howsh. Here, I haff had to improfishe, yesh?

Schultz restores his upper teeth and smiles a sane, proud smile. He makes a mock-shushing gesture and presses one palm to the leg of his desk, the other to the surface, and the two pieces separate, just a few inches, enough to reveal the hollow shaft of one of the table's steel legs.

Frederick approaches Schultz's desk, peers into the hollow to discover a masterwork of concealment. In cheery pharmaceutical colors, the leg is filled nearly to the top. Hundreds of pills. Within Mayflower's nascent anarchy, pills are already an appreciating currency, and here is an unwanted fortune.

Soon, I must find some way to dispose, Schultz says with a laugh and knocks on the table. *Or else, how to get into these other legs.*

2

Generally, in the first months of the new administration, Canon's staff has successfully concealed potentially disruptive news from the patients. Often, reports that would have been of no small interest—suicidal gestures, sexual congress, narcotics found in staff offices—were kept entirely from patients, even from most of the staff. Though two days have passed since Marvin Foulds's suicide attempt, and the psychiatrist in chief has yet to return, the structures he established, though besieged, are still in place. Once more, Canon's echelons, like Schultz with his desk, manage a major feat of concealment.

For there has been another suicide attempt, a fact that will be kept entirely from the men of Ingersoll, the women of South Webster, the girls of South House. But perhaps *suicide attempt* is too certain a term for what has occurred. It is perhaps the ineffectual nature of this particular gesture that makes it seem no compelling news to spread. Certainly, it seems to the few who learn of the attempt that the boy—one of the new admissions to North Webster—had meant to fail with such a slapdash act. Either he meant to fail, they believe, or else he had resolved to make his quietus so suddenly that he had not time to devise a halfway decent scheme.

A passing motorist found the boy, apparently unconscious, in a tangle of bedsheets, with which he had attempted to hang himself from the high oak post of the elaborate road sign for the Mayflower Home for the Mentally Ill, down on Mill Street. The boy had failed in his attempt, but his successful absconding down the hill, suicidal linens in hand, is perhaps the most salient portent yet of the dangerously accumulating chaos.

The boy had remained conscious for the entire episode. Perhaps wanting only to taste death's flavorlessness, he simply lay there, beneath the sign, within the sheets, trying not to move or breathe.

He looked enviously up at the trees, displaying their modest late season brilliance against the pitiless late afternoon light. *I could be happy right here,* he thought. *I could be a tree, a shrub, a blade of grass. It might feel quite nice to have people walk through me, to watch them drive past, all day long. Maybe what I want is not to die. Maybe what I want is only not to be human.* He shut his eyes tightly and tried to will his flesh to grow roots.

The possibility of his dendriform future, however, was soon disrupted. Squad cars and ambulances, responding to the motorist's call, split the grim quiet of the afternoon with their manic squawking, bearing the boy away, at emergency speed, denying him his wish of stillness. *Put me down,* the boy requested, repeatedly and to no avail. *Please. Just leave me at the side of the road.*

3

When Mass General phones Mayflower, the receptionist transfers the call to Higgins, who thanks the presiding emergency room doctor. Then Higgins places the phone on its receiver, leaves his office, swiftly traverses the campus, and passes through the three doors of South Webster to find Rita. Rita is standing in the common area of the women's ward, discussing one of her new patients' plans to write an opera. Rita excuses herself and walks outside with the doctor to hear his news.

As Higgins explains what has happened, Rita wonders what it might suggest that, in Canon's absence, Higgins has sought her out first. Undoubtedly, the staff has seen Rita talking to Canon with an unrivaled intimacy and frequency. Is it simply that Higgins thinks she has the boss's ear? By her proximity to the psychiatrist in chief, has she become the de facto number two, her response to a situation more determinative than that of Dr. Higgins, the de jure number two? And might this unspoken hierarchical arrangement imply that they know?

Maybe that would be for the best; the thought is dizzying and darkly thrilling. So many times, in the on-and-off two years—*how, my god, two years already?*—of their affair, Rita has imagined it, the freedom to at last relinquish the shameful secrecy that Canon and she have held tightly to themselves.

It is likely, she thinks, that there are whispers, whiffs of suspicion. She and Canon, hardly able to speak of their situation between themselves, have told no one. But there are other ways in which such knowledge transfers; lovers exude some hormonal plume, received by others in a place before language. Something as felt as her affair with Canon cannot be contained endlessly, can it?

Rita tries to calm Higgins, but he continues to fidget, continues to clutch at his hair, seems to be beyond her words. A tide of red rises radially from the rosy protuberance of his nose, as if Higgins's nose is a thing to which his face has become suddenly allergic. Rita senses, from her months spent overseeing similarly agitated men, that simply he needs to be touched. She lays one hand on the old doctor's shoulder, rubs the soft flesh of what was once a bicep, tells Higgins that she has to go find Canon. And that, in the meanwhile, they must try to keep this news to themselves.

We can be many things, Rita thinks. A twenty-four-year-old girl, with little faith in modern psychiatry, can suddenly become the chief authority at the nation's premier mental hospital.

Perhaps, she has sometimes thought, she is capable in this hospital, in this position, because she does not want it, has never aspired to it. Unbothered by ambition or by possible censure, she is lucid.

But she isn't just here for Albert, she thinks now, as she will still believe, years from now. Though, of course, it had been Albert Canon who first seduced her into the profession, flattering her with his inordinate attention in his abnormal psychology course, which she had signed up for simply to fulfill a curriculum requirement at Radcliffe. One day, in the third week of the semester, Albert had asked her to stay after class to discuss the first paper she had turned in. Rita had braced for his criticisms, but as soon as her classmates left, Albert spoke to her in an excited whisper, lauding her brilliance, asking her if she had considered psychology as a career. As she warmed to his flattery, Albert's compliments grew hyperbolic; he proclaimed the loss to the field of psychology should she choose a different career.

As that summer turned to fall, her after-class meetings with Albert became more frequent and more impassioned. She felt herself become pliable to his visions for her.

Albert, making a display of intellectual worship, excitedly received whatever came from her lips as if she perpetually revealed the hidden truths others had spent entire careers seeking but never finding. When, for example, Rita spoke of her tendency to blame others for her own failures, while seeing others' failures as no one's fault but their own, Albert remarked that she had just deduced one of the basic principles of social cognition, which had taken experimental psychologists years to describe. When Rita told Albert of her own inconsistencies, of her inability to see herself as she saw others, in any singular way, he told her of the exciting new theories of identity construction, and how her unique perspective could spur major theoretical advances, if she chose to apply herself in that field. Albert turned her abstract, ambivalent notions into his certainties: a great comfort to Rita, who at twenty-two had felt ambivalent about nearly everything.

Ambivalence: Rita felt forces at all times pulling her in their contrapuntal directions, had always experienced argument and counterargument in simultaneity, had seemed always to want everything: to be pure and base, to make love to boys and to resist all boys; to join up with the communists, the anarchists, and also to deliver tirades on the absurdity of children of comfort and privilege dabbling in communism and anarchy. She wanted to impress her practical parents with a practical application of her degree and become a lawyer; she wanted to shrug off all the expectations of her parents and move to Morocco to write poetry. She wanted to marry young, raise a family, prosper in the common ways; she craved absolute solitude, life nearest the bone, to sort things out for herself.

Often, she wondered how some of her classmates could speak of their futures with such certainty. She wondered if anyone actually experienced such certainty or if all lives were merely the midpoints between opposing impulses, carried forward.

And then there was Albert. Not only certain, but certain about all the things she was not. Certain, in fact, about her uncertainty. *This uncertainty you always tell me about,* he said, half-lover, half-therapist, *this fear of being no one. What you can't see, what is abundantly clear to me, is that this is simply the burden of a receptive and thoughtful intelligence. It is precisely this ability to see all the angles that will make you one of our most brilliant therapists.*

Our most brilliant therapists, Albert had said, as if he were on the ruling council of some exalted society.

But now two years have passed, and for all the grand visions Albert has presented her, Rita knows his limitations as plainly as she knows the coarseness of his hands, the hairs that sprout from his shoulders. For example, despite his dumbly persistent claims to the contrary, Rita knows Albert will never leave his wife, will never make his love for Rita public. Not for lack of love for Rita, or for any moralistic belief in the inviolable bonds of marriage. And certainly not out of any great sense of devotion to his wife. Simply, Albert would never make public this or any secret that might jeopardize his position, embarrass him, or—worst of all—thwart his ambitions.

Over time, Rita's tenderness for Albert has become rather the inverse of when they first began two years ago. When Albert speaks to her now, with all his familiar ambitions and certainty, it strikes Rita as not unlike a little boy dreaming of becoming a professional athlete or a superhero: in its optimism, its grandiosity, holding a kind of tender purity. But it isn't enough, this tenderness, for her to continue her affair, for her to continue in the strange position she has never felt fit her.

No, the truth is she is fascinated by something else, what psychiatry seeks to eliminate. Why could some people endure wars, famines, holocausts, while others lost their sanity in a comfortable world in which people spoke things that were not always true? Why, for some, does plain silence provoke such horror that profound, intricate hallucinations are required to compensate? And why, too, are poets so often mad?

Poetry, Rita wrote in her journal last week, *is Promethean. Madness is the fire poetry brings back to earth.*

Rita feels close to something essential about madness and about herself, about madness and something that madness conceals.

An intimacy with chaos: not just in her position, but in her affair as well. Something compulsive in her closeness to catastrophe is why she has allowed herself to continue with this man, who occasionally, as now, repels her.

Repels her. When Frederick came into the office and found the two of them, Rita could not quite read Frederick's face, silhouetted against the hallway light, but she projected into that dark oval her own repulsion, received the shame of the scene through his imagined eyes. And, in the days that have followed, that shame has only deepened. Canon had not come to find her after she ran from his office, had not told her himself of her transfer to the women's ward. He had let the orders come through Higgins, as if she were any other employee. The coward.

And, though Rita does not know the extent of it, does not

know that Canon ordered not one but three sessions of ECT for Frederick, this far more dastardly act does not provoke fury, as does her transfer. Simply, she is ashamed, for her part in what has happened to Frederick, for her relationship with a man capable of such actions. Her shame of Canon's cowardice conflating with the shame of her affair; many times she has wanted to go to Frederick, in Ingersoll, and plead with him to forgive her. But what would she say? It isn't a rational thing, an entirely explainable thing, this affair, her need to remain here. Her need, most shameful of all, for Canon. Repulsion, but also—no denying it—need: two years (*my god!*) of her ambivalence, incarnate.

But there are more important considerations now. In the two days Canon has been gone, something has ruptured within Mayflower. It began with the first true horror she has known here. That night, one of the most fascinating, most tormented, and kindest of the Ingersoll men had found a lighter and done to himself something impossible to consider.

(Was it only a coincidence it had happened just after she had been transferred off Ingersoll? Might Canon be right, at least in this regard, that the slightest disruption in care and authority can be devastating to patients?)

And though Marvin was taken, as per protocol, to Mass General, though the staff, as per protocol, have denied and obfuscated, she has witnessed the chaos pushing at the seams Canon so diligently tried to sew together with the sutures of his protocols. And now this, another suicide attempt, if halfhearted. Herself, the affair, Frederick, and her shame aside, Mayflower needs its psychiatrist in chief.

Rita knows, so well, Canon's weaknesses. She knows, for example, that in Canon's shame over Frederick's discovery, in the dark outcomes of his childish overreactions, he is simply waiting there, at home, for his mistress to come and convince him of how absolutely necessary he is.

4

Do you think there's anything you could have done differently?

What are you implying, exactly?

Nothing, I just wondered if you felt you should have done anything differently.

Of course not. Of course not! What could I have done? Differently? Differently? How differently?

Albert, Lara Canon said, already weary of the conversation. She is always so weary, his wife. Always so uncaring. Sometimes, though he'd never say it aloud and certainly never act upon it, Canon shames himself with a sudden impulse to shake her by the shoulders, strike her until she cares.

I was merely trying to suggest, Lara said, with the mock-formality she dons at any of Canon's emotional outbursts, as if all this might be recorded for later referral in a court of law—this, he has thought, can't be too far from her mind—*I was merely trying to suggest that if you could not have done anything differently, then you have no cause for regret.*

Regret? It's not regret. I saw something horrific the other night, Lara. Something incomprehensibly bad. I am disturbed, dear. Regret!

Poor dear, she said, as if her husband were complaining about any other rough day at the office: an insubordinate orderly, difficulty finding enough financing for the new parking lot. Why couldn't she understand? He had gone to the hospital and seen one of his patients with his face tattered, the flesh dangling and seared, still smelling of its own cooking. *Poor dear!*

The next morning, after dressing for tennis and making the boys pancakes, Lara came upstairs to discover her husband, awake but shiftless, still in bed.

Aren't you going to work? she asked.

How can I? Canon said. *His face. Christ, Lara, his face!*

But haven't you seen terrible things before? Lara countered. *In the war?*

Canon sometimes forgets this, the embellishments he has made to his war stories. Yes, he had been sent to Europe as he has claimed, but he never left England, never left the small room in which he evaluated soldiers. In that room, Canon had been responsible for ensuring midlevel officers were ready for combat, had been responsible for little more than administering a set of standardized tests of psychological well-being. He had, in truth, been little more than a nurse, making his routine evaluations just as the other nurses probed, measured, and inoculated the new recruits before combat. He had not, as he has since claimed, worked with the soldiers just back from the front, traumatized with stories that *made all our normal frustrations seem irrelevant.* In the story he had told his wife in their early courtship—he had wanted only to impress her in the moment; he had not then considered he'd have to live with these fabrications forever—he had been an angelic figure, striding ruined battlefields, leading men lost in their tenebrous terror back up to daylight.

Well, Lara said. *If you aren't going to work anymore, you'll have to start helping out around here.* Then Canon's wife looked to the apron she held in her fist, tossed it to the traumatized doctor, and informed him that today she was going to teach him how to knead meat loaf.

To his own surprise, Canon accepted her orders, like a child receiving his mother's punishments. Later that afternoon, suffering what he had told Lara *could well be a trauma-induced minor psychotic episode,* he was made to pick the boys up from soccer practice, circumnavigating his asylum, perched over Belmont. When he returned home, he insisted no one answer the phone that periodically rang, explaining he was simply not ready to return, not yet. And then dinner passed; even the kids did not ask any questions, even when he mustered a tear.

Canon will only consider much later that likely he accepted all of these indignities as penance for shame. He was, after all, a man who had been discovered in an affair, if only by a patient.

At the end of the dinner, citing the results of a recent physical examination, Canon's wife did not allow him to have dessert.

And so there he is now, the great reformer of the Mayflower Home, brooding as he sits on the floor with his kids, while the new inductees to the Mickey Mouse Club name themselves on the television.

Poor Canon. Perhaps it is true that he exaggerates his trauma only as a compensation for his shame. But still, there had been Marvin's face, slick with ash and blood, confronting Canon. And then there had been the call from Clarence Winthrop, chair of Mayflower's board of directors, panicked at the prospect of the home's most famous case study coming to a fiery end so soon after the board had installed Canon to Mayflower's highest office.

Winthrop and his board. Canon knows well, from a long career of ascendancy in academe, what is at stake for these men. Given the prominence of the family names under Mayflower's care, poor stewardship from the board could yield disastrous outcomes for the academic and political futures of its members. Marvin Foulds had not died, but the closeness of it was enough to require Canon to spend a perspiring hour talking Winthrop down from an emergency meeting of the board. It is as simple as that, Canon thinks. One more dropped lighter, one more purloined blade, and the board members could ruin Canon's career in a flailing attempt to rescue their own.

The doorbell rings. Canon calls to his wife that he will answer it.

5

And there she is. At first he panics to find his mistress on his doorstep, assuming she has come for a reckoning, now that they have been witnessed. Sometimes, he thrills and terrifies himself by imagining her words to his wife. *I was a student of his, Mrs. Canon, and at first I craved only his mind. But at some point the craving turned into something else, bigger, and I believe he took advantage of it. I know this is terrible for you and your family, but I thought you should know, Mrs. Canon, that I love him, that I—*

Where have you been? Rita says.

I needed some time away. That's all. You didn't see it, Rita. It was the most terrible thing I've ever—

Canon prides himself on the assiduousness of his considerations of all possible reactions, interpretations, and passions. But now, facing his mistress in front of his house, the possibility of a motive far truer than the one he has claimed to his wife and now to Rita strikes Canon with a magnitude typically reserved for divine revelation. Simply, Canon has been afraid, is afraid now, of what Rita will say to him next.

Something has happened, she tells him.

It was always a shameful thing, all that secrecy, all that dissembling, but now that this shame has been acknowledged by another, if only a patient, it will become unbearable. She will leave. For what is there to hold her to him? These last months, he knows they both have discerned a fading. The act itself, never unsatisfying, has just recently begun to feel borderline perfunctory. *Perhaps it's for the best,* he has tried to tell himself. After all, how many times has he resolved to end it? Better to live, as he instructs his patients, at the surface: exposed, all needs spoken of directly and publicly. Better to end it, of course, and to live honestly. And yet, to contemplate a future without Rita—the thought sparks love's opposite, kindles dread.

I know, Canon says. *I know. But I don't see why it necessarily has to change anything. I mean this, thing, we have.*

Not that, Rita says. *Something else.*

As she explains what has happened, Canon sees Rita through a strange lens, the way certain moments, such as Marvin Foulds's face the other night, can appear as if photographed, as if Canon is a small boy glimpsing a picture book depicting his potential future. She is beautiful, in this heightened moment. *They need you,* she says.

It's only been two days, she continues, *and look what's happened.*

This loss, this fading, can be overcome. But first he must identify the source of the bleeding, before he can stanch the loss of passion. Being discovered by Frederick is only an obstacle; the usband in the alleyway behind the house, carrying on a rsation with the dumpster rats. Under advice from the rd counselors, Irit drove her husband to Mayflower. And during the week of observation his doctor recommended, eft. Irit simply took her husband's place in his plans. With- a word to Schultz, Irit left, knowing that her husband ed the help of these doctors, and that he would never allow o go on her own. She left for Bolbirosok, her suitcase heavy a loaned fortune in German currency, the kind that still value.

When Schultz eventually, briefly emerged from Mayflower, it all over. There was no credible news, no correspondence for nths and then for years, until it was clear what had happened. As before, as with the death of his parents, all objects again gan to speak more loudly with their compensatory words. A nic landscape that Schultz could no longer pretend to ignore. hultz's colleagues at Harvard soon returned him to May-ower. He hasn't left since.

There is something wrong with my head, Irit says in Yiddish, in chultz's dream. *I don't feel so good.*

Now Schultz sees the lesion rising, right in the center of his wife's brow. It opens rapidly, already revealing skull and brain, but rit doesn't seem yet to understand the severity.

Maybe I should see a doctor.

No, no, Schultz says, and still the hole expands, cleaving her brain.

She is trying to speak Yiddish still, but as the lobes of her brain separate, she slurs, producing other sounds that are perhaps re-lated to the language that has obsessed Schultz. But Schultz can-not focus on what she is saying, cannot pause to consider her words. The hole grows still, burrowing straight through her

true loss comes from some other place. A place that remains maddeningly obscure.

And I need you, Canon says.

Rita herself cannot name her reasons. For the hospital? For Canon's sake? For love? She surprises, sickens, enlivens herself as she takes Canon's hand and gives it a quick pump with her fin-gers.

From his pocket, he removes a crumpled pack of Lucky Strikes. In his abject state, he bought it just this morning and there are only two left now. His wife despises his smoking. Canon lights up and the warm vapors rattle his lungs; his tongue tastes the slow exhalation.

All right, all right, he whispers. *Tomorrow. I'll be back tomorrow.*

Already, in his mind, Canon anxiously revises his protocols.

6

When occasionally Schultz does sleep, his dreams are still in a postlapsarian tongue, the Yiddish of his youth. His dreamworld is never a purgatory. Either his dreams are heaven or they are hell.

Schultz and Irit had escaped the war, just barely. They had es-caped the horrors of which others had told them, horrors that seemed impossible to believe, until all reports continued to con-firm them. On the first day in that comfy Cambridge apartment bestowed by Harvard, Schultz woke in bright sunlight, his wife sleeping beside him. Her belly had just begun to convex with their son. Since the start of her pregnancy, she had lost control of her gases. And that first Cambridge morning, she awoke with a fart. He laughed to himself as she darted upright at the rupture. *It's nothing,* he told her in Yiddish, *just bad dreams.* She scrutinized the new foreign apartment, and then reclined into the sunlight. She smiled, kissed his hand, and said, *The light comes in nicely here.* Schultz pressed himself to her, and, over the next hour, they made love.

Presently, in his fit of sleep in the starched sheets of his bed at the Mayflower Home, Schultz is making love to his wife in the safe, sunny room, the war distant and impossible, the future, their family, growing between the friction of their bodies. This is heaven.

And then there is hell, but it does not at first present itself that way. In the radiant postcoital glow, Schultz and Irit go out into the day. Outside the sunny cocoon, however, is not the new strange city of Boston, but the town that Harvard paid for them to flee, their childhood town of Bolbirosok in the time before the war. They pass the familiar faces: Kogen, the Mohel. The grocer, Shmuel Block. Menachem Mendelsohn, Irit's father. Irit and Schultz wave to each, on their way to Hadassah's Cafe for a breakfast. They are contented and oblivious; there is so much beauty to receive this morning that they do not need to make conversation. But. Schultz looks more closely at those familiar faces and bodies, and discovers each is wounded.

At first they appear as only small red risings, bug bites, pimples at the worst: on Kogen's hands, on Block's cheeks. A pinprick of blood on the shirt of Reb Mendelsohn. As Schultz and Irit continue toward the diner, Schultz watches their wounds expand and multiply, like a slow-motion film of the people of Bolbirosok riddled with invisible bullets. All those faces, the

faces of his childhood, each looking to [...] Schultz is distracted by his wife's hand, tu[...] own urgency, and he turns away from the [...] just as they succumb to their wounds, fallin[...]

This is a dream version of how Schultz h[...] he has tried to stop himself from imagining [...] since. All those bodies, all those faces, opened [...]

On the strength of his scholarship, the ling[...] of Harvard had arranged an exit permit for Sch[...] through the University of Vilnius just as such [...] come nearly impossible to obtain, even with m[...] been a great debate; at first Schultz and Irit had [...] people of Bolbirosok—Irit's parents most strid[...] gued that their refusal of the offer would not only [...] be a great disrespect to the others, who could d[...] such an escape.

If you stay, Irit's father told the couple, *you will [...] part of this family.*

And so they left. They left, but always planned to r[...] always planned to return when things got better, bu[...] got worse, and then worse still. Soon, their letters [...] longer to reach Bolbirosok.

A small community of Jewish exiles in Cambrid[...] hopeful stories of buying family members' passage to [...] but there was no way now to send money. The only [...] others agreed, was to go there with tremendous sums a[...] mination, and hope for the best. And so this was what [...] resolved to do, returning to Bolbirosok to rescue one ge[...] of Irit's family, as Irit remained in America, to birth anot[...]

Maybe it was the tension, or maybe it was pure chanc[...] morning, just two weeks before Schultz was to leave, Irit[...]

brain, and now he can see to her skull's far wall. Irit has begun to convulse; her face is fearful, and soon she will collapse. Schultz reaches out to his wife, as if his hands pressed to her can slow the spread of her wounds, but she is just beyond his reach. He tries to get closer to her, to run to her, but his distance increases with his effort to reach her. He lunges, but now she is so far away, her face barely legible, the hole now tunneled straight through, allowing a gap of light in the center of her forehead, like a literal version of what a Hindu's red dot signifies.

I'm scared, she says, just before Schultz wakes with a start in the starchy friction of his hospital sheets. Schultz vows again to stay awake as long as he possibly can.

7

You and the girls are all that ever could keep me in some semblance of a normal state, my grandfather writes in another faltering attempt at a letter to his wife. *Without you now, I either harden into ice, or else I turn to vapors.*

Vapors, Frederick thinks. It is like that now, his awareness diffuse. Or maybe more like radiation, some charge thrown off by solar flares. He knows he has felt this way before, many times, but its familiarity never comforts him. Charge after charge: he cannot quite discern if he is excited or terrified. He thinks of hoboes wandering Boston Common, raving with Jerusalem syndrome. He rises from his bed, leaves the room, and paces the hall, but his bodily motion only adds to the energy, each step another push to the swinging of his mind, which seems about to vault the top bar. He puts one hand to his heart, to measure its pace. *Katharine.* He wants only to hold himself to her. He wants to clutch on to her, as he has before, to keep from floating away into that peripheral place. That place of near visions and half-whispers that he sometimes receives.

The silence of the hall seems somehow louder now, as if the walls were thrumming with an obscure power. Frederick wonders about the private sounds that obsess his roommate.

8

Dinner comes and goes, and then more pills. Now that he is in bed again, the Miltown has begun to obscure his thoughts, and Frederick writes a simple memory:

> *We kissed. Then we walked from the USO to the harbor, a silly ro-*
> *mantic idea on such a chilly night. We stood behind a chain-link*
> *fence, ships obstructing all views of the harbor except for cracks and*
> *slivers in which the moon reflected oily. This time you leaned in. I*
> *was taken aback, literally. Then I tried to stand where I was and to*
> *be equal to it.*

Citing his unceasing restlessness, Frederick asks for a second dose of Miltown, which the Crew Crew boy grants him. He lies in bed for an hour or two, trying to will the tranquilizer, a blackness gathering at the base of his stifling atmosphere, to accumulate into the pure darkness of medicated sleep. But another half hour passes, and still Frederick is restless, still there is that dreadful imminence. Frederick interrupts Schultz from his notations and asks for a couple pills from the desk leg stash.

Be my guest, Schultz replies. *But you know how these things muddy the brain.*

Frederick gratefully swallows three, then four, and finally he finds himself on the other side of brief sleep—or, more accurately, *unconsciousness*—waking in his bed in the late evening, the sky outside the same blue-black as the crows that maunder there. He sits up in his bed as a boy opens the door, *checks,* and closes it again.

Frederick waits for that foreboding to reassemble with his wakefulness. But minutes pass, and there is nothing. The luminous sheen of things has dulled away. Now there is only the starched sheets, the scratching of his roommate's pencil, a boy making his inspections, the cinder-block walls housing the meaningless fact of Frederick. When it switches, it can switch this quickly.

Frederick—so often contemptuous of the doctors and their vague diagnoses—allows himself some comfort in the term they have given to his condition. *Manic depression,* he thinks, *this is what it means.* The chemicals in his brain go one way, and then they shift and go the other. Only, just now, it does not feel like science. It feels, in this moment, like a dark revelation. Frederick knows he has deluded himself, just as people everywhere allow themselves their fantasies. Frederick's enthusiasms, his notions, his writings have all been only noise to cover this. But now he will be strong enough to see things clearly, as they are. My grandfather will look straight into the darkness, even if it only continues to expand, even if it blots away everything else.

ANOTHER

POSSIBILITY

1

There is no more money, Katharine.

In the silence that follows this proclamation, Katharine pictures her father as he is now: in his house by the ocean, watching the fog roll in over his cabana down on the beach at the base of the hill. His biggest problem, his daughter's mad husband aside, is where to acquire the evening's lobster. And there she is, a woman alone in a clapboard house, on the far side of Mount Washington, winter beginning to make itself known, ice-glazed pinecones strafing the windows. She has carried the phone to the kitchen table, the veneer of which is balding from her work, the central office of the enterprise of trying to hold her family together. My mother and her sisters have left for school, and so my grandmother has resumed the business she still tries, as best she can, to make invisible to her daughters.

Katharine sits with her first book of S & H Green Stamps open on the table before her. Later, she will spend dull hours trying to fit her expenses to the government allowance, she who, as a child, rang a bell for servants to come. How is she expected to know how to navigate times like these? Sleet has begun to give way to snow; the window next to her is quickly becoming a fuzzy opaque rectangle.

Katharine and her father remain silent. The green refrigerator drones; the lightbulbs buzz in a stained-glass lamp on the serving table; the radiators groan and hack. Outside, a branch dislodges and passes the window as shadow play.

Katharine knows that only a hundred miles to the south, where her parents live on the coast, the weather differs drastically. She must endure winter's dreadful clamp, while her parents receive only its tinge, blown inland by sea breezes.

But, still, what right has Katharine to expect them to suffer as she suffers? It is an irrational requirement, she knows, to feel that our parents must share and then redeem our suffering. It is irrational, Katharine tries to tell herself, to perceive her parents' well-being as a slight to her. Truly, why should she expect her father to abandon the comforts and securities he has built through a lifetime of hard work for the seemingly boundless project of containing Frederick's chaos? After all, Frederick, in his various ambitions and failings, must have already sapped nearly a third of her parents' savings. Hasn't her father already been tremendously generous? Shouldn't she be grateful for what her father has already paid, not resentful of what he now denies her?

Well, that's not exactly true, she says.

Yes, Katharine, her father replies. *Presently we have enough to support ourselves. What would you have us be, homeless?*

Tears catch in her throat. Katharine rarely cries, but there are certain notions, certain people, that seem to bypass the normal ways she receives the world, entering her sinuses directly.

For a moment, Katharine's anger flares but shifts. She is furious, not only with her father, but with Frederick. Genius, tortured Frederick! He is allowed to fall apart, and still he commands awe. Still Katharine's cousins describe her husband's tormented brilliance. What would happen if Katharine allowed herself such indulgences? For she also has thoughts that are not entirely rational; she also, at times, finds the life she has unbearable.

Look, her father says. *This is not a hopeless situation. I would never let anything happen to you and the girls. But he just isn't getting better, at least not in that cushy hotel.*

There is literal red in Katharine's eyes now. She briefly imagines slapping her father's face. The morning after Frederick was first hospitalized, when she called her parents, had her father not delighted in rising so nobly, declaring that he would make sure Frederick got the best treatment, that he would make sure Katharine and his grandchildren were safe and cared for?

This, he had said, *is what money is for.*

Just such a catastrophe had, in that moment, validated his years of prudence and denied pleasures. Had there not been a barely suppressed delight in his tone when he called Katharine to discuss the paperwork sent to him by Mayflower, paperwork that would ensure—should his money keep coming—that his daughter would remain separated from that mistake of a husband?

It's no hotel, Daddy.

Your husband is ill, her father declares. *But maybe what he needs is not the comfort of Mayflower, but the harsh reality of a public hospital. A hospital that, I might add, we wouldn't have to pay for.*

At the mention of the state hospital, which her father now invariably brings up in these discussions, the face again materializes: the face of Oakey, the face of—let's call a spade a spade—the village idiot. As a child, Oakey was the placid town's one spot of mayhem, positively supervillainous by tranquil Graveton's standards, with a short criminal career that included two bridges set on fire, a dozen dead rabbits hanged from the school yard trees, and one schoolteacher's calf permanently disfigured by hotfoot. At seventeen, Oakey had been taken to the Kirkbride State Hospital following his expression, via fifteen stones hurled through a bedroom window, of his dissatisfaction that Molly Mitchell, a Graveton High sophomore, had not returned his affections. Three weeks later, Oakey returned to Graveton, the adolescent slumping of his shoulders straightened, his beatnik black outfits exchanged for khakis and collars, his formerly devious face slackened into the sack of features that will now forever hang from his skull. The state of New Hampshire, in balancing the costs and benefits of long-term psychotherapy against the simple application of an ice pick to his frontal lobe, chose lobotomy.

It is worse than death, Katharine thinks. In ways, what the state does to those it cannot fathom is worse than murder.

Do you know what they do in those places? If you become too much of a burden? They stick a pick in your brain.

I don't think that's so. Not always, certainly. And, anyway, from what I've read, those procedures can have remarkable success. There was a story in the Globe *about one young man—*

I'm not going to argue with you the merits of a lobotomy. I'm just asking for you to help me.

And now the fire passes and flares in my great-grandfather. A fury so immaculate that it cannot, for ten, fifteen seconds, catch to language. He stutters angrily for a long moment before finding the words: *Help? Help? Do I need to remind you of all I have—*

When they hang up soon thereafter, agreeing they both need to calm, again nothing has been decided. Will he simply stop paying the bills? And then what? Frederick was checked in by the state police; he can come home only when his doctors decide he is ready. Without her father's money, Katharine knows the only possibility is that he will end up in state care, the ice pick poised. His failures and her burdens aside, doesn't Frederick at least deserve her defense?

Mustn't there be another possibility? Couldn't they all—all those doctors, and nurses and psychiatrists and police—be convinced they are wrong? Who says their understanding of sanity is sane?

These are the kinds of thoughts that Dr. Canon, among many others, has told Katharine can be greatly detrimental to a loved one's progress. But isn't this how indoctrination always works, an entire deferral of your own judgment to a higher authority, whom you are instructed not to question?

But surely, Katharine tells herself. Surely they must be right in some degree. The minds in that hospital are some of the country's greatest. The poet Robert Lowell and the mathematician John Nash, among many others, choose Mayflower for their breakdowns.

No, no, of course they are right, she tells herself, pulling a box of Lorna Doones from the pantry, taking a bite. His drinking, his women, his tirades, the anorexic failed sailor in her bed. Katharine thinks, *He is sick.*

Katharine looks at the phone on its cradle and considers making the call she has told herself, many times today, that she will not make.

Over these last weeks, Katharine has spoken with Lars Jensen many times. Last time, she nearly wept and said things that still feel impossible to attribute to herself.

Lars again asked to see her. *I don't have any intentions,* he swore.

She has denied his offers to meet four or five times over, but each time less assuredly. Lars, playing sensitive, is also persistent. Lars senses an opening, as does Katharine. They both sense that all it will take is one or two more sessions of Lars's sweetened assertiveness.

For Katharine has begun to wonder exactly why she resists

Lars's advances. Frederick has taken other women many times over; is it not simply pathetic, her fidelity to some notion that her husband clearly abandoned years ago? Just two and a half years into their marriage, when Katharine had discovered Frederick in the first of his affairs, she still had never considered the possibility she now considers. Lars never had Frederick's charms, but she has begun to consider what else, more enduring, Lars might have given her in that now vanished, other life. Katharine knows Frederick has taken many other women, but she also knows that for her an affair would mean something entirely different. Frederick discarded women like scrap paper while brainstorming. Trying to rewrite himself, he wrote on them until inspiration dimmed, or another notion redirected his consideration. One kiss at a dance nearly twenty years ago, and Katharine has never kissed another man. She cannot lie to herself about what meeting Lars would mean.

This could still go away, Katharine thinks as she climbs the steps of her house on the way to the bathroom upstairs. Simply, Frederick needs to come home.

She has no need for the toilet but sits on it anyway. She simply needs the smallness and the quiet of this room. She breathes in the smells of toothpaste and vague mildew; she wonders about a leak under the sink. She examines the tiny tiles of the floor; she thinks of the impossible patience required to lay them all there, one by one. Her marriage is failing; the possibility of another future is opening. But still, doesn't their past—the one-time simplicity of it, the life that was, occasionally, what they wanted it to be—deserve at least one more fight?

Perhaps all the doctors are right. It is even likely that they are right. But she must see for herself. Frederick's treatment, Dr.

Canon and Dr. Wallace have explained, requires complete removal from his normal life, absolutely no contact at all, until he is ready. But it has already been months since she had that single, terse conversation with Frederick. Shouldn't she at last be allowed to speak with her husband once more?

2

Just this, just this, Canon thinks.

Rita is wriggling against him on the psychoanalytic divan. Canon feels himself now joined with her, speaking a nonsense lascivious language with two tongues.

When the phone rings, Canon immediately decides to ignore it. Rita, beneath him, slows a bit, and on the fourth ring, she speaks in plain English.

Shouldn't you?

Not now, Canon says.

It could be important.

If it is, they'll call back.

The phone silences, but only for a moment, then obstinately begins ringing again.

Christ, Canon says.

You need to get that.

As he crawls off and toward the phone, Rita grasps for her discarded uniform.

Shit, Canon whispers.

It might be an emergency, Rita says.

Yes? Canon mutters into the phone, and turns to the window. *Katharine Merrill?*

Of course Canon convinces Katharine. After her stubborn insistence with the operator and with Higgins, when Katharine finally succeeds in getting Canon on the line, she is no longer certain if she has called to plead for her husband's release, if she has called to demand to speak with Frederick, or if she has called only to seek Canon's reassurance.

Of course, I understand, he tells her. Of course she is plagued by doubt. It is an element of Frederick's illness that allows him to open this doubt in others.

Canon, in the persuasive, authoritative voice he has honed through years of study and months of practice, remains as vague and hopeful as a fortune cookie's fortune. *Even I did not expect for him to need to stay here so long. Frederick's condition is much more complex than I anticipated, but it shouldn't be so much longer,* he says. *Not so long at all. I am quite confident.*

However, Canon's success, in this moment, is not what matters. Or, rather, it is not what is important now, from my vantage, nearly five decades later. For the history of my family, the important moment is not this conversation, but what occurs just next to it. A simple awareness dawning upon the woman slipping into her underwear on the divan. From where she sits, Rita can discern the tones of Katharine's desperation. Not the words themselves, but the way in which Katharine speaks them. The quality of Mrs. Merrill's voice transmits that desperation into Rita's receptive shame. Maybe, Rita had tried to convince herself, her inexplicable need for Albert was justification enough. But now Rita thinks of Frederick, and she turns her back to Albert.

1

Each man in the ward has his own name in the language that speaks only to Schultz. Unlike the failing languages, no two names are the same. Canon's name is similar to the sounds produced by a hungry stomach. Frederick's is a sharp sustained note, with bass beating beneath it, a sound Schultz has not yet been able to get his own tongue to replicate.

It is strange, how the names of random others suddenly come to him; Schultz has not yet entirely deciphered the system by which they are revealed. It makes some sense that the revelation of certain names is a result of their close physical proximity or of their constant, background presence. President Kennedy (a wistful grunt) or Khrushchev (like an elongated cough). Each of the patients in the neighboring boys' ward contributes a whine to that kitten's cry that the building always emits. But why do certain other seemingly random names—a grocer he has never met in Back Bay, a construction worker downtown, a lady selling gloves in a department store in Danvers—suddenly reach his perception? Why do these living names speak to him, suddenly revealing the entirety of these men and women he has never met? And also, why, recently, have the names of the dead begun to speak? Thomas Edison (*lalaaa*), Lincoln (*ca-oola*), the hospital's namesake, the merchant John Mayflower (*haaaaahaaaa*).

From the graveyard down the hill in Belmont, the names of

the dead sometimes speak in chorus, a sound coincidentally close to the trill rustle that often accompanies graveyard scenes in films.

Schultz chides himself for occasionally diverting his studies to a personal end, but he cannot help scrutinizing the sonic matrix for her name, his murdered Irit. Alas, he still has not heard it. Not entirely, at least.

But if the names of the dead can speak to him, then that further complicates the vexing question of this language's origin. If the dead can speak in it too, then does that lend credence to the theory of the True Torah in which Reb Mendelsohn believed? A text that dictates the universe, written at all times by a High Author? Schultz likes to think of himself as a man of science, but he feels at the precipice of something else. Is it courage or is it foolishness to believe in what he cannot know for certain?

For the most part, Schultz has remained as skeptical of the kitsch and claptrap of the Bible and its notions as he was as a boy in Bolbirosok, studying the Torah.

You are telling me, he would ask Rabbi Grossman, *that Baruch HaShem smote this man, Onan, for spilling seed? Rabbi, I don't know how much time you spend talking to boys my age, but by this logic there shouldn't be a Jew left in all of Lithuania.*

But, over the years, has Schultz begun to revise his position? Perhaps it is in no small part the influence of Irit, always contextualizing present issues with biblical parables, embarrassing Schultz in front of their Harvard friends, who scowled at her persistent faith and counterquoted from Kant, Marx, Nietzsche. Still, Schultz believes so little of the Torah. Not literally, at least. He has always seen that book as a series of metaphors, at the same distance from the truth of things as the languages men speak are distanced from the true language. But perhaps, in that way, it's all true. That which cannot be perceived by those without this form of perception must be explained in details people can understand. Though Schultz has not yet made the proverbial leap, the notion still occurs to him: perhaps each story within the Torah is molded after another, truer story, that can be told only in the lost, true language.

2

Nothing. Not one thing we don't know about.

It is Monday morning and Canon has ordered every one of his employees, all the way down to the kitchen staff, to an emergency meeting. He gesticulates dramatically, speaks vehemently, does not allow himself to sit, produces a performance perhaps subconsciously imitative of that of Alec Guinness in *The Bridge on the River Kwai.*

We have to be better than accidents, Canon tells them. *We have to search, every day, in every drawer, under every mattress, so that not even an accident will give a patient the kind of possibility that that lighter gave Mr. Foulds. We must know about everything. What the patients track in on their shoes.*

At this point in the meeting, much of the staff undertakes the imaginative act that everywhere joins psychiatric patients with their caretakers: with enough will and creativity, what object is entirely safe? What thing could a determined man or woman not use to bring about his or her end? If one had the will, a book's pages could be crumpled and jammed into the trachea; a pen could be driven deep into an eye socket; a simple wall could crush a skull's contents.

3

The Crew Crew, Visigothic in their late teens and early twenties, pillage room after room, per the new protocols. They do not pause if the patients they find inside are sleeping or engaged in some private act, they merely walk to the patients' desks, as if the desks were their own, and then search every drawer, hold every book by its cover, shaking the binding loose in an attempt to dislodge potential contraband.

These things are not yours to rifle through, Schultz informs the two boys rattling his journals.

The Crew Crew boys don't respond but turn to each other and share a supercilious smile. Frederick, observing the scene, composes a thought to write later in his own tussled journal: *The history of catastrophe is populated by such young men, empowered by leaders with frightful ideology. We should be glad they carry only charts and reports, not guns.*

4

The men of Ingersoll are assembled now for group therapy, and the session opens with clamor, vociferous protests of the Crew Crew's raids. Canon attempts to evade the questions, deflecting them back to his patients—*but why is it that authority bothers you so?*—until the group's protests resolve into the familiar rallying cry, furious questions and invectives about the fate of Marvin Foulds.

Why in God's name won't you just tell us what has happened—

Though he does not join in with the others, Frederick smiles. He is glad for the cacophony that, for the moment, is louder than his own agony.

Something in Canon nearly rises to the surface, but he catches it. He crosses his legs and watches the scene with a decent imitation of dispassion. He pulls his cigarettes from his white coat, lights one, and then takes a long Bogart pull. Then Canon gestures to the Crew Crew at the periphery, who remove each protesting man, one by one, as Canon—beneath the clamor—consults his notes and makes his normal therapeutic inquiries: *Bobbie, perhaps it would be more productive to talk about your feelings of alienation . . .* It is only in the session's last moments—when Lowell, Stanley, Bobbie, and three of the catatonics have been pulled away—that Canon can be heard.

Mr. Merrill, Canon says, meeting Frederick's eyes directly for the first time since that night in solitary. *How are you feeling today?*

Frederick smiles an inscrutable smile.

Welcome back, Frederick says.

Canon must catch himself once more. And then, once more, he performs his well-practiced act of transcendence.

5

Frederick has known a variety of insomnias. There is the ecstatic insomnia, the universe too brightly electric and too loud to admit sleep. There is the insomnia of dread, the possibility of impending horror requiring nightlong vigilance, a febrile, inextinguishable wakefulness. And then there is this insomnia, similar to the dreadful, but somehow more archetypal, insomnia in its purest form. This is the insomnia of the meaninglessness of things, which includes the meaninglessness of sleep. Every object, room, and person is pregnant with the promise of decay. The mind is kept awake for the same reasons it is kept alive, arbitrarily. A happenstance of nature, electrons gathered to animate the inanimate for a time, to carry the dim flickering flame, day and night, until inevitably it goes out.

Every five minutes, the door swings open with a dull utterance of *checks,* which seems a dark existential metaphor, in some way Frederick is too exhausted entirely to grasp. And so Frederick lies in bed now, the darkness of the ceiling the only truth, as his roommate persists in his scribbling. *It doesn't matter,* he wants to tell Schultz. *Sane or mad, what you are doing does not matter. Go to bed. Relinquish. Relinquish.*

But Frederick's contemplation of the blackness above him is soon punctured by light, opening at an angle wider than the

Crew Crew's routine checks. Frederick turns to find Rita in the doorway, raising a hand to greet him. Schultz hardly looks up from his notebook, offers a friendly *Hello,* his pen barely pausing on the page. Rita comes to Frederick's bed and sits.

Well, there, Frederick says.

Did I wake you?

What do you want?

Rita doesn't say anything for the moment. She looks down at her hands, as if trying to devise the optimal configuration for her fingers.

I, well. For one, I came to tell you that they're transferring Marvin from the hospital. To the infirmary here. He's doing better.

It's not that Frederick isn't grateful for the news but, in the midst of this insomnia, the news seems to belong to a place that he has left.

I'm glad.

Better, but his burns are—

Forever.

Terrible.

A long silence now. But not the silence that Rita, walking to Frederick's room, had imagined. Not a clenched silence, as she failed to find the words to explain herself, to apologize for what Frederick had witnessed, and the traumas that her ridiculous affair have caused him to suffer. That apology, at least in this moment, is subsumed into something else, a darkness that Frederick radiates, as powerfully as the hallway's tubes fluoresce. Rita has always been unusually receptive to others' moods; the energies of others transfer to her as cleanly as the motions of billiard balls.

Sometimes, Rita thinks, she is little but this: no person, merely a permeable membrane that absorbs the language, the passions, the glooms of others. Others are themselves; she is an amalgam of them. Frederick's despair is so total, such a boundless, word-less thing, a smothering black oil spilling over her perception, that when she does begin to apologize, it is a relief to speak.

I also wanted to tell you I was sorry.

Frederick remains silent. If only for the comfort of her own voice, Rita speaks again.

It's just, with Albert, I don't know. It started back when I was only— I know how he can seem, but there's so much about him you can't know. You should have known him before. I know he doesn't mean— I mean—

From the darkness before her, the place where the darkness collects into a human-size shape in the covers, Frederick's voice emerges.

It doesn't matter. Things happen. I understand.

Rita gives a half-laugh of recognition, *things happen.*

Frederick grunts, or perhaps it is just his breathing.

Your wife called. I was, well, in the office, and she called. She's worried about you.

Katharine?

Yeah. Rita says. *Katharine.*

Katharine. It's not that her name cuts through his mental morass, or that this news in any way encourages him now. But amid that swampland—with its wicked desiccated trees, its noxious gases bubbling at all times from the turbid depths—her name is the promise of a house there in the distance. A door with a single warm bulb reflecting across the marsh. The marsh is tolerable if one joins it, if one kneels into its decay and waits for it to make its inevitable claims. But what the light of the house in the distance promises is, by contrast, heartbreaking. Katharine. This insomnia is an absence of feeling, or else agony reduced to its faintest, minimalist components. But Katharine's name is pure

THE STORM AT THE DOOR 225

feeling, even if, at this moment, plain torture. Frederick sits up-right, for the first time in hours, and finds himself pleading with Rita.

I won't tell anyone. Can't you explain that to him? I'm not angry, not at you or him. Of course I understand. Who could understand bet-ter than I could? But you have to tell him. There is something dark now; it's like exhaustion that you can't resist. This darkness. I don't know. And I don't know. Will you just explain it to him? That I won't tell. That I don't care. That I must go? That I must leave? That Katharine is the only—

Rita finds herself nodding at Frederick's pleas, not in agree-ment—she knows even she is nearly powerless to persuade Canon in that way—but in recognition. At this moment, she too knows the agony of the house in the distance, its impossibly dis-tant promise.

The only what? Rita asks.

I'm not sure what the right word is.

6

It is the next morning: a rare fall day, the unfiltered sun surpris-ing everyone with its announcement that warmth is still possi-ble, inspiring Bostonians to plan one last sweatered weekend in the lakes and mountains to the north, while there is a chance of the weather holding.

Has Frederick too begun to switch once more? On the march back from breakfast, he feels, intensely, some nameless need. It is a strange, objectless demand; for a moment he even thinks it is the coming of a sneeze or else a sob, but none materializes. It is some need caught between his sinuses and lips, like a craving for a kiss, but then he decides that even an imagined kiss would not sate it. There is a panicking foreignness to it, like some new form of hunger. Like hunger, but it also seems to have something to do with violence. Frederick clenches his face as the line of men ascends to Ingersoll House, but the sensation doesn't cease until he is inside, when it is replaced with other considerations.

Frederick is near the rear of the line, and so he does not learn of Canon's new decision as soon as the others. By the time he enters the lobby of Ingersoll, he finds that some revelation has silenced the room, except for Stanley, shouting nonsense into his hands. The men are stooped curiously over a cot placed just behind the sofa. They lean in and rear back, like a pack of dogs trying to eat an overly heated dinner. Frederick approaches the cot, but already he senses what he will find there. Intravenous drips dangling above, bloodied bandages concealing most of his face, there is Marvin. Marvin's one uncovered eye is closed as, in shame, he pretends to sleep.

Just then, like a play that was set to commence as soon as its audience was in place—has Canon planned it this way?—the infirmary's doctor, Wilkins, enters Ingersoll, white coat flapping, retractable pen clicking, assisting nurse in tow. The nurse holds a bright orange wastebasket and a fresh roll of gauze.

Wilkins lowers himself to Marvin's ear, and speaks to Marvin in the megaphonic way that the young often address the old. *It's time to change your bandages, Mr. Foulds!* he says, loud enough that the words faintly echo off the far end of the corridor.

A hardly audible whimper rises from Marvin, as the nurse begins at his feet, unraveling. At the first glimpse of his exposed

THE STORM AT THE DOOR 227

shin, burned now to a strawberry's porous red, Frederick surprises himself by speaking.

Why on earth would he be here? Shouldn't he be in the infirmary?

Dr. Canon felt he was well enough to return, Wilkins replies. *The important thing is that nothing distracts from Mr. Foulds's psychiatric treatment, especially now.*

Frederick, like many of the others, suspects Canon's true purpose for this display. Even still, in this moment, Canon succeeds. As the incendiary Marvin, the martyr rebel, had irresistibly compelled the other men, the extinguished Marvin seems equally to repel them. For the rest of that day, and the night that follows, the men confine themselves to their rooms, while the common room remains empty, except for a babbling television and a psychotic burn victim, alone on his bed.

7

It is so simple, Frederick writes in his journal. *A leap, a slash, a squeezed trigger. This is what the doctors fail to grasp. The ridiculous simplicity. Its elegance.*

8

Robert Lowell's eyes have regained their focus. Just descended from a week of *up days,* Lowell has restored his gaze to the things set before him. It is Lowell who devises the plan.

The next afternoon, a Crew Crew boy pushes open Lowell's door, *checks,* and then startles to find more than half the Ingersoll men crammed into the narrow space.

Poetry seminar, Lowell explains.

Oh? Are you reading anything new? the boy asks earnestly. The power of Lowell's celebrity, even here.

Sorry, Lowell says. *Patients only.*

The Ingersoll men, for the first time in days, laugh en masse. Even Frederick, leaning against the corner like a catatonic, receives the pleasure of this, the laughing, the whispering, the conspiring.

. . .

As with every detail of their daily routine, there is a protocol for what foods patients are allowed to carry back with them from the dining hall. Fortunately for Lowell's scheme, fruit is included on this list of permitted snacks: three items per man, but the staff must first inspect and confirm that the skin of each piece is unbroken, to make sure the fruit isn't used as crafty conveyance for contraband. And so, this night, each man takes his permitted three, the kitchen staff only mildly suspicious of the Ingersoll men's sudden passion for produce.

When they are assembled again later in Lowell's room, the poet devises a way to achieve the desired effect with a collection of pencils, the crimson blanket his wife brought for him, and the large seashells Stanley has been allowed to keep in his room as mementos of the time his nephew took him for a weekend trip to Cape Cod, six years ago.

They wait until the middle of the night, when the orderlies will least expect it, when the scene will have its greatest poignancy. At precisely 3:00 A.M., as the two Crew Crew boys read in the administrative office, nearly every door inside Ingersoll opens, the men emptying into the corridor. The Crew Crew kids startle at the beguiling scene, their madmen risen like nocturnal apparitions.

9

One of the boys grasps Frederick by the arm. *What's going on?*

You're welcome to come and see, Frederick replies. The boys share a dubious gaze and set down their books to follow behind.

Soundlessly—except for a few stray giggles—the men gather around the cot, making an enclosure of themselves. Lowell stands just before the head of Marvin's bed, stoops and whispers into Marvin's ear.

Ms. Diablo, Lowell says. *Ms. Mango Diablo, it's time to go onstage.*

Marvin wakes with the semblance of a startle that his scorched body can manage. Only the fingertips of Marvin's right hand, the whole of his left hand, and his right eye are free from bandages. His eye widens with the discovery of the men assembled before him.

What? What's going on?

Lowell turns his gaze to the expectant, grinning faces.

We have a surprise for you, Lowell says.

A surprise?

Sure.

I must look like a monster. Like a mummy, Marvin mutters. *A living dead thing.*

Frederick considers the perfect precision of these words. *Living dead.*

It's not so bad, he manages.

Then Marvin closes his eye and speaks.

Whatever it is you're planning, he says. *Will you do me a favor first?*

Of course, Lowell says.

I want you to see. Under the bandages. I haven't seen yet. But I want you to look so I can know by how you look at me. The doctors only look at me like a patient.

Frederick, like all the men assembled, has not been able to stop his imagination from filling in, hideously, what the white bandages conceal. He almost begs Marvin to reconsider, but then he looks to Lowell, who nods knowingly. As Marvin reaches his unburned left hand to the bandage's end near his temple, Bobbie cries out.

Wait! I mean, wait. Isn't it bad for the burns? I mean, couldn't they get infected or something?

I'm scared too, Marvin says, and then begins the unraveling.

It takes a long while, his hand slowly orbiting, which only adds to the horror. With a fearsome yelp, he peels away a final panel of gauze, revealing the wound his face has become. Is any sight as horrible as a burned face? The features boiled and congealed into a cooled red-black porridge. It seems impossible at first, like a Hollywood monster's makeup. A monster's mask, but made more hideous than anything Hollywood could conjure, with the reality of the single human eye, adrift in that mess. The men either do or do not gasp, they either cry out or are silent: it doesn't matter to Marvin, receiving their horror, which mutes the moment.

I need you to kill me, Marvin says. *I need to die. How? How? How? How am I supposed to be this thing? This monster? I don't even know how to be myself.*

Marvin's one open eye begins to water, oozing its salty secretion into his burns. And then Marvin screams out, a fundamental sound, which, if Schultz is to be believed, is perhaps a word taken from the true language. It is the true name of anguish, and it opens pure anguish, its measureless fathoms. The men are there together, in some silent unreckonable space, as endless as their conditions. Their conditions, given names, but immeasurable. They are immeasurable, indecipherable, unfit for this world. Perhaps, my grandfather thinks, they are where they belong.

But Frederick tries to remind himself that they have come here for a purpose that is good. They will do what they have come for, and right now, in this moment, that is enough. Frederick looks back to Marvin, who delicately restores the bandages to his ruined face.

We brought something for you, Frederick says and gestures to Lowell, who reaches into the laundry sack at his feet, removing their communal creation: a seashell bra bound with shoelaces, Lowell's blanket fashioned into a passable skirt, and, the masterpiece, a towering fruit headdress.

Behind his bandages, Marvin's face seems to shift. The men work gingerly, dressing him in this ersatz rendition of the costume Canon took from him.

Oh, boys, he mutters and grunts as he draws his breath to

muster a respectable line or two of "Bananas Is My Business," before losing his breath. The men applaud.

And when the applause subsides, the Crew Crew attempt to intervene. *All right,* they say, sensing Canon's displeasure at the scene. *Everyone back to their rooms.*

Oh, not just yet, Lowell says. The men turn to Lowell, curious about this unexpected component to the scene he has plotted. *Gentlemen. If you would be so kind. I'd like to read something I've written.*

The Crew Crew boys begin to object, but Frederick has come prepared. He shoves his fingers into his pockets and reaches out to shake the hands of the two increasingly irate boys, depositing into their palms balled-up napkins containing twenty-five of Schultz's pilfered Miltowns apiece. Fueled with institutional power, the Crew Crew boys sometimes seem an inhuman force. Pure, dumb, masculine will. But sometimes, Frederick remembers, they are only boys. They both look at what Frederick has left in their hands, and widen their eyes at each other like children awarded candy, who cannot quite believe their luck. Then they remember themselves, they try to restore their glare at Lowell, at the others, but quickly retreat to their office.

And so, just after 3:00 A.M. in the common room of a mental asylum, to an audience of schizophrenics, borderlines, and manic-depressives, Robert Lowell reads a poem from his *Life Studies.*

At his desk down the hall, Schultz turns his attention toward the men. For once, Schultz stops scrutinizing his sonic universe, and simply listens to Lowell speak.

WAKING IN THE BLUE

The night attendant, a B.U. sophomore,
rouses from the mare's-nest of his drowsy head
propped on *The Meaning of Meaning.*
He catwalks down our corridor.
Azure day
makes my agonized blue window bleaker.
Crows maunder on the petrified fairway.
Absence! My heart grows tense
as though a harpoon were sparring for the kill.
(This is the house for the "mentally ill.")

What use is my sense of humor?
I grin at Stanley, now sunk in his sixties,
once a Harvard all-American fullback,
(if such were possible!)
still hoarding the build of a boy in his twenties,
as he soaks, a ramrod
with the muscle of a seal
in his long tub,
vaguely urinous from the Victorian plumbing.
A kingly granite profile in a crimson golf-cap,
worn all day, all night,
he thinks only of his figure,
of slimming on sherbet and ginger ale—
more cut off from words than a seal.

This is the way day breaks in Bowditch Hall at
     McLean's;

the hooded night lights bring out "Bobbie,"
Porcellian '29,
a replica of Louis XVI
without the wig—
redolent and roly-poly as a sperm whale,
as he swashbuckles about in his birthday suit
and horses at chairs.

These victorious figures of bravado ossified young.

In between the limits of day,
hours and hours go by under the crew haircuts
and slightly too little nonsensical bachelor twinkle
of the Roman Catholic attendants.
(There are no Mayflower
screwballs in the Catholic Church.)

After a hearty New England breakfast,
I weigh two hundred pounds
this morning. Cock of the walk,
I strut in my turtle-necked French sailor's jersey
before the metal shaving mirrors,
and see the shaky future grow familiar
in the pinched, indigenous faces
of these thoroughbred mental cases,
twice my age and half my weight.
We are all old-timers,
each of us holds a locked razor.

—Robert Lowell

EXHAUSTION

OR

FEAR?

1

Is it her worry or just exhaustion? It seems that every time Katharine so much as blinks, another dream state is suddenly available to her, suggestions of color and faces and sound, advertisements for potential dreams. The membrane between conscious and unconscious has suddenly become porous. Maybe, Katharine thinks, madness is only exhaustion at its extremes.

Katharine is in her dim Graveton living room, sitting in Frederick's armchair, just as he would sit: cigarette in hand, the house hushed and still, the chaos only in her own skull. But, unlike with Frederick, her own dread is reasonable.

The clock ticks on the mantel; Katharine doesn't let herself look at the time. She will keep herself from looking at the time for as long as possible, but she knows the terrible truth: it must already be well after midnight. Upstairs, three of her four girls are in bed, but Susie is still not home.

As Katharine has taken Frederick's place in the armchair, so have the girls taken his place as purveyors of family crises. Last week, Rebecca did not return home until morning from a date with Jeremy (she is grounded, but, with only Katharine to enforce, grounded in the way twine could anchor a jetliner). Yesterday, Louise, trying to bolster an argument that she did not need to study for her math exam, underlined her point by kicking in the bedroom door. Even little Jillian, last week, hid in the coat closet and did to a box of chocolate chips what a junkie would do to a fresh score. And now Susie, Katharine's vice pla-cater, her partner in rosy assessments, is more than two hours late for curfew. Could Susie possibly just be flaunting Katharine's rules as her sisters have begun to? Or must it be something worse?

Katharine takes a long pull of a Lucky Strike, holds the fumes, releases. The only light in the living room enters sloppily through the impressionistic poured-glass windows. Katharine watches the snowfall, the weather rendering the streetlight a creamy orange. The snow is early season snow, loose and heavy, and only switched over from rain at eight this evening, but al-ready the window's base is pillowed white. Where is her daugh-ter?

Sickened with nicotine and with worry, Katharine pushes her cigarette into Frederick's ceramic tray. The cling of vapors on her clothes is nauseating. A metonymic smell, stale smoke, the smell of Frederick's capitulation to his compulsions, the sour stench that remained with his regrets in the morning, the poison still pushing out of his pores.

Katharine closes her eyes for a moment, and the detritus im-agery of her subconscious projects onto the backs of her eyelids. Faces, nearly. Colors, nearly. Susie's voice, nearly. Shut eyes, sleep, now seem to promise the opposite of what they ought to.

Katharine thinks, *I am also going mad.* She thinks, *I am also im-prisoned.*

Imprisoned. That is the word for it. A more subtle imprison-ing than her husband's, but no lesser.

An imprisoning, for what crime? Perhaps, as others say, Fred-erick is also blameless, simply cannot help himself. But at least there are nameable incidents, choices that Frederick could have not made, impulses she still believes—is it unfair of her?—that he could have suppressed, if he had really tried. He could have not drowned his better reasoning in bourbon, night after night. He could have not changed into George Carlyle's raincoat, could have not exposed himself to the passing traffic.

Katharine has done exactly what anyone would say she ought to have done, but it has yielded only this: an anxious middle-aged mother, mad with worry, snuffing out cigarettes in the empty living room of a house they can no longer afford.

The snowfall has reached full saturation; it is like the Milky Way now, so many particles that they all smear together into a single spectacular texture. Katharine thinks of the ropes that the farmers up the road tie between their houses and outhouses in the winter, to guide them from door to door in such weather. Each year, two or three farmers fail to secure these tethers and so freeze to death, lost just feet from their back doors. What is she supposed to do now?

Katharine goes to the kitchen and dials Lars. She does not consider what she will say, or what she will ask of him. The idea of the phone ringing in Lars's house, of another person waiting there to receive her, is a tremendous relief, a telephonic life pre-server cast out. One week ago, Katharine finally caved to Lars's persistent pleas to see her, but with a caveat. She would agree to meet him, she said, but not for a month. This was her way of both agreeing and not agreeing, setting the date a month in ad-vance, and then informing Lars she would not speak with him until then, to be certain it was what she wanted. *My capacity to please others is endless,* she had said with an eloquent self-awareness that so impressed her she later recorded it in her jour-nal, a thesis statement for her being. *I need to be sure this is what I want. That I'm not just doing it to make you happy.* The date is still three weeks away, and Lars has kept his part of the agreement, at least so far. When he answers the phone, Katharine panics and hangs up.

More than two and a half hours late now. Should she call Lars back and tell him to come help her? Should she call the parents of Susie's friends? But which friends? Katharine has been so pre-occupied this fall that she does not even know the names of some of the girls with whom she sees her daughter walking home from school. Should she call the police?

Katharine goes to the front hall closet, removes her mink coat (a gift from Frederick in better days), and pulls it over her robe. She slides her feet into her ankle-high, fur-trimmed boots. Considerable patches of her bare white legs remain exposed.

2

Outside, the familiar shapes of Graveton have metamorphosed into a cloud-dream. It reminds Katharine of when she had Rebecca's first pair of baby shoes bronzed; first they poured a thick plaster over the booties, in which a bronze replica was cast. Graveton, abstracted with snow, seems readied to produce a replica of itself.

The snow pauses for a moment, for Katharine's first steps out the door. But then, as if her entrance reminds the weather of its purpose, the snow begins to fall heavily enough that the few feet she can see in any direction become suddenly intimate, a mobile enclosure of static. She walks toward Main Street by instinct, on what seems to be the sidewalk but could also be the street. Susie claimed to be going for a dinner at Archie's, in the opposite direction, but Archie's would have been closed for hours now. Katharine does not consider where she should go, but her instinct is to head toward the center of things.

In the milky orange oblivions between the strange snowy renderings of Graveton's houses, Katharine loses her place. The snow, holding the streetlight, is more and more radiantly orange, and when she blinks it away, there are still, in her exhaustion or fear, that almost red and almost blue and almost yellow, mighty colors that vanish as they begin. Incandescent orange, the suggestion of other colors, and then, in a flash, the snow whites around her.

Headlights gain with a suddenness that feels final. But then they simply pass her and vanish. Katharine tries to decide if this was a near-fatal encounter, or only a car passing as she walked into town.

In space, John Glenn said on the news the other night, there is no up and no down. Our notions of place are tethered to the constant force of gravity. And it seems to Katharine that some constant force, the thing that has held her to earth, to her home, to her town, to her family, has come unbound, and she could be anywhere. Her daughter could be anywhere, could have been crushed by rising lights, as Katharine was perhaps just nearly crushed. Underneath the snow there are still streets and sidewalks and houses, still that constructed geography, but right now it seems that there is no such thing as forward.

Another car passes, less terrifyingly this time, and Katharine becomes aware of the figure she must strike, the snow matting her hair to her scalp, her robe and mink billowing to press the cotton of her nightie flat to her body. A madwoman. She shivers and realizes she is tremendously cold.

In front of her, the orange deluge begins to whiten again. Twin lights rising slowly, two expanding cones. At first she thinks it impossible that a car could come from this direction, but concludes that she must be at an intersection. Alpine Street? Park? She tries to decide which way she should dart to dodge the coming car, or maybe she should remain where she is? She is frozen there, with a deer's paralysis, until the twin lights loosen from their parallel beams. The headlights come unstuck from each other, the car gone cross-eyed. Katharine either mentally or actually gasps as the twin beams focus upon her and halt. And then, the lights turn upward to illuminate the faces of Susie and her friend Jacquelyn with such suddenness it is as if the snow were a magician's confetti in which they have been conjured.

Mum? Susie asks. Susie and Jacquelyn lower their flashlights and step toward her.

Susie, Katharine says, as if to confirm this reality. It seems she might blink it away, might close her eyes and open them again to find her daughter replaced by some chromatic burst, the suggestion of some featureless face.

But they persist there. Susie and Jacquelyn are now in this space with Katharine, everything beyond particulate and flickering, as if they have entered a scene from a silent film, stained orange to resemble dawn.

What are you doing, Mum?

Katharine wants to tell her daughter how scared she was, and how that fear ignited something. The almost colors, the near sounds. To normalize the moment, she raises her voice. In

Katharine's few moments of actual rage, the force of her own voice nearly crumples her, but now she performs only an imitation of parental scolding.

Susan! Where were you? I have been trying to find you. Where were you?

The answer is obvious: the girls' mouths are rashy from kissing boys, and the cigarette reek, which vanished when Katharine left her living room, has returned. So, kissing and smoking. Likely in the balcony of the town hall's theater; she knows kids sometimes sneak in there at night, for those purposes. She should yell at her daughter, and ground her. There is a simple script to follow, a lecture on the dangers of boys, impulsivity, ruined opportunities.

My mother, like my grandmother (and also like me), seems constructed of matter at the same harmonic resonance as a human yell; fury has the same effect upon her as a soprano's high note upon a wineglass. But Susie must know the falseness of Katharine's anger; she does not cower or seem on the verge of shattering; she is only startled, nonplussed.

Mum? I was just. We were just—finishing dinner? We were just coming home. I must have lost track of time?

The doomed futures opened to us at all times, the one path from which we must never stray; Katharine knows what she ought to tell her daughter.

C'mon, Jacquelyn, Katharine says, her voice sinking back into its honeyed warmth. *Let's get you home.*

It's really coming down, Jacquelyn remarks, testing Katharine's restored softness.

Katharine turns to watch the snow for a long while, longer than she knows is quite appropriate. She closes her eyes, and still her exhaustion montages inside her. When she turns back to Susie, her daughter looks at her with what seems acknowledgment. Not sympathy, or apology, but an eagerness to accept.

At this moment, in the spacelessness of the snow, it seems that they could go anywhere, that they could not go home, that they could be freed from the town and the history the snow has buried. Katharine nearly startles at the thought of that freedom.

Gosh. It's hard to see where we are, Susie says.

Maybe there is a simple and proper way forward that Katharine could discern, if only she focused. Maybe a right and clarifying direction is there, just beneath things, like the colors she can nearly see, the sounds she can nearly hear, the snowbound infrastructure. Maybe, but Katharine no longer knows which way it is. Katharine knows only that either she can fail her decisions and plans or else they will continue to imprison her. Katharine can no longer bear that prison; in this moment, my grandmother knows she will fail her husband.

3

In her bed the next morning, my mother wakes early, two hours before dawn, as she often has in the months that her father has been gone. Her father has his own form of insomnia, charged and restless straight through to morning, and Susie worries what this shared affliction of sleeplessness might imply. In ways, however, she thinks that her particular insomnia is crueler than her father's, waking her to be present for the loneliest, unclaimed hour that is not quite night and not quite day. Susie once read a poem in English class called "The Skunk Hour," a name that she thinks of often, as she paces her room in this time fit only for crepuscular animals that waddle outside. Susie rises from bed and tiptoes the pine planks of her room, as silent as the Skunk Hour wants her to be.

Silent and pacing, Susie thinks of her mother standing there in the street, her nightie snow-dusted and flapping beneath her mink. Illuminated by the twin flashlights, her mother seemed deliberately arranged for operatically dramatic effect. Had she clutched a penknife in her fist, bloody from her adulterous husband, the image would have been complete. Her ethereal and tranquil mother, who has always been able to absorb others' abuse with bullet-trap imperviousness, suddenly transformed into that haunted heroine. Susie clutches at her hair, shamed to consider that the tipping point was her own gleeful curfew violation.

Susie wonders how she could have allowed herself that selfishness. But maybe she is not entirely to blame. Her mother, after all, has encouraged her sisters in their self-indulgences; at times, it has seemed to the girls that this parental laxity is a rightful and fitting compensation for having a father in a loony bin. Susie knew her curfew, but also knew how her sisters had broken similar rules with little more than a halfhearted scolding. Generally, it seems what her mother wants most is for them to have fun.

And Susie was having fun there, at the empty theater of the town hall. As the hour of her curfew whizzed by, Susie split a cigarette with Dickie Clayton, a nerdy boy, who she had believed might be capable of a Clark Kent transformation with the simple removal of his horn-rimmed, tortoiseshell glasses. After the cigarette burned to a nub, Susie, cavalier as Ava Gardner, stomped it between the rows of plush seats, then pulled away Dickie's glasses. But the unencumbered face was not what Susie had hoped; without the glasses' magnifying effect, Dickie's eyes receded to two narrow, deep-set slits, and he looked at Susie with the expression an old man might make on all fours, feeling the ground for a dropped pill. But Susie kissed him anyway, only her third kiss ever, Dickie's mouth opening so eagerly into hers. A thoughtless place, where she could think nothing about her family.

When their mouths separated, Dickie bowed his head and blinked up at her, with girlish timidity.

So, Dickie said.

So—

I've been wanting to ask you.

Yes? Susie said, in a tone she felt certain would provoke what seemed his sentence's inevitable conclusion: *do you want to go steady?*

How's your dad doing?

Had this been the point? The reason that even poindexter Dickie Clayton would kiss her? At school, all the kids seem finally to have learned where her father has gone, and a couple have even loaded that fact into their wicked arsenals. Last Tuesday, as Susie leapt mightily from a school yard bench, that jerk Tom Neuberger exclaimed, *Look! One flew over the cuckoo's nest!*

Susie never responds to the other kids' questions; she imitates her mother's demureness and, as with her mother, the intrigue surrounding her has grown, granting her a tragic sort of mystique. Is it possible Dickie invited her to Town Hall, kissed her for this reason? Did he think that his kiss earned him that intimacy, that he could be the one to know Susie Merrill's secrets, about which everyone was curious? Or was she being paranoid? Susie patted the side of Dickie's face, as she might a puppy's, and told Jacquelyn it was time to go.

They can't lie to themselves anymore, as her mother says.

But what if her father never gets better? Or what if he comes home and does something even worse? What if he is truly sick and only getting sicker?

Maybe they can't lie to themselves anymore, but what else can they do? It is the Skunk Hour of their family, and Susie wants to say to her mother, *what else can we do but keep on as we have?*

In history class last week, Susie watched a newsreel of Mahatma Gandhi. *We must be the change we wish to see,* Gandhi said. Susie knows others, her father more than any, can think her mother naïve and simple, but now Susie is thirteen, practically a young woman, and so she knows she must help her mother, convince her to find reasons to hope.

It's all about how you see it, Susie thinks. That's what makes a thing true or not. Her father is no madman in a nuthouse, he is only an exhausted man in a quiet place called Mayflower. He has treated them terribly, but he was so exhausted. Susie knows that she herself, when exhausted, is capable of much she would not believe herself capable: rage, pettiness, teary fits. And they must remember that her father is not only the problem he has become. He is also the famous party thrower, the famous adventure seeker, a water-skier extraordinaire, a gourmet of the grotesquely thrilling: whole suckling pigs, flocks of stuffed pigeons. In the past, Susie's friends and her cousins often told her of their jealousy that Susie gets to live each day with the great entertainer.

Her father has made his family tremendously happy, no matter what people think or say about him now. Others may see it as childish, but she knows belief requires much more of us than does despair.

Yes, Susie thinks, that's all she can do, all they can do. Her mother once believed this, she knows; her mother once explained herself in almost exactly those words. Susie must make her mother believe it again. And should her father never come back, or should he come back only to tear everything apart again, still Susie must keep on believing and believing.

My mother is only thirteen now, but she knows things are not as simple as they might appear. Adulthood might seem a plain and bountiful field from the distance, finally to offer no harvestable crop, only a labyrinthine maize maze, carved by some ancient, vanished prankster. But, then, maybe Susie's naïveté is an asset. Maybe, uncomplicated, she can see how simple things ought to be, how simple they can be, if only her family could insist on a better life.

I will not be born for another twenty years, but my mother is now already thinking of her corrections, how she will do things differently, when it is her family, when it is us.

Hoping her resolutions will quiet her thoughts, Susie climbs back into bed and tries to will herself to sleep. Failing that, she watches the sky out her window. The snow has stopped, and as the sky lightens to a sidewalk gray, she tries to see whether or not the clouds have cleared.

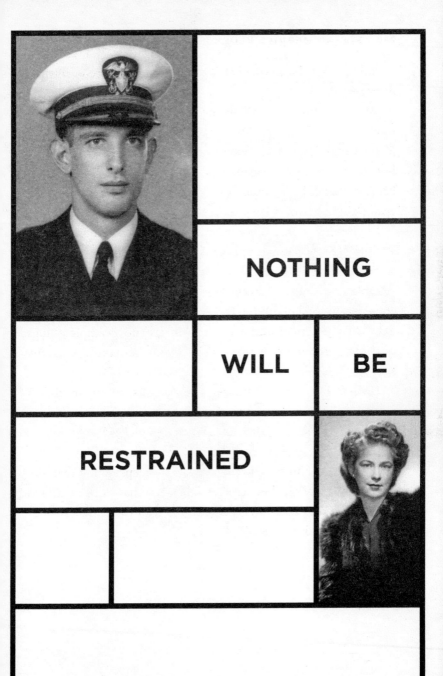

NOTHING

WILL   BE

RESTRAINED

1

High above Belmont, sullen clouds unburden themselves of hail, which falls upon Madhouse Hill, assaulting the Upshire windows in discordant percussion. In the surrounding trees, squirrels dash about their late autumn needs: mating, stockpiling acorns, collecting bedding for the season to come. In the tunnels beneath Upshire, gas burns to force vapors through the iron ribs of the radiator that clangs in the psychiatrist in chief's office, a demanding small presence in the room, like a restive puppy. My grandfather sits before his psychiatrist, who is also his judge and jailer. Frederick's journal is in Canon's hands.

The hail, the autumn, the squirrels, everything else continues, and here is Frederick, a balding man in rumpled slacks and shirt-sleeves, in a mahogany office filled with Victorian knickknacks, a tacit prisoner prosecuted for the crime of attempted truthfulness.

Would not the world and I suffer immeasurable loss for my capitulation to "sanity"? Canon reads from Frederick's journal.

Canon, upon learning that his plan to display Marvin as a dire cautionary example had backfired, upon learning of the reappearance of Mango Diablo and of Lowell's reading, issued the order he immediately understood he should have issued long before. Yes, he knows that writing therapy can be helpful; it is true that the written word can allow powerful revelations to emerge from the otherwise illegible depths of the subconscious. But, equally, writing can be—as Canon now sees that it is for so many men in Ingersoll—an escape, an indulgence to distract from the truth that therapy seeks to address. And so, the day after Lowell shared his poem, Canon had directed the orderlies to seize all the men's journals and papers. Canon knew the men would object; he could predict their rage. And, exactly as expected, they had risen in protest, with fists as well as words, when the Crew Crew conducted the literary plunder. But Canon will explain that even this he has done only to achieve his highest aim: for the patients under his care to see the truth clearly. To see the truth with no imaginative act, no metaphor, to obscure it. To see the scarred fact of a burned body, not the abstruse transcendence of Lowell's poetry.

And yet it was Frederick, who knew Canon's secret, whose journal Canon read first, and frantically. As he had feared and also expected, there it was, in plain words: the secret he had done so much, for two years, to conceal. *Could Rita actually lust after that flabby blowhard? Could she love Canon?* Frederick had written. *But then why else would she touch him?* Plain words written in a journal that anyone might have read.

I don't know, Frederick says. *I wrote that a long time ago.*

Our words define us, do they not? By giving words to something, we can make it so.

Frederick slumps in the sheeny leather chair; he tries to close in on himself once more. He tries to gather around himself his depressive, obliterating blackness, the nihilism that makes Canon's judgments—and the months and months of imprisonment and ongoing financial burden to his family they promise—bearable, merely another example of the meaningless absurdity of all things. The hail beating at the window, a squirrel slipping

from his copulative act and falling to his death, a man indefi-
nitely imprisoned in a madhouse for glimpsing an act of sex—
none of it, at its base, explainable. All of it is simply what
happens. Frederick feels that it might require the strength of the
Crew Crew to restore him to Ingersoll.

2

In Lowell, Canon's theft of the journals stokes hellfire. It is nearly
enough finally to drive Lowell from the hospital altogether.
Lowell is, after all, one of the voluntaries, who still has that
power Canon cannot take away. But Lowell is eager for the fight,
to confront the chief's plain and absolute wrong, to use his elo-
quence and reputation and rage to earn back for his fellow patients all that has ever made Lowell able to endure his eely
electric blackness.

Schultz surprises the others by seeming to be unmoved by the
loss of his journals. But, for Schultz, all he has written amounts
merely to study. The journals themselves are unimportant; what
is important are the words they have allowed him to acquire. His
journals are like a Berlitz language guide, abandoned now that
he has arrived in the foreign place to find himself speaking almost fluently. What remains to be learned, he will learn through
direct experience. With or without his journals, his work still
nears completion.

. . .

When Canon appears for the afternoon group therapy session in his standard self-satisfied calm, the protest flares, immediately.

Where are our books? Lowell asks in a voice straining with mock civility, the fires rising. *We have a right to write.*

Write to right! squeals Bobbie in pleasure, either at the protest or at the homophony.

Then, before the circle of his Mayflower Screwballs—all picking, scratching, muttering at the objects of their psychoses and neuroses—Lowell delivers his protest, occasionally lifting a straight, firm hand before him, striking an image that looks to Frederick like a vaguely demented variation on a Norman Rockwell painting.

I have sat by and accepted all of your deluded stratagems, Lowell says. *But this, well, it is no simple dumb tyranny like the rest. This, I hope you can see, is simply dangerous. Without our journals, what will we have? The blood will be on your hands.*

Lowell continues, enumerating famous writers (Hemingway, Woolf, Zweig) who have ended their lives when they became unable to write, quoting several poets on the absolute imperative of writing (*If I don't write to empty my mind, I go mad*—Byron). Canon receives all of this like an attentive, purely rational academic, betraying nothing beyond curiosity. Eventually, as Lowell's voice drops with the gravity of his Puritan patrimony—*and all that will happen will be yours to take to the grave. You will see what you have done*—Canon interrupts, speaking in the tone of merely a colleague engaged in simple rational discourse.

Your knowledge of literature is extraordinary, Canon says. *It's no wonder that universities hire you to share your knowledge. But I hope you can understand that I was hired because of my expertise, my knowledge. If you can't trust my judgments, then I don't see how you are ever going to make any progress.*

Lowell opens his mouth, but no more words come. Fury silences the poet, and he lunges for the doctor. Two Crew Crew boys intervene, of course, restoring Lowell to his chair, pressing the poet into Canon's audience with palms on Lowell's shoulders. The others cry out, in protest, in solidarity, in fear, or in defiance. Canon allows a moment for the welter to untangle. He knows better than to attempt to answer his patients in their tones, knows better than to attempt to speak over them. Eventually, with the assistance of the two additional Crew Crew he has brought to this predictably contentious meeting, order is restored, as is a semblance of quiet—with the exception of the catatonics still bickering with whatever it is within themselves they bicker with.

Don't you see, Professor Lowell, Canon says, *that it is selfish of you to disrupt the work that all of these men have to do here?*

Canon is proud of himself for this bit of improvisation, the success of which is measured by Lowell's silence. In the wake of this reprimand, however, is the silence not only of the one problematic patient but of the group. The outrage their silence transmits pushes upon Canon, is hot against his face.

Canon, determined yet to make a cautionary display of Marvin's self-imposed injuries, has insisted the burned man's cot be placed within the therapy circle. Until this moment, Marvin has not spoken; he has been discounted as likely unconscious. But then, from this tensed silence comes a voice, raspy and searing, like the hiss a match makes when extinguished in water.

Don't you see, Marvin says from his cot, *that escape is all that makes any of this bearable?*

For a beat, Canon is as silent as the rest. Of all the protests and the accusations, it is this, the half-whisper of a burn victim, that at last seems to sway the moment to the patients' favor. *Reframe,*

Canon tells himself, mentally quoting *The Mental Asylum. And if that fails, shift the subject.*

And how are you feeling today, Professor Schultz?

Schultz, with the serene smile of a bodhisattva contemplating a butterfly, turns his attention to Canon.

Me?

I've taken a look at your journals, Professor. And frankly there is a lot I don't understand. A lot that concerns me. But sometimes, I see, you mention your wife who has passed away. Irit?

Had Canon, Frederick wonders, believed Schultz would react at all differently? Or had this been the point, another of Canon's dumb displays? At the utterance of her name, Schultz's face fills with something uncontainable; an irrepressible sound erupts from his mouth.

Discount Professor Schultz. Believe him psychotic. Believe all of his theories no more than schizophrenia. But, as when Marvin bellowed his anguish the night that the men of Ingersoll came to him, when Schultz now screams in his found, fundamental language, he speaks into collective being what is within him. Stanley begins to weep; even Frederick, obscured in nihilism, perceives the coming of tears. Schultz speaks the true name of mourning, a mourning for not only what Schultz has lost but what all the men of Ingersoll have lost: the old Mayflower, onto which this dystopia has been superimposed; the men's other lives, from which they have been exiled.

Schultz is not conscious of the Crew Crew lifting him and pulling him to his room; he is not conscious of the passage of time for over an hour. Time, for the time being, is as fragmented as memory.

3

The hospital is the same and it is also different. It's 1962 and it's also 1945. A friend from Harvard, an anthropologist, has come to take Schultz to the symbolic funeral that Dr. Wallace believes might help bring Schultz a measure of closure. The anthropologist drives him to a dim, incensed room, where his friends have hung what pictures of Irit they have found in Schultz's office. People try to speak with Schultz, but he cannot hear their voices, not above that other language. He does not try, as he once tried, to ignore the words that speak only to him. Instead, he is searching the other language for her true name, but there is still only her human name. Irit. At a gravestone in Temple Israel's cemetery in Wakefield, a gravestone on which his wife's name is written, a gravestone that marks nothing but earth, a rabbi delivers the Mourner's Kaddish. But Schultz cannot hear the Kaddish. To the chagrin of the rabbi, Schultz cannot recite the Kaddish. All of this death, opening more and more of that other language. Schultz has lost everything, and in its place another language rushes in. His mother, his father. *Kokowa, Seekowa.* Irit's parents. *Hakenda. Makoola.* Their names rise up together, chanting with the name of their lost town of Bolbirosok, *Choogama! Choogama!*

It is 1945, but it is also 1962 and 1935. The kittens cry across the Depression; the widow Abrams makes her whistling sound. His roommate's name resonates from down the hall; the obliterated town of Bolbirosok still chants its name. *Choogama! Choogama!* The atmosphere above chimes its sharp *ah,* the stars beyond, *Om.*

And then, at this moment, all sounds converge into the voice that spoke on the day of James Marshall's suicide, on the night of the Phoenix. The death-voice speaks, louder and louder, as if in anticipation, as if a crowd eager for a famous musician's first song. And then there is silence, and they are there.

Ookalay. Belooka.

They are transformed in some way, but it is unmistakably them. *Ookalay.* Irit. And *Belooka.* At last, for the first time, Schultz sees his son. His boy is here, with him, in Boston.

Belooka. His Isaiah.

Ookalay! Belooka! Here they are, but only for a moment. He speaks their names, and they return for the moment of speaking, but then they fade along with the words' echoes. *Ookalay! Belooka!* Schultz's vocabulary may be near complete, he may now have all the words he requires, but to complete his project, he now knows, will require the leap his Irit made unquestioningly, so simply, at all times. It is not enough to know; he must also believe.

It's 1962, but it's also 1935. Schultz sits with Irit and Reb Mendelsohn in that seemingly indestructible wooden study. Reb Mendelsohn reads to his daughter and his future son-in-law the story of Babel from the Torah. *And G-d came down to see the city and the tower, which the children of men had built. And G-d said, Behold, the people is one, and they have all one language; and this they begin to do: and now nothing will be restrained from them, which they have imagined to do.* Schultz is decided.

4

Frederick, wanting to give his roommate time to himself, spends the balance of the afternoon in the Quiet Room at the far end of the corridor, a room not unlike the solitary one in which he spent three days, but without cushioning on the walls or a lock on the door. But perhaps he has sequestered himself here not only for his roommate's sake; perhaps Frederick simply craves the silence and the solitude of these close walls. How, he wonders as he lies on the room's single mattress, has he ever managed to be all that he once had been? A father, a husband, a business-man. Restoring himself to any of that seems, at this moment, as unlikely as tethering himself to a stone, jumping off a bridge, and expecting not to drown. Even the walls of this asylum and the absurd protocols of Canon and his Crew Crew could never be a prison as absolute, as inescapable, as the airless cell of himself. Maybe it is for the best that Canon took his journal, so he can finally give up the false notion that he might explain himself. For the best that now he is not allowed to write; words too are only false shelters, shoddy lean-tos, blowing apart in the mea-sureless desert.

Frederick is surprised to find himself waking, twilight in the hallway windows. He must have slept for at least four hours.

Before the door to his room, Frederick pauses. He hears no sound coming from within, and so he expects to find Schultz ei-ther in a rare state of sleep or, more likely, returned to his chip-per work, making his notes mentally, now denied his journals.

Instead, Frederick turns in to his room to find the professor in an avid state, bounding toward the door. When Schultz's eyes meet Frederick's with urgency, when Schultz's hands clutch Frederick's arms, it seems as much of a surprise to Frederick as witnessing a paraplegic simply rise from his chair to go take a leak.

It is time for me to say what happened. You will listen to me, nu?

Frederick does not want to risk disrupting the rare moment with any reply. He nods.

It is true, what he says, of my Irit. It is true she is gone. But there is something he does not know, something no one knows, and I will tell it to you now. A secret, yes?

Schultz walks to his desk, and removes from the lap drawer a framed sepia photograph of a comely, dusky young woman smiling in Harvard Square.

This is my Irit, yes? he says, tapping his fissured fingernail against the glass. *A beauty.*

Very beautiful, Frederick says earnestly.

May her name be a blessing, it has been almost twenty years.

Wow, Frederick says, then chastises himself for this reply, but still can think of nothing sufficient to say. Before, the mere mention of Irit's name has driven Schultz to maniacal paroxysms; how, now, can he speak of her so simply?

Schultz, grasping with both hands the image by its frame, locks his elbows and projects the photo toward Frederick's face.

You must look very closely at my Irit's belly, yes? One might mistake it for too many sweets, but I'm telling you, Irit had the body of pencils.

As Frederick scrutinizes the photograph, he discerns the unmistakable nascent swell. He thinks then of the time, making love to Katharine, he felt the first undeniable fact of their future family, the firm and rising evidence of what their love had made.

A child?

My son, Schultz replies, nodding.

Your son?

My Isaiah, Schultz says, and then both men fall silent.

My Isaiah. He survived.

Isaiah. A third presence seems now to have entered, one larger than either of them, larger than the room. Or maybe not a presence, but a void. Not only the void of Schultz's lost wife and son, but the void of all that has been lost, a void that also holds Katharine, Jillian, Louise, Susie, Rebecca. All that is necessary but gone.

I have told no one. When he comes back to Boston, I do not see him, because I am in this place. I am here, and I do not know what to say to him. Years pass. What to say? I was ashamed. I am ashamed.

Silence.

My boy, Schultz says. *He wants to see me. But never can I let him see me here. In this place.*

Frederick and Schultz share a gaze; their eyes widen with the recklessness of the thought. A possibility, one that Frederick has not allowed himself to consider, suddenly presents itself. *Katharine,* he thinks. *My girls.* It is a crazy idea, he knows. Likely it will resolve terribly, with a de facto sentence measured in years. But after Canon's reading of his journals, his time here is now interminable anyway, and this idea, at least, is something other than that nothingness. Really, what choice is there?

My grandfather nods.

5

Do you ever wonder what is behind the locked door? Marvin asks.

Frederick, in a chair pulled up to his cot, has told Marvin, and only Marvin, of what Schultz and he have begun to discuss.

It surprises Frederick that Marvin should mention it, that anyone else has considered it, the knobless door near the end of the hall, with its rusting lock.

A long, long time ago, when I was still a boy, Marvin says, *I don't know why they stopped, but they used to take us down there. Below this whole place there are tunnels. Every building has one, connecting to the others. It was how we used to get from place to place in the winter. It's funny. I remember that the winters were more severe then. I don't see how that can be true.*

Tunnels? Frederick asks. Before Canon, Frederick remembers, the older orderlies, among themselves, would sometimes make vaguely mischievous references to the Tunnels. The Tunnels, he had assumed, was either the name of a nearby pub or else some subterranean crawl space, in which the orderlies and nurses sometimes shared a surreptitious cocktail between shifts.

Tunnels, Marvin repeats. *They connect everything. This building to South Webster. My old house to the cafeteria. The cafeteria to a door beyond the front gates.*

Huh.

Once, this was years ago, I lived alone in that house. This was before they had checks all the time, when we could still roam about as we pleased. They used to give us our own keys!

Ha! Really?

I don't think you understand. Keys. I had my own keys, Marvin says. *When they kicked me out of my house, I buried a box.*

Frederick is smiling now.

I can't guarantee anything, but the lock on that door looks pretty old, huh?

Frederick nearly yelps a giddy laugh.

It sure does look old, he agrees.

6

To get to the box was a simple thing, far simpler than Frederick had expected. Canon may have issued his revised protocols, but he has not stanched the spread of dereliction that had opened in his absence. Daily, the patients now manage a thousand tiny transgressions: pills slipped down shirtsleeves, unapproved food brought back to the halls in exchange for a few pilfered Miltowns, even—it is rumored—a couple of conjugal visits in South Webster, purchased with who knows what. When Frederick learned of Marvin's buried box, his mind had run over the texture of his daily schedule, feeling it for weaknesses. Perhaps he could ask for special permission to take a walk, but at best he would be allowed the walk only if another patient also wanted to go, and then only under the direct supervision of a chaperone. His greatest chance, he reasoned, would come when he passed Marvin's old cottage—presently in the slow process of conversion into a building for arts and craft therapy—on the march

264 STEFAN MERRILL BLOCK

back from dinner. On the way to dinner, the Crew Crew were always alert, vigilant for potential outbursts of their patients, irritable with hunger. But after dinner, the walk was often a placid stroll, the men sated and drugged. Typically, in the last weeks, the Crew Crew shared cigarettes and laughed on these walks. Once, Frederick had witnessed them pass a flask among themselves.

Under the cover of the dark, with the Crew Crew both relaxed and increasingly derelict, it was simple for Frederick—who managed to keep his faculties by furtively tucking his pills up his nostrils—to slide behind a tree when no one was looking.

And so, presently, the Crew Crew and the men of Ingersoll continue the slow procession onward, leaving Frederick behind. Frederick watches two security boys patrolling along the side of the Depression; he knows he does not have long.

Frederick approaches the spot Marvin described to him, the cottage's southwestern cornerstone. He kneels down to it and shoves the block with his palm. And then there it is, within a hollow of the masonry: a tin lunch box, which—slightly breaking Frederick's heart—displays a rusting image of Carmen Miranda. Frederick rests the box on his thighs and opens it to discover, as promised, the key chain, a considerable roll of twenty-dollar bills, and the third object, about which Marvin made Frederick swear promises.

There's something else in the box, Marvin told him. *My father brought it to me when I was a boy. What did he expect me to do with it? I can't let myself think of that. Well, you'll see. Just please leave it there, and put the box back when you're done. Promise me.*

Okay.

Promise me, or I won't tell you where it is. You're going to want to get rid of it, but you have to promise. Promise.

I promise, Frederick said, but already now he considers breaking that promise. It is, as he should have suspected, a pistol. Frederick thinks of Marvin's unburned left hand, what he could do with it, as soon as he is well enough to make his way back to his box.

Frederick examines the pistol, military-issued. He hasn't held a firearm since his faltering naval service, and the sudden weight of it in his hand surprises him.

He's never considered it, not really. Yes, he has starved himself to near death, has gotten himself so badly drunk, before driving home, that even a straight line was a tremendous effort. Still, whenever he has heard the news of a suicide, he has thought *Cowardice!* in the same instant, unthinking way that the sight of the inordinately beautiful spurs him to the word *vapid!* And perhaps, he thinks now, he has been right, perhaps everyone must walk the same tenuous bridge over the same rushing water, but most have the fortitude not to look down.

But, then, maybe he has been the cowardly one, so often prostrating himself before death, but hoping that it, not he, would swing the final blow. But now the gun is in his hand, and Frederick thinks again, *it is as simple as this.*

The traffic rumbles and hisses around the base of the hill. Autumn flowers still manage to bloom in the garden below the cottage's bay windows. The moonlight, blue and vivid, casts the otherworldly shadows of a movie-bright night. The dying grass dampens his pants. These things are not on top of him now, pressing with the weight of their demands. Nor are they beneath him, seemingly assembled to allow him some revelation. Sitting here, gun in hand, for the first time, in a great while, he feels in between.

It is as simple as this. You put a pistol to your head and you squeeze. The static continues. Still there will be birth, life, death.

Still moonlight and flowers and girls and families. Still love and resentment. But a single squeeze and you enter it in a different and unknowable way.

He is not serious, not really. He wants only the closeness of it. To know he could have that power. He spins the revolver, until one of its three bullets disappears behind the barrel. Then he presses it to his temple with his palm, and feels the pressure of its metallic kiss. Something within him accelerates.

Words come to him, a common construction, but incontrovertibly true. *I have failed,* Frederick thinks. And then, there is the same foreign need as before, the need that is not quite for a sneeze, or for a kiss, or for a sob. He moves the barrel of the gun to where his face seems to crave it.

Even if he manages to escape, to make it all the way to Katharine and his girls, could he possibly convince his wife that he belongs there with her again? Could he possibly persuade her to convince whomever she must: Canon, the police, the board of Mayflower? How many times, already, has he convinced Katharine of his contrition, of his renascent ambitions, of his lucidity, and then failed again? Again and again, he has failed, in the average, boring ways. He has thought only of what her love promised him, what the love of his girls promised him. But the promise was reciprocal, and he has failed it. Not because of his thwarted ambitions, or even, directly, because of his infidelities; Frederick has failed because where others can sustain, can believe in something they spend their lives constructing, he cannot remain anything for long. He has never found a way for what is within him to coincide with what is beyond him.

His palm is damp on the handle; he realizes that he is now lying down, in a patch of the dying grass, looking at the stars through what is left of the leaves.

Insects, trees, animals, people, all carrying on with the same inexplicable imperative: live, live, live. Bats, leaves, grass, a man crying out from Ingersoll. Everything will continue still, without him. *Katharine. Katharine. My girls.*

No.

Frederick has broken many promises, and he will break one more. Scuttling away in a crouch, he rounds the corner to the cottage's rear, where it overlooks the fall of the hill, dense with bramble, at the base of which car headlights etch the shape of Pleasant Street. He grasps the revolver by the handle and breaks his promise, the pistol landing somewhere in the inscrutable dark brush.

7

When Frederick returns, walking right up to the front door like some sociable neighbor dropping by, he is admitted by the Crew Crew boys, who, stunned at his escape, inform him that they could make his life hell. To expedite their empty scolding, Frederick tries not to smile. Worried the keys might give themselves away with a jangle, Frederick palms them in his pocket. Back in his room, he dangles the keys before Schultz, like a sixteen-year-old proposing a joyride.

For fear of word reaching the Crew Crew, Frederick and Schultz agree they cannot make the farewells to the other men that they would like to make. The two simply offer Marvin their thanks (*Good-bye,* he replies, in a wistful, conclusive tone), gather a few of their things, and wait for the Crew Crew to complete the final round of checks. At 6:00 A.M., the orderlies return to their office, to complete the paperwork before the morning shift arrives. Marking their forms, the boys fail to notice Frederick and Schultz creep out to the locked door. Frederick pulls the keys from his pocket and inserts one after another, until, a quarter of the way through the chain, one fits and turns.

8

The Tunnels. Some lined with dusted decay, others given over to the storage of abandoned attempts to rein in madness. Perhaps some of these objects are no more ridiculous than Canon's modern, Freudian notions, but in their historical remove, they would be laughable if they were not so horrific. The rotting wood of cold-water chambers. The rusting shackles of ancient confinement beds. Rows of glass jars, holding the dust of what were once thousands of leeches. A considerable collection of laudanum elixirs. A profusion of decaying douche bags. In a room just beneath Canon's office, Frederick and Schultz pass a storage closet where a bit of early dawn light just manages through a half-buried window above to allow a glimpse of dozens of shelves lined with human skulls. Stony way curves into dim stony way, some leading to dead ends, where the original architects perhaps believed buildings would one day rise. Frederick and Schultz pace these corridors now, trying to navigate, by their whirling internal compasses, the way that leads out.

Before returning to Ingersoll, Frederick had considered, just for a moment, making this escape on his own. He worried for his obviously delusional roommate, and what he might do once free. Though he betrayed no skepticism to Schultz, Frederick did wonder at the veracity of his roommate's story of his son. But Frederick reminded himself that this place has failed Schultz as surely as it has failed him. Perhaps it was even a heroic act, liberating Schultz from Mayflower, where his obsessions seem only to deepen. But down here, in Mayflower's labyrinthine Id, it is Schultz who takes the lead. Frederick does not have the perspicuity now to consider how Schultz marches through these tunnels with the beatific certainty of a vision quest, not the anxiety of a long-overdue family reunion. In these convoluted, dark passageways, in this fearsome funhouse of Victorian curios, Frederick is grateful for the professor's confidence that guides them.

There, at the end of another corridor, is a doorway, rimmed with sunlight. Sometimes, a moment arrives this way, chance offering up an immaculate metaphor. Behind Frederick is convolution, dark way after dark way, a subterranean netherworld, all musty and moribund, ignored by most but still existent. And here, just now, that darkness is shot through with the first rays of daylight. It is like when Frederick walked out on the White Paper Company after they failed to promote him, like the three or four times he has abandoned his attempts to write a book. The self-mercy of relinquishing an impossible project. There will be a new project now. He will go to Katharine, and he will convince her. And then, together, they will convince whomever else they must convince. In this new clarity, he will do these things.

Schultz, at this moment, knows the converse of Frederick's

pleasure, the incomparably more complex satisfaction of accomplishment. He has completed his toiling decades, and now he alone is responsible for what he has wrought. From its place off of the eastern horizon, the sun exposes itself to the city of Boston, which is suddenly luminous.

9

Freedom! But the exultant feeling does not last long. Scrambling down the hill into Belmont, Schultz and Frederick are not yet pursued by anything other than the idea of pursuit, but they nearly stumble, time and again, as they search among the denuded trees and granite boulders for any sight of their would-be captors.

The two calm slightly once they reach the sidewalk opposite Madhouse Hill. In the time before Canon, the men of Ingersoll sometimes went down into Belmont, when the old orderlies would take them for a movie or an ice cream, like an elementary school field trip. But they had let themselves be treated as children then, leaving the navigation entirely to the authorities, as they concerned themselves with one another and the looks given by the people in town.

And so now, without exchanging words, Frederick and Schultz simply walk along the road in a direction chosen at random, determined only to increase their distance from Mayflower. The appearance of a bus shelter, just down Trapelo Road, seems at first a mirage, too wonderful to be true.

They sit on the shelter's bench and then attempt, in whatever strained nonchalance two escapees of a mental hospital can muster, to wait like any other pedestrians. To their relief a bus arrives and they board.

In the suburban morning hush at the back of the bus, Schultz turns to Frederick and speaks. *You will come with me, yes? My son will help you. To get where you need to go.*

Frederick will later wish he had spent more time considering Schultz's offer. But at this moment, stunned by the success of their escape, he forgets whatever vague semblance of his own plan he might have had; he is grateful for any plan, even a schizophrenic's.

Where is he?

Downtown. I know the building.

Frederick nods.

He will help you. You will see.

They are bound eastward on Interstate 90, and when the highway rises to a squat summit, they receive another clear view of Boston.

He's there, Schultz tells Frederick. *My son is in that tower.*

Frederick, not entirely aware, simply thinks he now has the answer for his roommate's previously inexplicable fascination with Boston's colossal new tower.

He was so certain, Frederick will later try to convince himself. He was so certain of what he would do that Schultz would have found his own way there. But, still, Frederick will know that it was he, not holy-eyed Schultz, who was responsible for navigating the series of transfers that brought them to the T station at the tower's base.

10

They emerge from the subway to the awesome sight. For Frederick and Schultz, as for all New Englanders with eyes trained to the low altitudes of brownstones and carriage houses, the steel and glass monolith astonishes.

Any flicker of doubt Schultz may have had is extinguished by what now stands before him. This city scene is near deafening in his strange perception: the cars speeding past with a *gareeej,* each of the passing men and women transmitting his or her own unique name, while the magazines they hold *fiffififif,* the cigarettes they smoke *keeee.* But there, before them, is the tower, singing out to Schultz, like a prima donna's voice cutting through a preshow murmur without the warning of a rising curtain. It has taken thousands of years, humanity has nearly obliterated itself many times over on the way, but at last they have done it again. It is a thing made by people, but of the same name as the universe in its totality. *Om.*

Still anxiously vigilant for pursuers, Frederick expects the tower's lobby to be populated with skeptical and stern security guards. Instead, what they discover upon entering are only a few passing pedestrians, overwhelmed to silence by the glistening magnitude of the space: the polished marble floors, the immaculate steel elevators, the spotless glass, all so modern as to seem anachronistic, as if this were not a room in the present, but a room in which the future will take place. Schultz surges ahead of Frederick.

Don't you want to check the directory board? Frederick asks, but

Schultz does not respond, merely continues to the bank of elevators.

Frederick just barely makes it into the elevator car with Schultz before the doors close. But Schultz doesn't notice as he scrutinizes the panel of buttons. He pushes the button with the highest number, fifty-two.

Really? Frederick asks. *He's on the top floor?*

Schultz doesn't answer. He cannot hear Frederick; this building is too loud with the name of what people have finally achieved once more. Each faultless slab of marble, each poured steel girder, each pane of glass, all coalescing into an *Om* in perfect harmony with the cosmos. *And now nothing will be restrained from them, which they have imagined to do.*

His son isn't here, Frederick knows. But what can he do now? Schultz's increasingly audible mutters already draw the quizzical gazes of the two other men sharing the elevator. Frederick senses that, if he tried to derail Schultz's mission, Schultz would react in some exaggerated way. It wouldn't take much—a walkie-talkie, a phone call, a couple of police officers—to restore them to Mayflower. When the doors open on thirty-five to let out the others, Frederick nearly resolves to force Schultz out as well, but he decides against it. He decides, instead, to allow Schultz to pursue whatever he has come to pursue on the top floor, where Frederick will try quietly to cajole him back to the elevator. And then what? Perhaps he will simply hand Schultz a few of Marvin's twenty-dollar bills, then set off on his own for the bus station and New Hampshire. The elevator dings at floor fifty-two.

11

Soon, the scene that now opens will be a lead story in the Boston papers; soon, it will be the great news of the weekend to come. On a Friday morning, in the city's newest tower, two escapees from the Mayflower Home arrive on the top floor, near the doors of Top of the World, Boston's new restaurant in the sky, in which men and women bearing Boston's proud names—those Winthrops, and Kennedys, and also Lowells—breakfast atop their city.

Schultz immediately darts from the elevator and away from Frederick with a swiftness that Frederick would not have thought his old body could muster. Schultz seems to know precisely where to find the emergency stairwell, down a little corridor to the left of the restaurant. Schultz and Frederick bypass the rattle and chatter of breakfast service, but many of the diners will soon invent stories of seeing the men, with their crazed expressions.

Shit, Frederick says. *Shit.*

Schultz is already in the stairwell. Frederick, trying not to further rouse suspicions, lags behind in the corridor, following Schultz as swiftly as he will allow himself.

Frederick pulls open the door to the fire escape and lunges to the stairwell's railing. He looks down to find only the surreal evenness of an orange glow illuminating the stairs' descent, the lines of which converge at a great distance far below. Schultz is nowhere to be seen, and Frederick's first apprehension is panic, a primal heat rising, all his movements now dictated by instinct. Schultz, he believes, has fallen into the dim orange abyss, and

Frederick begins rushing downward to—what? Race down fifty-two floors to undo a fifty-two-floor plummet? They are not rational, these motions. Frederick is already down to the forty-ninth floor, when he pauses. He breathes through his nose. The smells of fresh paint and plaster mix with his own heightened, acrid scent.

Taking two and three stairs in each bound, Frederick returns to the fifty-second floor, and passes it, surges up the one additional length of stairs with a swiftness that borders on flight. At the staircase's end is an opened door, an image like a surrealist painting: the dull, industrial space of the stairwell opening to a pure void, the blue and white infinity of the sky. Frederick passes through the portal and lowers himself onto the rubber membrane of the roof's surface. He does not bother to check whether the door has an external knob, does not bother to prop it in case it locks, which it does. But it doesn't matter; soon, others will come for him.

Turning the corner, the stairwell's entrance no longer obstructing a clear view of the roof's far side, Frederick finds him. There Schultz stands, only feet from that infinity.

Schultz doesn't say anything for the moment, feels no more obligation to respond to Frederick's plea that they go back down than he would to answer the wind tussling the bush of his hair or the seagulls circling nearby.

Strangely, Frederick feels himself calm. He does not try to force Schultz, by yelling or by intervening with his own body. Since their escape, Frederick has felt frantic and unbound, his plans vague, his goals unlikely. But here now—with all sounds muted by the wind, with the entirety of Boston before him—is a soothing sense of conclusiveness. Here, in this moment, it somehow seems as if this sight may be the entire reason they have escaped, as if there could be some revelation in the closeness of that wholeness. Perhaps Frederick has not merely followed Schultz on an insane errand, for lack of better plan. Perhaps it is, instead, the ancient question about the mad, the question about prophets: insanity or vision?

Nothing, G-d said, *will be restrained from them.*

The *Om* of this tower, equal to the *Om* of the universe, is a blank page on which Schultz could write any future in the resurrected language.

Schultz had meant to say other words. The wounded world is spread there before him. With Frederick as his witness, he had planned to speak in his true language, and begin to heal it. Schultz understands that whatever he says now will be. But he cannot help it; first, he must speak only to heal himself.

Irit, he begins, in Yiddish. *Isaiah.*

Ookalay.

Each letter spelling her different aspects, filling her in before him.

Belooka.

One syllable, his lost boy's face, then his arms, then his hand outstretched.

Schultz does not think now of all his years of work, his culling of all the names, his comprehensive project of transliteration, what he has accomplished, what it might allow. Schultz can think only of his wife, and his murdered unborn son he has just seen, for the first time.

Ookalay. Belooka. They are present, not just in aspects, as in memory. They are now as present as each bolt, each steel beam, each pane of glass beneath him is present.

Ookalay. Belooka. But they stand back from him still. Why? Irit will not allow their boy to run to him, holding him by the wrist. She stands there, in that infinite space, saying something that is inaudible to Schultz. In the true language there is no true name for *I don't understand,* and so Schultz says this in Yiddish. Irit is speaking, but Schultz cannot hear, and so he says in Yiddish, *I cannot hear.* He says in Hebrew, *Speak up!*

Ookalay, Belooka. Louder, he says. *Louder, Irit!*

He knows he must go to her. It requires that leap. She always made that leap, which analytic Schultz never allowed himself. She believed while he remained the skeptic. With faith, she always leapt: not just for G-d, but for love, for her family, for her family's lives while Schultz remained in Boston, cowering within his own visions. It was she who kissed him first.

Ookalay. Belooka. Schultz knows there is still one word left. There is one word he does not yet know. He knows this is the word, the last word, which Irit is speaking to him. His own true name. But to hear it he must go to her; he must make that leap. It is not a test, not exactly. It is simply the truth. To hear the name that creates him, he must leave physics and reason, and what it was he thought he wanted to accomplish, and he must go to her.

Ookalay. Belooka. He closes his eyes, and she is still there, on both sides of his lids. He leaps.

Irit lets go of his son's wrist, and Isaiah's hands grasp Schultz's arm. Irit comes to Schultz and puts her mouth to his ear. At last, Schultz can hear.

There are the seagulls flying above, the busboys clearing tables below, the society women kissing familiar cheeks, the workers toiling over their business, the class of schoolchildren pulling up

in a bus to tour the new tower, a red smear of him on the pro-
truding ledge thirty or forty feet below. And much, much farther
down, what was Schultz is obscured by the gathering crowds.

My grandfather stands at the edge. The distance is great and
unreckonable and seems to be growing still.

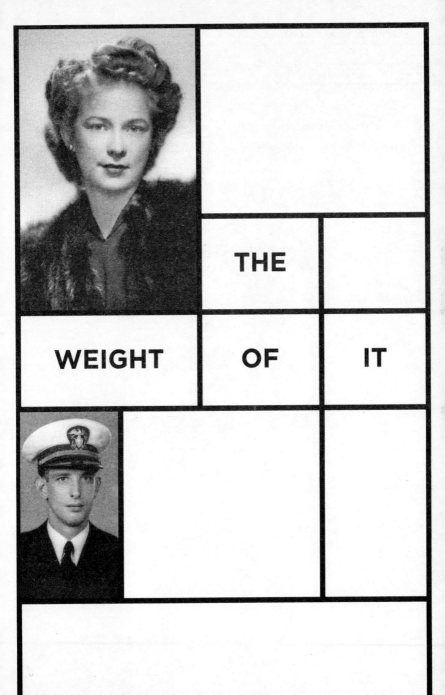

THE WEIGHT OF IT

1

On its perch in the kitchen, the phone rings.

For the last week, my grandmother has allowed herself to use the phone only when it is she who dials; she has told my mother and her sisters to do the same, to ignore all ringing phones.

Those awful, pushy creditors, Katharine has explained. *They just keep calling and calling, and I can't bear to speak with another.*

Her daughters are still girls, but even they seem to see through this dissemblance.

The phone is ringing, Mum! It's ringing! Rebecca calls from her room upstairs.

Don't answer it! I told you not to answer it!

But Muuuum, this is so weeeird!

I don't want to talk to those people. Now listen to me, I said don't answer it!

But Muuum, what if it's Jeremy? Rebecca says.

You can call him later. Don't answer it!

Mum!

Fortunately, the phone finally silences.

This is BS! Rebecca yells.

Tough toenails, Katharine says to herself.

Katharine knows she must not let herself speak with Lars again. Maybe he will stick to his pact not to call until the night they have agreed to meet, but likely he will not. She is to meet with Lars one week exactly from today, but Katharine has stuck to her plan not to speak with him until the decided-upon date, in order to sort things out for herself. She wants the decision to be her own, but still, even in the ringing of an unanswered phone, she can feel his needs. In certain moments, Katharine is certain she will meet Lars, certain she will capitulate to everything he wants of her; other times, she is certain she will not.

An hour later, the postman slips the mail through the front door's slot. Sorting through it—third and fourth warnings of debts with a few car advertisements thrown in, as if in attempt at humor or cruelty—Katharine does not at first perceive the significance of the thick manila envelope, even after she reads the return address of the Mayflower Home scrawled onto its top left corner. It has been just a week since her father called to inform her he has stopped making his weekly payments to Mayflower, and still that news resonates in all her thoughts. How will it be after her husband is lobotomized? Or, possibly, will the cessation of payment compel Dr. Canon to release him? Mayflower has played such a prominent role in her internal life that at first it seems not unusual an artifact of it would crop up here in her mailbox. But then, she realizes, this is the first piece of mail she has received from Mayflower in all the months of Frederick's hospitalization. Katharine feels herself quickening.

A bill sent to her, now that her father refuses to pay? But the package is too thick for a bill. Maybe his file. Maybe her father had phoned Dr. Canon to tell him he would no longer be paying, and Canon, in a fit, decided to forward to Katharine all of his reports on Frederick's progress, or lack thereof.

Katharine lays the envelope on her kitchen table, pulls out the papers it contains one or two inches, no more. This glimpse is all she allows herself to see of it: maybe forty or fifty pages, written in an erratic version of Frederick's script.

Katharine stands, turns to the phone, and dials Lars Jensen to tell him that, on second thought, she would like to see him tonight instead.

During the brief conversation, which consists of Lars reciting a list of suggestions in a memorized way (both flattering and vaguely dispiriting to know how thoroughly he has considered the details), the package lies open on the kitchen table before her, Frederick's letters just peeking out from the envelope. She does not know why, precisely, she refuses to allow herself to read, just as she can't know exactly why she has phoned Lars. With only her children for company, Katharine has been alone with her mind for months, dizzying herself with its spiraling movements. But now she does not allow herself self-scrutiny.

Lars will drive the three hours from Exeter. Lars tells Katharine he will meet her at the house, if she wants, but that maybe she should hire a sitter for the kids, and choose some other place. Katharine agrees and phones the sitter, a smart high school girl with a stutter, who will come at six.

Just going to dinner with the ladies, Katharine explains to her daughters (Rebecca predictably protests that, at fourteen, she is old enough to look after her sisters). *But we have some catching up to do. Might be late.*

As she prepares her face for her—what? date?—with Lars, Katharine surprises herself by nearly beginning to cry. She whispers her husband's name, and then tries to correct herself. Katharine tries to think of Frederick's failures, but there is only the terror in his eyes, the ice pick poised. Katharine clutches herself with both hands. He is alone in a mental hospital now, in part by her own doing. Or is it by her doing? And how, so many pages? What has he written? She cannot bear to contemplate the weight of it.

Katharine stands. It is time to go meet Lars.

Might be late, she tells the girls again, on her way out the door.

My mother and her sisters surround Katharine, begging her to settle their disputes before the court of Mum retires for the night. The sitter shrugs at her apologetically. Katharine attends to the quarrels evenly, calmly, firmly, as she has learned she must, and leaves.

SILENCE

AND SOUNDS

1

It happened on a Friday. Much of the staff, eager to put aside the working week's institutional grimness for weekends of boozy frivolity, did not follow the local news and so did not hear of Schultz's death until the next week began. Rita, too, did not learn the news until Monday. But then why, for Rita, was that relentlessly beautiful weekend so vaporous with dread? A hazy oppressiveness, like a premonitory mourning, fogged every frame of the movie she went to see on Friday, clouded the space between her and a boy she agreed to meet for dinner on Saturday (it would never work, it was too sad, the boy's unvarnished enthusiasms, glistening against her gloom). Was it that she knew, in some instinctive way, that the events of the last weeks were now bound, irretrievably, to some dark outcome?

Whatever the reasons, when Rita finally learns the news through the static of her transistor radio that Monday morning, it seems to her that somehow she already knew. Still, Rita rushes to dress, and drives half-recklessly up to Mayflower, parking in front of Canon's office. Before she shuts off the engine, she pauses in her seat to wonder why she has hurried here. Climbing out of her car, hours before she is due for work, Rita realizes the truth: even though she has come to despise aspects of him, even though she has decided—or perhaps not decided, the awareness simply has come to her—that the affair is over, she knows she has come for Albert's sake.

She tries his office door, finds it locked, and so she slips her key into the latch (*you are one of only three people with this key,* he once told her with a sexual exuberance). When she enters, she thinks the room is empty, but then her eye catches on the dull texture of his tweed coat in the far corner.

Albert is seated on the divan, his hands covering his face. He glances up to Rita without surprise. He seems to expect Rita here as certainly as he nightly expects his wife to come into the bedroom. He turns away, cradles his face, and speaks.

We have done incredible things here. There were still cows wandering around this place, for chrissake. I will not let one man destroy all the good we have done.

Rita remains silent, and so Albert lowers his hands and faces her.

You know how much good we have done.

Rita nods, but vaguely. Vaguely, and this slightest faltering of her assurances is enough to flip on Albert's rage, the next words coming fast and moist with his spittle.

If you don't think we have done good here, why have you stayed?

In this surreal aftermath moment, Rita briefly considers trying to explain it. Instead, she only tells Albert that she's been wondering that herself.

Albert's face takes on a strange aspect, something she has never exactly seen before. It takes a moment for her to comprehend the fact of what she is witnessing; it is not verified until the evidence trickles across his face.

Out of instinct, she reaches for him, smearing, rather than wiping, his tears. Out of her mouth come platitudes—why is it, she wonders, she always transforms into this glib counselor at the sight of tears? *I know you have done your best,* she concludes.

Albert nods at this, inhales his bottom lip, and produces a string of disembodied words, *I— This— How— But— Are—*

To quiet him, Rita puts her mouth on his.

Neither Rita nor Albert acknowledges it, at least not in words, but there is a bloodless awareness of departure to the final attempt that follows, like the handshake that the high generals of warring armies must make to seal their truce. Her body is not receptive, his not giving, and after five minutes of awkward attempts, Albert pulls away and apologizes, citing a stomachache. They will never try again.

2

That afternoon, Canon shuts his office blinds and removes his emergency pack of Pall Malls from the desk drawer. He lights one, the little glow in the darkened room both a slight comfort and a sad metaphor. Canon does not allow himself to reflect on his situation at large, does not count his failures, with Rita or with his patients. Instead, he thinks of what Frederick Merrill wrote in his journal.

It is so simple. As the failure mounts on all sides, as he sits there in the shadow of his shameful valley, Canon perhaps allows new considerations. One could scale those walls, one could scrape and climb to the light far above, where others seem to live so

290 STEFAN MERRILL BLOCK

simply, and perhaps never make it. One could spend a lifetime climbing that faltering climb, Canon thinks, or else simply open the fearsome door that presents itself at the valley's nadir. But it would take great courage to do either: the resolute constant courage of the climb or the sudden drastic boldness of opening that door. Canon thinks of Professor Schultz.

3

And my grandfather? There he is, as he knew he would be if apprehended, returned to solitary. Nearly accounted for now is that void in my family's history, that absence that stretches between Frederick's naked romp on Route 109 and the pages that my grandmother received, the pages she would keep in the attic for years, until, one day when I was seven, I would find her sitting before the fire, contemplating their incineration.

The gap is nearly accounted for, but not just yet. For now, my grandfather paces his small cell in the solitary ward, banging at the door to ask to speak with Canon and, failing that, to be let out to the bathroom.

Frederick has spent three days in solitary, but he is yet to be provided the fateful paper and pencil. In his little room at this moment, instead of letters and words, there is only the wordless horror that Schultz's death unbound. When he is allowed the occasional trip to the bathroom, Frederick tries to speak with the orderlies, at least to speak with someone.

I had no idea. He told me his son was there. How could I have known? There will never be anything as horrible. How could I have?

But, after a tiresome afternoon and evening of Frederick's frantic pleas, which the Crew Crew boys in the solitary ward could no more tune out than they could ignore a baby's urgent crying, they yell at him to shut up until he finally does.

And so there my grandfather is now, left to silence. Or not silence exactly, but the calls of the other men and women in the solitary ward, echoing. The muffled noises of other patients, and a faint ringing in his room that may or may not be produced by the single lightbulb caged to the ceiling.

4

He's in such a fragile state. He could be a great danger to the other patients. Not to mention a major distraction.

The next afternoon, Canon attempts to explain his reasoning to the two investigators hired by Mayflower's board of directors (in institutional euphemistic terminology, the board calls them *consultants,* these two bearded, balding men whom Canon knows well from their reputation in the academic literature). The two men look at each other, and then the one with the mole asks how long, then, will they have to wait to talk with Frederick. When Canon again explains that Frederick is in a very troubled state, and that reliving the incident at this moment could be catastrophic, the two men look at each other again.

Canon provides the men answers as best he can, deferring to minor staff failings, the unforeseeable way in which his patients escaped, the statistical fact that almost no mental hospital is entirely free from suicide. That, despite all the planning and order in the world, some things are simply uncontrollable.

Uncontrollable: the word lingers putridly after the *consultants* finally go. How long can he hold Merrill from the board's investigators? Or should he simply let him talk? But undoubtedly Merrill would try to blame Canon and his approach, would try to link Schultz's suicide to what had transpired in Canon's group therapy session the day before. But, Canon asks himself, what does he have to hide? All the empirical scrutiny, his careful study of failure in mental hospitals shows . . .

Higgins knocks at Canon's door and enters to deliver the news of another bleeding of Canon's authority. That morning, Higgins tells Canon, Robert Lowell woke with the others, dressed for the day, waited for the morning orderly's next round of checks, and informed him that today he would be leaving.

I'll bring him here, Higgins says. *Before he goes.*

Canon shrugs. It is a great effort even to reply to Higgins, but Canon can see his subordinate is nonplussed to the threshold of vertigo, and so he manages, *If he wants to ruin all he has accomplished, leave him be. We have to focus on controlling what we can.*

Really? Higgins says.

Canon will see Lowell just once more, as a taxi comes to bear the great poet back into the city. Canon will watch the scene from his office, assuming Lowell cannot see him behind the bright reflections of daylight on his window. Just before crouching into the car, Lowell will turn to Canon in Upshire and offer what at first appears a salute. But then, Canon will see, it is a salute made only with the middle finger.

5

The next morning, Rita and a Crew Crew boy named Pete relieve the evening shift, and then conduct checks. When the two reconvene in the office, Pete starts in with the only conversation on the staff's lips that week: Schultz's suicide and its aftermath. This is how Rita learns where Canon has put Frederick.

Rita considers confronting Canon, but she knows better than to try to argue with him. Even now, Canon would never allow Rita to persuade him to her own notions of how he ought to handle his patients. Instead, Rita concocts a plan of her own.

At the end of her shift, Rita, fearless of Canon's censure, goes directly to room 108 of the solitary ward, through the window of which she can see Frederick, half of him on the room's single thin mattress, half of him splayed on the linoleum floor. When Rita first opens the door, Frederick hardly raises his head from the mat to greet her; a long line of saliva is drawn from the corner of his mouth.

Frederick, she says.

He doesn't reply. And so Rita enters the room, crouches next to him, and lays down her offering, paper and a soft charcoal pencil (she fears what he might do with a pen). Frederick looks at the objects strangely, as if deciphering their purpose, and turns, closes his eyes, retreats back into the corner, into the Miltown.

When Rita touches him, gently at the back of his scalp, he turns to her and his eyes elucidate.

Write, she tells him.

Write? he asks, as if the word were not English.

To your wife, she says. *I'll send it. Tell her what happened.*

Frederick thinks, *What happened?*

. . .

The solitary ward is staffed with one orderly for every two patients, and even Rita, Mayflower's de facto number two, cannot
offer the company, the touch, the conversation she senses might
help restore Frederick to some semblance of reality. But by
stealthily altering Frederick's prescriptions, Rita is able to whittle
down his Miltown to levels lower than when he was on Ingersoll. She is also able, twice a day, to replace the pencils he breaks
or crushes against the wall, the paper he tears and crumples. It
reminds her of newsreels she has seen of researchers administering a new medicine, for which they hold the highest hopes, to
diseased primates in their laboratory cages. For two days, she
passes the little window to his door, hoping for the best. For two
days, he seems simply to belong in the place where he is.

And then, on Wednesday evening, she looks into Frederick's
room to find him seated on his mattress, crouched over the floor,
applying pencil to page. When she enters the room, he tells her
that he is going to need more paper.

Frederick does not sleep that night, or the next. It seems to
Rita as if he has stored up on sleep, in these last days, for the purpose of this output.

Only for a moment, when Frederick asks about sounds in his
silent room, does she doubt her project.

. . .

When Rita arrives at Frederick's room that Friday evening, she
finds him sleeping on his mattress, the pages nowhere to be seen.
She unlocks the door and enters.

Frederick darts upright with a sudden, wide-eyed awareness, as if ready to overtake a predator.

Sorry, she says. *Sorry to wake you. I wanted to know—*

The pages, Frederick says.

Yeah.

I was afraid someone might take them, he explains, reaching under the mattress and producing a considerable stack.

Will you read them for me first? he asks.

But they're for her.

I don't know if they make sense. I tried to make sense. I can't tell anymore. If they make sense, send them. If not, throw them away.

I'm sure they—

Please, he says.

Rita doesn't say anything more, and so Frederick says *thank you*.

That evening, as dusk gives way to proper twilight, Rita sits on a bench on the edge of the Depression, and reads in the orange glow cast by one of the Victorian lampposts.

6

When Rita has finished reading, she walks up the opposite side of the Depression, enters Upshire, slides the key that only three people possess into the door of Canon's office, and copies Frederick's home address from his file onto a stamped envelope addressed to Katharine Merrill. Then she returns all of Frederick's charts and clinical jargon, walks to her car, and drives into town. Rita slips the envelope into the first mailbox she passes

Poetry, Rita thinks, is not the result of some divine madness, some awareness gifted from the gods. Poetry is what makes madness, for a time, vanish. Love, language: for a time, another place.

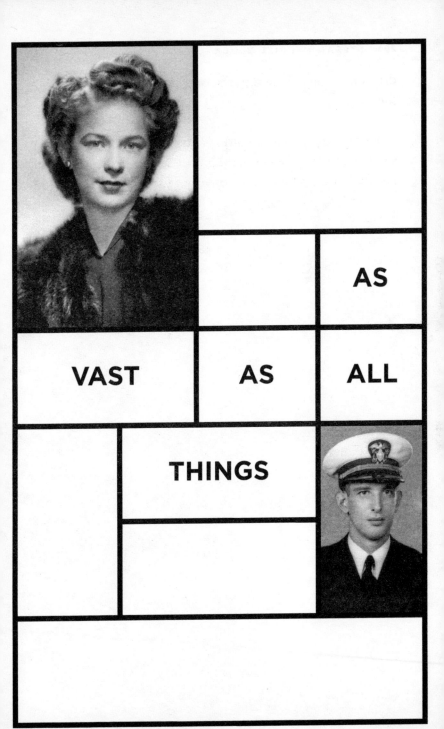

VAST AS

AS

ALL

THINGS

1

As Katharine turns her Ford Country Squire into the place Lars and she have agreed upon, the darkened lot behind Graveton High School, she finds Lars already there, leaning against his car, waiting to receive her. He wears a leather jacket; his thinning hair is Brylcreemed, his face freshly shaven. Now in his forties, he looks like a shoddy imitation of himself at his prime. Like a cheap bouquet of silk roses, Katharine thinks. If Katharine were to pass by him in the market, she likely would not recognize him. His face might strike her as a sad implication of time's passage, similar as it is to a greatly aged version of the face of a boy she had once known.

Katharine, he says, more to himself than to her, as if savoring the word's flavor.

Lars, she says, extending her arm mechanically into the charged space between them. *So nice to see you.*

Lars scrutinizes Katharine, finds neither intent nor apprehension, only her placid, unreadable face. But she was always so inscrutable, wasn't she? And, after all, she has shown up here, hasn't she? Mustn't that be an expression of intent?

Let's go somewhere, Lars says. *C'mon.*

Katharine nods and climbs into his Oldsmobile, with its traces of Lars's children—petrified french fries, crushed aluminum toys—littering the backseat.

Lars's weathered face, the detritus of his children; here she is, a married woman with four children, in a car with a middle-aged man, with two children of his own, the two of them linked only by a teenage romance, abandoned half a lifetime ago. What is she doing?

Katharine watches the trees erupt and then vanish from the headlights and tells herself to stop thinking. That the whole point of this, of tonight, is not to think, not of Frederick, or of his pages waiting for her on the table, or of her children and what they require of her. As they cruise in fourth gear, Lars rests his hand on Katharine's leg, and she doesn't usher it away.

Katharine wants not to think, wants—only for a moment, just once—to transcend her endless cycling considerations and re-considerations, but she also knows that it wouldn't take much. Just a simple capitulation. All she would need to do now is give in just a little. Katharine's father has already cleared Lars's way (could her father possibly also be responsible for Lars's suspiciously convenient reappearance?). If only, just now, she accepted his hands, his mouth, his body, Lars and her father would take care of the rest. She could earn permanent residence in that rosier land of Lars's Norman Rockwell existence. And Frederick would be sent where her father wants, the state hospital with its frugal enthusiasm for the lobotomy. She may feel only a lonely woman grateful for an evening with this nervous, affectionate man, but Frederick's fate is held in the space between her hand and Lars's.

The Oldsmobile's tires sing on the country roads, bound north. Eventually, thirty miles from town, they approach the Squaw Lake Diner. Lars steers into the parking lot.

Remember this place? he says, his words slightly hollow of sentiment, coming from a carefully considered script. *We came here on our first date all those years ago. I don't think I'll ever be as happy as when you held my hand that night. Come on, we're going to order the same thing. Peanut butter and bacon sandwiches, remember?*

What is she doing? Does she really think that Lars's former love for her, now mutated into his private mythology, could persuade her?

I don't know, she says.

Lars has imagined the evening so often that he is prepared with just what to say if any possibility comes to pass: hesitancy, ambivalence, passion. But when Lars now delivers his reluctance rhetoric, it comes out not precisely as he has practiced. The words all rush at once and clog up on escape; the speech, by its middle, reduced to a slow drip that just barely manages to trickle through the dumb orifice in the center of his face. But by the end of his monologue, Katharine has reddened as Lars sputters, *we—can—find—the—courage—in—each other.*

Katharine doesn't want his speeches or plans. What she wants from tonight, from Lars, is the opposite of plans. Here she is, trying to act on impulse, agreeing to this evening with Lars because of its imprudence. She wants, just once, what Frederick has allowed himself so many times: thoughtless movement into a night; a willfully cavalier confrontation with chance; the possibility of being, for the night at least, foreign to herself and her commitments. But already she is something else; already she is made into a character in Lars's story of how he will be remade. She will later wonder if, at a younger age, she might have been able to muster belief in Lars's visions for her. Romance, after all, had once seemed this way; a kiss had once seemed an opening to an utterly transformed future.

302 STEFAN MERRILL BLOCK

I won't be part of some fantasy of yours. You're a married man. I'm a married woman. This is ridiculous.

As Katharine watches Lars's face recalibrate to her new judgment, she does not regret what she has said, nor does she pity him. Instead she slumps with a friend's feeling, a weighty empathy. His quivering, the compensatory bolding of the righteousness in his gaze: this ancient pain, which Katharine now inflicts upon Lars, as Frederick has so many times wounded her. Likely, Lars will argue with her. He will denounce her faulty reasoning and her misrepresented intentions. But the real sadness Katharine receives, which she wishes she could describe to Lars, is that no one has done wrong. It would be so much simpler if one were right, one wrong. But Katharine, like Lars, has only done what felt right for the moment, and in doing so passes to Lars a fire that Frederick has many times ignited in her, as others have set to Frederick. An ancient flame, a super-Olympic torch relay with a fire we have passed back and forth among one another, ever since some togaed ancient first invented heartbreak and kindled this ever-burning.

Lars is at least comforted to find he has language even for this, the darkest of the evening's possible outcomes.

Ridiculous? I'll tell you what's ridiculous. Denying our true selves. How we live, that is what is ridiculous.

You sound like you're sixteen years old.

Well, maybe a part of me has stayed at the age that I loved you.

Could he actually mean this? In a way, she realizes, yes. Yes, at least in this present moment. Katharine, too, has known moments like this, in which all time is compressed into a simple story of thwarted love. Never mind what Lars must have felt when proposing to his wife; never mind his love for his children.

And never mind the other women he might have loved. For this moment, here in his Oldsmobile, Katharine is to Lars as vast as all things. If only it were as simple as that. If only we could remain that vast, capable of delivering what we seem, in these compressed moments, to offer one another.

I don't think I'm hungry, Katharine says.

Pitiable, deflated, the words that come from Lars when they return to the school parking lot finally come unrehearsed.

There's no way I can convince you?

I'm sorry. I know I might have led you on. But it's not as easy as you think.

Lars searches his mind for other speeches, contingency plans he must have scripted and is now forgetting. But the truth, he sees, is that they are only what they are: two sad middle-aged parents, falsely hoping the fantasy that they had concocted at the origin of their adulthood could somehow mend them now.

Is it the sadness of this realization in Lars's face? Or is it only her own desperation? Katharine plunges her fingers beneath the surface of what remains of Lars's hair, and soon they are kissing.

No, not desperation. It is, instead, a curiosity. But Lars's mouth on hers is just a mouth on hers. Katharine pulls away, and leaves.

2

Jillian and Louise are at full tilt when she returns home. They barely acknowledge her as they run laps through the rooms, chasing each other in a shrieking conflation of rage and delight. Katharine walks to the kitchen table, where her husband's papers are still where she left them. She sits.

Yes, the Frederick she loves perhaps exists only for moments at a time: a dybbuk, a false thing. But, sometimes, he has held her entirely. My grandmother pulls the pages out of the folder and reads.

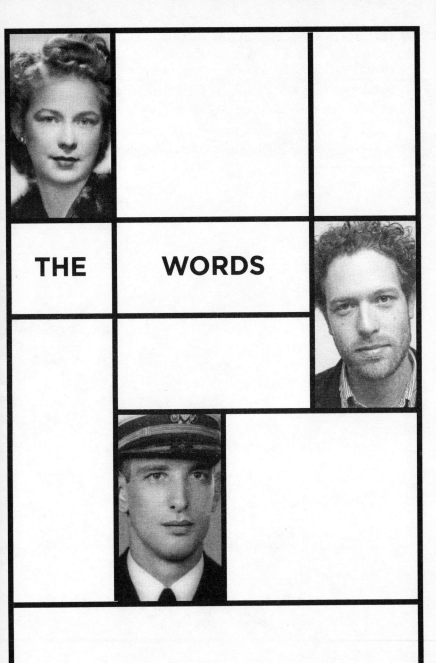

THE WORDS

1

In the soil of a New Hampshire forest, on a summer day of 2007, the words are no longer words, now only particles of ash. At a Massachusetts pencil factory, on a spring afternoon of 1959, the words are not yet words, only a few inches of charcoal in a rod. At the bottom of a milk crate in a cluttered attic, on a winter morning of 1976, the words fade slowly on yellowing paper. Inside the glow of a Franklin stove, on a July day in 1989, the words curl into one another, embrace one another with their sloping appendages, as they incinerate. Ascending the chimney of Echo Cottage in a plume of white, they could have been anything.

2

On a November night of 1962, in a solitary room at the Mayflower Home, my grandfather looks at the whiteness of the paper, on which he does not know what to write. For months, he has tried to worry out of his notebooks an intricate, irrefutable argument, a plea, poetry. But he has awoken to something else. He was in a false place, he thinks now, a false place of words and reasons, of cause and effect.

But now he knows death. The things he has seen. He does not belong here, perhaps. Perhaps it is only Canon's fear that keeps him here. But he also knows that he belongs here or doesn't belong here, just as much as he belongs among the living or the dead. This is merely what has happened. So he now has no plea to Katharine. He does not now know if he is guilty or guiltless. He has tried to make sense of things, to make sense of himself. He has tried to conclude whether the electrified notions just beyond the edges of his excitement are true, or if the truth is only the common sounds, muted tones. He has tried to figure out if there is power thrumming in the walls, or if Rita is right that there is only silence. He has tried to accomplish what those in his hospital are supposed to accomplish. Again, as with Katharine, as with his daughters, he has failed.

The whiteness of the room and of the paper. What else is there to say? This is how time passes now. The whiteness, the sounds of other patients, and the droning of something electric in the walls. The uncounted hours passing, punctuated by meals and movements of bladder and bowel. And though he doesn't know what to write to Katharine, what else is there? At least for a moment now there are words with him in the room.

3

Five days later, the words are in my grandmother's hands. They articulate themselves within her, one after the other, for the first time. For her remaining decades she will be able to navigate these pages from memory, almost as surely as she navigates her bedroom in the dark. But now she simply reads them.

Katharine has tried to convince herself that she is only a sane woman married to a sick man. She has tried to convince herself, again and again, but she has never been able to believe it, not really, not for more than a moment. The chaos of alternatives always overtakes her.

And here now, in her hands, is another.

My grandmother tries to remind herself of all she has suffered, and what she has learned. But, in this moment, with her husband's strange and beautiful and desperate words, she can't help herself.

4

The words, in the summer of 2007, are carbon in the soil outside Echo Cottage, just beyond where I sit on the upstairs sleeping porch, on which I have set up a portable table and a loose-legged wooden chair. It is the lake at its best hour, as the sun starts to settle. My parents are downstairs, visiting with relatives over sangria. Beyond the screen windows, the lake presents itself at a seemingly impossible angle, somehow canted toward me, like the floor of a ballet studio in a Degas painting. It is the second day of what, despite its squeamish connotations, my family persists in calling a *three-day blow,* seventy-two hours of ceaseless wind, the whitecaps heaving themselves in linear patterns, whipping the lake's surface into a mad cursive, as if the waves might, at any moment, arrange into legible sentences. On the table in front of me is a blank page.

At the top of a bookshelf in Echo Cottage, there is a picture of my grandfather, at about my age, dressed in his naval uniform, ready for the war. A few times this summer, I've held his portrait next to me in the mirror, and then considered our similarities. At the far side of my mother's life, far behind this sunny summer with a family of her own, there is something dark but obscured, which I clearly resemble in superficial ways—and also, I know at twenty-five, in other ways too. One night, over sixty years ago, on the deck of a ship in the South Pacific, something in Frederick shifted and he could no longer eat. One night, four years ago, in my crumbling university apartment, something shifted in me, and I couldn't sleep for four days straight. When I spoke with a doctor, just once, about my strange, objectless insomnia, her tentative diagnosis stunned me, as if she had just named a relative of mine she couldn't have possibly known. *Bipolar disorder,* she said. Manic depression. My grandfather's supposed affliction.

Frederick and I are at a great distance but we are also profoundly intimate, on opposite sides of my mother's willful decisions and best efforts. Frederick presented my mother with the problems; my mother has tried to give her corrections to me.

My mother has told me that one night, when she was thirteen, she made a resolution, one of many in her life. I know not to underestimate my mother's resolve. Now in her fifties, she still possesses a formidable gift to come to decisions and then to remain faithful to them. Three years ago, for example, she decided to prohibit all gluten from her diet, and no trespassing gluten has entered her mouth since. When I was nine, she decided she could provide a better education than my oversize, work-sheet-papered elementary school, and she spent the next five years homeschooling me. And decades ago, during her father's hospitalization, my mother decided that if she were to have a family of her own it would be different, clarified of her parents' confusion. And, as ever, my mother kept to her resolutions; she and my father raised us far from her history, in a bright Texas house in which we would always be visible to one another.

But maybe resolutions and plans can never be shelter enough from the unforecastable meteorology with which chaos and history assail the present moment. I've also thought that through deliberate will and close consideration I could bring order to that discordant history. That, with enough effort, I could finally write our family's story, the one I'd heard only in attenuated echoes. I've interviewed Frederick's surviving acquaintances; I've read everything I can find to read about my grandfather, his hospital, and the affliction I may or may not share with him, a nebulous condition he himself may or may not have had. I still don't know if whatever it is within us that flares and fizzles is an illness or just the way we are.

I scrawl the names *Frederick* and *Katharine,* and underline both twice. My inheritance? It sometimes seems there is only this: only the poor passing facts of what happened; only two people, Frederick and Katharine, who succeeded and failed, who found love and lost love, who woke and slept, who lived their lives. Beyond the facts of a few books and conversations, I cannot know what my grandfather suffered in his hospital, or what my grand-mother endured as she waited for him, what their stories could explain about my family and also about me. I can know only the letdown of a few weighty facts, and the coarse, loosely spun the-ories we weave to net that fall. The same is true of my family's other side: the Blocks are from a Jewish shtetl called Bolbirosok, which the Nazis destroyed. Nothing and no one can unburn our history.

I look at the page for a while, and then I look up to the shore beyond Echo Cottage.

Having spent twenty-five summers at Echo, I've mytholo-gized every inch of it. The water shed behind the house that is home to a witch, who, if you listen carefully and are under the age of ten, you can hear whispering for you to enter; the spot over the staircase that chimes when thumped, which could only mean that somewhere behind the ceiling my great-grandparents stashed a small treasure of jewelry; the L-shaped room in which my mother developed polio one night when she was three and which therefore is thought to be haunted by an evil spirit. Echo Cottage is only a common thing, a humble house on a lake's bay, a dense forest just behind. But it is also like a living library, com-mon things holding other places we know are not quite true, and yet, for moments, seem truer than the drab and hushed room.

Here is the simple fact of this place, Echo Cottage, a creaky, musty house, in which I sit uncomfortably in a chair at the edge of a government-protected forest, many of its animals tagged and inventoried. But here is also another place. Here is another house, in a wilderness.

The sun slips behind one of the clouds skittering across the sky. The sleeping porch, which had just begun to orange with the late afternoon, is suddenly the pale blue of the room at dawn. From the bed behind me, I pull off one of the blankets my grandfather invented, rendered from paper by-product, and I draw its abrasive stiffness over my shoulders.

Maybe, sometimes, when my younger cousins run down the path outside, the particles of what were once my grandfather's words are stirred, and I inhale them. Once the words were held in soil, which birthed trees, which were felled and incinerated for the charcoal in which my grandfather wrote; to soil they have returned.

And yet. Now burned and gone, the words can become whatever we need them to be: another place, not quite real, outside or within what happened. Another place, in which we can all be together, all be present to explain ourselves to one another as we cannot in all other places.

There are the words my grandfather writes, the words my grandmother reads. In the end, they will not be enough, but for a moment they are.

SOMEPLACE

ELSE **ENTIRELY**

1

On a morning in late November 1962, Katharine looks at her clock. It is only ten. The girls won't be home from school for six hours.

She hefts the garage door, and then settles into the vinyl seat of the station wagon. She is so certain now that it takes several miles before she recognizes the rareness of this certainty.

Perhaps she could be happier in many other ways. She could be happier as any of the other people in the Fords and Chryslers and Chevrolets passing by; she could live in one of these austere farmhouses, with their sated, milk-fed families. But chance and her decisions have fixed her to this: a woman navigating a wintry, windswept morning to a mental hospital, where she will demand her husband's release. Katharine passes through the foothills of Mount Washington.

Minutes and then hours pass; sleet gives way to rain, then to tranquil clouds, and finally to sun. Katharine tells herself to remain focused and purposeful, despite the somniferous drive. But she finds she does not need to discipline her purpose: thinking of her husband and his pages she has read, purpose, irrepressible as sickness, rises inside her. As the sleepy simplicity of the Spaulding Turnpike convolutes with Boston's mad visions for its motorways, Katharine tells herself not to panic.

. . .

She has never seen it, not in person. But there it is, much as she has imagined it, if even a bit more idyllic. The Mayflower Home for the Mentally Ill, perched atop its hill, with its paradoxical grandiose beauty.

The station wagon rattles to a stop in the parking lot behind Ingersoll. Katharine steadies herself, knows from years with Frederick how her purposefulness can dissolve so easily into more solvent wills. Katharine has not considered her appearance until this moment, but now she thinks of the importance of projecting her argument without stray hairs or smeared makeup to undermine her assuredness, her lucidity. She twists the rearview mirror and tries to divide her face into the parts that might require a reapplication of cosmetics, but she can see only her eyes. Her argument is valid; her anger is warranted; her certainty, for once, is untainted. From the passenger seat, she clutches the envelope holding Frederick's papers and pushes open the car door.

Katharine comes to a green, where the land dips, forming a wide bowl in the center of the campus. On the bowl's lip, she receives a clear view of the city beyond, the urban geometry just slightly smeared with smog from this distance. She does not allow herself to pause and consider the wistfulness this provokes, the city of her youth before her now.

There, at the far side of the green, is the campus's most imposing building, a Georgian mansion. The ornate building seems clearly to house the administrative offices. She tries to decide whether she can plead her case there, or if she should look for another building, in which visitors are received. The decision, however, is soon made for her, because there, jogging to greet her in the center of the green, is campus security, a thick, grave boy with a crew haircut.

Madam? Excuse me, madam?

Katharine does not know why, exactly, but she at first ignores the boy, simply keeps on, toward the mansion. But he soon reaches her and walks alongside, up the far slope.

Madam? Do you have grounds privileges?

Excuse me?

Let's get you back to your room, he says, leading her by her upper arm. *South Webster?*

Oh, no, no, she says, and knows that she should laugh, that the show of humor would prove her sanity, but she can't summon it.

I'm here to see my husband.

Your husband?

He's a patient. Frederick Merrill?

Look, if you're a visitor, you're supposed to have registered at reception, he says and guides her, his hand on her shoulder, his fingers just slightly pressing into her armpit. Katharine feels that if she acts out now, if she says a word out of place, she could end up in one of these wards, as simply as had Frederick.

The boy takes her through the mansion's three sets of doors, and eventually they approach a dowdy receptionist, to whom Katharine begins to explain she has come to see her husband. The receptionist looks dubiously to the boy, who nods, as if in confirmation of Katharine's sanity. The receptionist interrupts Katharine's speech—*I have a right to speak with my husband, and I demand*—as she presses a buzzer and speaks Katharine's request in an affectless tone to whoever might be on the other end of the intercom.

And, within moments, there he is. Dr. Albert Canon. Katharine requires a moment of adjustment; this man, standing now before her, seems to bear no relation to his looming largeness in her thoughts. Here is only an aging man, his features, from flaccid belly to sagging expression, appearing to experience, more acutely than others', the pull of gravity. It seems even an effort for Canon to raise his eyes to meet hers.

. . .

When the suicides came, after Schultz's death, they came both rapidly and seemingly without reason, patients whom Canon had never even considered to have suicidal tendencies making their swift and decisive ends. Taking care with each step, a boy in North Webster managed to succeed where the other boy in his ward had failed. He slipped away on a walk to breakfast, and was found minutes later, dangling from one of Olmsted's handsome elms, his nervous system still sputtering out in his legs.

Two days later, a woman in South House revealed her months of Miltown pilfering. Perhaps she had been planning it all along, perhaps not. Either way, a possibility, displayed by others, suddenly came to her, and she had all the pills that she required.

But the most horrific of the suicides was Stanley's, employing three belts to tether his head into a toilet seat. On his knees, he pulled the belts as tightly as he could and locked them in place, drowning himself in the shallow pool.

. . .

Mrs. Merrill, Canon says.

Katharine was ready for a fight, was ready to remain resolved against his arguments, but she was not ready for this: to find herself inexplicably pitying this man.

Canon is exhausted. During last evening's emergency meeting of the board of the Mayflower Home, he could not rise in argument, in his usual self-assured rant, against the reprimands as those eight dour men turned against him, teeth bared in that uniquely New England mode of self-righteousness. Much was said, and Canon at first tried to respond, but eventually he began to drift, to acquiesce.

We've begun to look for a replacement, Clarence Winthrop concluded.

A replacement? Canon said. For just a moment then, he felt the fight within him, a furious listing of his accomplishments. But then he paused.

Canon has tried to make something new from his years of close study, protocols crafted to hold all of these patients in a state where he could impose reality upon their delusions, and rescue them all. But patients have died; Rita has left him; his peers have turned against him. Over the last few days, Canon has begun to fantasize his return to his small windowless office at Harvard, a room in which he can fill papers and books with his notions, where the chaos of others will not betray his conclusions.

I'm here to see my husband, Mrs. Merrill tells him.

Mrs. Merrill—

I have a right to see Frederick. I've read his papers, she says, lifting the envelope before Canon. *This place isn't helping him.*

His papers. *Rita,* Canon thinks. But then, now, what does it matter, this final betrayal? Give him his office, his research, and leave others to do as they will.

All right, he says. *All right.*

Later, after Canon returns to Harvard, he will present a paper summarizing his time at Mayflower, a quasi-successful attempt to restore at least part of his academic prestige. *It is crucial for psychiatric professionals to remember,* Canon will write, *that, however clearly delusional they may seem to us, patients hold their idiosyncratic perspectives dearly. Even if patients are overtly paranoid or delusional, it is critical not to disturb their worldview too entirely or too quickly. For, once stripped of the defenses of their delusions, they are delivered to an immensely confusing world.*

As Katharine and the orderly cross the campus toward the solitary ward, her clarity is submerged by something weightier, something profound that overtakes her. Her heart rises against her breastbone; she thinks she is afraid.

They reach the doors, then more doors, then the fluorescent-lit hallways of solitary. No, not afraid. That first night at the USO dance, Frederick leaned in to her, without warning. The thunderclap of a first touch; just when Katharine believes finally that noise has subsided, it again finds some new and distant obstruction to silence, some new object off which it echoes back to her.

The orderly opens a final door.

2

And then there is Frederick. He is suddenly reduced. Suddenly, he is magnified. She has thought of him in many ways, but there is the actual Frederick, only a man with his knees curled to his chest, his hair shooting out at angles, his eyes scrolling. He seems briefly not to recognize her. Frederick looks at her various parts—hands, then feet, then hair, finally her face—as if she were a sentence in a foreign language that he must parse before he can translate.

But then there is Katharine. It is like a door thrown shut to a storm; the sudden silence is dizzying. *Katharine.* She had nearly become something else, an abstraction, only a name for all he had lost, for all that had become impossible. Irreconcilable, that she should be separate from him now, only a person, standing in front of him.

My grandfather stands. My grandmother nearly begins a step toward him, and halts.

She says, *Hi.*

Hi, he says.

They are locked there for a moment, like two animals who have come upon each other in the wild, each trying to gauge the threat, each watching the other for movement. And then they do move, both at once.

Later, riding home from the hospital, Frederick and Katharine will try to think of what, exactly, to say. And someday soon they will fight again. Frederick will again be called off by some nameless calling; Katharine will spend years adrift in the baffling geography of her past, all the alternative routes she might have taken. And eventually they will vanish from us entirely, receding into our possible explanations that we can imagine but never know.

But let it last, for another moment. There they are, my grandfather and my grandmother, kissing.

EPILOGUE

Those blessèd structures, plot and rhyme—
why are they no help to me now
I want to make
something imagined, not recalled?
I hear the noise of my own voice:
The painter's vision is not a lens,
it trembles to caress the light.
But sometimes everything I write
with the threadbare art of my eye
seems a snapshot,
lurid, rapid, garish, grouped,
heightened from life,
yet paralyzed by fact.
All's misalliance.
Yet why not say what happened?
Pray for the grace of accuracy
Vermeer gave to the sun's illumination
stealing like the tide across a map
to his girl solid with yearning.
We are poor passing facts,
warned by that to give
each figure in the photograph
his living name.

—Robert Lowell

WHAT

HAPPENED

1

In the weeks after he left the Mayflower Home, Frederick craved quiet. He sequestered himself in his study in the days but would join the family for dinner, when he would carry on lucid conversation, his speech neither effusive nor grim, merely that of a father asking about his girls' days.

That winter, as ever, the town of Graveton constructed an ice rink in the field just beyond the Merrills' house, and the children of Graveton came to skate. As he had in winters before, Frederick turned the speakers of his stereo toward the ice and played records for the skaters. Traditionally, Frederick would have been the first on the rink; he would have made himself an arctic Pied Piper, would have hoisted one of his daughters onto his shoulders and sped about the periphery. Or else, if his mood dimmed, he would have pointed the speakers back inside and played a mournful sonata, shouting at the children whenever their noise overtook his stereo. But now, in that time after his release from the hospital, Frederick played only light and joyful albums, Broadway tunes and Christmas carols, as he sat at his desk, his gaze alternating between an open newspaper and the children outside.

Frederick, once so intolerant of the musty obligations of fatherhood, now pleaded with my mother to spend long afternoons reading with him in his staled study. When my mother would grow antsy with a thirteen-year-old's restlessness and ask permission to leave, a watering of her father's eyes drew that particular tincture of pity, resentment, and guilt—that placater's feeling—a genetic extract that my mother had inherited from her mother. Frederick had settled, but into this fragile configuration his daughters had never witnessed before.

Eventually, at my mother's goading, Frederick joined his daughters on the ice. Before, he had maneuvered his six feet, six inches with assurance; before, his massive size had seemed the corporeal expression of the enormity of his character. But now his body betrayed him. With a few skittish steps onto the ice, Frederick began to teeter. Like a once-proud tower lumbering awkwardly at its implosion, down he crashed. He clutched his sprained ankle, and when finally he uncurled himself to let my mother help him to his feet, his face was moist and red.

Without the spark that could also set him ablaze, Frederick fizzled. But my grandfather was manic-depressive, and eventually there came a great reversal. When finally his energies began to return, they became, as before, incendiary.

Frederick found work as a freelance consultant for one paper company after the next. Within a short time, the family moved twice, to Mississippi, then Alabama. The company in Alabama offered Frederick a permanent position, but still he wanted to move, and Katharine, as ever, accommodated. All the moving was dispiriting to my mother and her sisters, as they repeatedly abandoned best friends and boyfriends and any notion of home. But, Katharine and the girls knew, insatiable Frederick needed regularly to free himself from confinements; at least this way he did not also free himself from them.

To Frederick's wandering, weary family, a job offer in Singapore in 1967 had been an easy sell. Singapore, in its foreignness, had seemed perhaps just what they needed. And for a time, that rare thing happened: their life in Singapore, more or less, equaled their hopes for it. This was a happy time, by all accounts, my mother and her sisters in the American School, the family wealthy by Singapore's standards, living in a gated house on a hill ringed by a monsoon drain that resembled a castle's moat.

But soon my mother left for college in America, Frederick's work grew monotonous, and he began drinking more heavily. There, again, were his old voracious cravings: the women, the bourbon, the unreasonable plans. Night after night, Frederick would fail to come home before dawn.

2

On Halloween night 1968, Rebecca was in Florida for college, and my mother had just returned to America for her freshman year in Boston. Of my aunts, only Jillian and Louise remember the night, and their memory is much like the rest of our family's knowledge of Frederick, a few glimpses outlining the absent figure. They remember waking to the ringing of a phone, the in-house line, and knowing, at that hour, that something must be wrong. Louise and Jillian went into the living room to find the police with their mother.

Mum was crying, Louise said. *She told me what happened.*

The closest I have to a precise account of what happened that night, and what led to it, are my mother's secondhand memories of my grandmother's story:

Late that night, Frederick returned to the home's outer gates. He searched his pockets but could not find the key that interfaced with the gates' lock. And so he yelled up to the house, at two in the morning, for Katharine to come let him in. For a while, Katharine lay still in bed, not exactly to punish him, she'd later explain, but to let him calm.

And so, there Frederick stood, at the ten-foot gates, shaking them and calling up to Katharine, who lay there and thought, *Let him wait.* Years before, she would have been ashamed for him, ashamed for herself that the neighbors might hear. Years before, she would have tried to protect her children from the sounds of his rage. But at the moment it seemed that finally all the masks had come off. They had tried again for happiness. Again, it had seemed so simple. Again, he had failed them. *Let them hear.*

Gradually, the ruckus quieted. When Katharine felt assured that his tantrum had passed, she rose from bed, put on her robe, and descended the stairs.

When she opened the front door, the misty lime phosphorescence of the Singapore night rendered the scene illegible. But then, as her eyes adjusted, the set stage became apparent: the driveway, the gate, the road, her husband nowhere to be seen. She felt for her keys in her pocket, pulled the front door shut behind her, and descended toward the gates.

The shock she had, my mom has said to me, more than once. *Can you imagine that? I wasn't even there, but I can't stop myself from seeing it.*

In this moment, it is only a few steps my grandmother takes into a night. A walk down a driveway, a moment that occurs as all moments occur. And yet, for me—not to be born for fourteen years—the scene is mythic, every step resonating through decades.

There is my grandmother, walking down the driveway. She is at the gates now, her lips pressed firmly as she unlatches the lock. She walks to the street, where the pavement is pale green and empty in both directions. She turns back to the house, but as she nears the gates, she pauses. There, in the ditch to the right of the driveway, is the strange and terrible sight: her husband's legs jutting from the drainage moat. Frederick's legs—still, stiff, and perfectly erect—as if he were held in that ditch by the inverse of gravity.

The sight must have seemed too absurd to be credible. Could she have wondered if he was playing a game? Might she have laughed? Might she have expected him to spring out of the ditch and berate her? Did it seem to her then that, finally, he had completely lost his mind?

There is my grandmother, calling Frederick's name, waiting for his legs to move. There is my grandfather, rigid, upended, motionless. Katharine calls and calls to him, but Frederick does not move. And so Katharine walks to the ditch and reaches for his ankle. She tugs at his sock, but upon release, the leg only snaps back into its vertical position, like a tree limb disturbed. She cannot know what has happened to him, but she knows that his body has become something else now, no longer exactly his. The name for what has happened ignites and flames through her; through the flaring of her self, it takes Katharine a long while to see to the plain wick, the word *death*.

My grandmother turns, runs up the street, house to house, begging neighbors for a telephone, her first instinct to protect her children from this horror, that word.

I made a sound then. A primal, deep scream, my mother told me. My mother was a quarter way through her freshman year of college when my grandmother called with the news.

A heart attack, Katharine told her daughter.

For the most part, her family and friends accepted this explanation, nodded in grim recognition of the name Katharine gave to the cause of her husband's death.

I hate secrets, my mother wrote me in an email a year ago. *Mum would always allude to secrets, but she'd never really tell us anything. Like what happened with Daddy's heart attack.*

One evening, twenty-five years after my grandfather's death, we sat with my grandmother on the front porch of Echo Cottage. She had slipped on a stone the week before, resulting in a tiny fracture to her tailbone. After this display of her fragility, health was a primary topic of conversation that summer. As we watched the sky just begin to redden over the lake, my mother interrupted a long silence by sharing her decision to go in for an EKG, to make sure she didn't share her father's heart defect.

Oh, Susie, my grandmother said. *You shouldn't worry so much.*

But isn't it reasonable? Daddy was forty-six when he died. Only a few years older than me.

Your heart is fine.

But didn't he seem fine too?

You don't have anything to worry about.

It seems to me like I might.

Susie, my grandmother said, rocking forward on her fractured tailbone to lay an emphatic hand on my mother's leg. *Believe me. You have nothing to worry about.*

An admission that Frederick's death was something other than a heart attack?

After Frederick died, the life insurance company refused to pay out on my grandmother's claim, citing insufficient disclosure of his history of mental illness. Would his psychiatric history be relevant if his death had been caused by a simple heart attack?

And then there is the way my grandmother found him there in the ditch, stiffened long before rigor mortis could have set in, which a doctor has told me might be suggestive of head trauma.

Soon after his death, without any autopsy, my grandmother ordered my grandfather's body cremated. When the authorities contacted her to deliver his ashes, she had them forward his remains to his mother, in New England. Katharine, of course, had abundant cause for a grief-stricken anger with Frederick. But if it had been a heart attack, if his death was entirely blameless, would she have denied his ashes? Was there, instead, a reason for her to be furious? Or guilty? Had he, perhaps, been calling her for help? Had he cried wolf so often, called out in his despair so many times, that she could not hear his real urgency this time? Or had his cry simply been one last howl at the life he had finally decided that he could no longer bear?

After Katharine had managed to escape the predations of the creditors who pursued her after Frederick's death, after she had managed to gather her children and her few things and fly back to New Hampshire, Frederick's mother one day arrived at Katharine's door, holding the box of her son's ashes. My great-grandmother asked her daughter-in-law to help her spread Frederick's remains in the ocean. Frederick's mother suggested that a quiet, intimate ceremony might provide Katharine and her daughters with some measure of closure. My grandmother declined, sending her mother-in-law to do with her son's ashes whatever she wished.

How could my grandmother—generous and accommodating to a fault—perform this final act of apparent heartlessness? Was it a sort of payback for some other heartlessness, which she had concealed? Had my grandfather allowed himself to commit that profound cruelty, that final selfishness?

3

One day, when I was ten years old, I nearly tackled my grandmother.

It was a February morning of 1993, in our glassy house in suburban Dallas, where my grandmother had come to stay for the winter. I had gotten up from bed early that morning, and my mother had told me she would make a quick run to the grocery, while my grandmother slept upstairs. The sound of the garage door closing, however, woke my grandmother, who soon came down in a panic. When I told her my mother had gone out on an errand, my grandmother declared that she had to go out and find her.

I don't think that's a good idea.

My grandmother ignored me. Shoeless, in a flannel nightie, she started for the door.

She's just gone for a minute. She'll be back soon.

I don't think so.

I know so, I countered.

Before, Katharine had been a living archetype of the Doting Grandmother. But now she told me to go to Hell, and swung open the front door.

Just months before, my mother had been comfortable, while running errands, to leave me in my grandmother's care. But my grandmother's was a swiftly progressing form of Alzheimer's, and now I stood near the door, restraining her with my arms, nearly toppling us both, before she finally capitulated.

Though she still had moments of clarity, it seemed my grandmother no longer could live on her own. Throughout the next year and a half, her daughters, along with a young woman my family hired in Katharine's New Hampshire town, took turns looking after her. Katharine spent the summer of 1995, as she had spent nearly every summer of her life, at Echo Cottage. At the summer's end, she moved in with my aunt Jillian's family, a half hour to the north of Echo.

One day early that September, my mother called my grandmother at Jillian's house. Katharine was fretful, but at a loss for the words to describe her concern. *There is something that just isn't right. There is, I don't know, something there. And I just worry, you know?*

Even on bad days, when Katharine could not remember her husband's name, she still spoke in obscure, generalizing ways of trauma and loss. And yet, for the nearly three decades following Frederick's death, Katharine took no new husband, no new boyfriend.

A year earlier, Lars Jensen had reemerged again, phoning my grandmother's house while my aunt Louise was staying with her. Katharine had refused to take his call. Katharine was bereft but wanted no salve for the absence she often could not even name. Still, her anxiety, on the fourth of September, 1995, seemed to my mother different from her ordinary sadness.

· · ·

There is the sound. From the basement of Jillian's house—at four in the morning, on the fifth of September—the sound of a falling.

The sound wakes my six-year-old cousin, who then wakes my aunt Jillian.

Mommy? I think something fell down the stairs. I think it was Indy.

But Indy, the family's Labrador, lies at the far side of Jillian's bed, where he cocks his head at the predawn commotion. And so Jillian rises and walks down her hallway. This scene too will become mythic, but now it is just a moment. Jillian walks in her robe as her mother, one night in Singapore, walked in her own robe, but also like a hundred other times Jillian has risen to inspect noises.

Maybe something fell off a shelf? Maybe a raccoon got in somehow? Could it possibly be burglars, out here in the woods of New Hampshire? The door to the basement is open. The staircase it leads onto is dark.

Deep within that darkness, at the bottom of the steps, is the sound of struggling breath. My aunt touches the switch, lights the scene, and reveals the fact of what has happened. At first, she feels that she can take it back. She can turn off the lights and turn them on again, and there will be nothing. She can crawl back into bed with her husband and explain that it must have been the wind. But she descends the stairs, and the scene persists.

Jillian tries desperately to will it away. She says, *Okay, you're going to be okay.*

Already she is imagining her mother's recovery, the close call, how they will all have to keep a closer eye on her from now on, but that will be it. *It will be okay,* Jillian tells her mother, and then she yells for her husband to call an ambulance.

· · ·

Four hours later, I opened my eyes to find my mother, in tears, seated on the corner of my bed, explaining that my grandmother had had a good, long life.

Likely, my mother told me, my grandmother tripped on something and fell against the door to the basement, into the space beyond. Or maybe she pushed open the door—in the midstages of Alzheimer's, in the dark—and walked confidently into what she believed to be the bathroom, to discover that the floor had abandoned her. Instead of cold tile under her feet, there was nothing at all. Nothing but blind space, and a falling.

An accident, a terrible accident, we said at her funeral. We had flown up to New Hampshire. It was the first time I had seen Echo Cottage in the fall, frigid autumnal gusts denuding it, in broad strokes, of its summery magic.

But at least, this way, her mind was spared. At least, this way, she died still herself.

. . .

One morning, three or four months after my grandmother's funeral, I sat opposite my mother at our kitchen table in Texas, eating the breakfast she had made for us. My mother looked out the window for a long while, her fried eggs coagulating. I asked her what she was thinking. She turned to me, her eyes glassy and narrow, and admitted that sometimes she still wondered exactly why her mother had fallen down the stairs that night. She would never say that my grandmother's fall was in any way deliberate, and we can't believe that it was. Still, my mother sensed that her mother, even in her confusion, grasped her situation, understood the troubles her worsening disease would impose upon her family. After all, she knew better than anyone the burdens of her husband's hospitalization. Perhaps anxious and deliberate Katharine had at last allowed, even courted, recklessness.

What Mum hated more than anything, my mom told me, *was to be a burden.*

4

A misstep. Or a pang in the heart. Or recklessness. Or a decision. The unknowable act, and then gravity. My grandparents reduced to bodies, their lives forever reduced to our stories. The full truth of how they lived and died split open and bled away.

There is my grandfather, his brain sharing his skull with the concrete. There is my grandmother, on an emergency helicopter ride, high over the land in which she was born, grew up, spent most of her life. They have both fallen into some other space.

That space, just beyond our understanding, like my grandfather's months at his mental hospital, or the truth of what my grandmother silently endured, or the lost words of my grandfather's pages: a vacuum punched open, which still draws our compensations that will never quite suffice. That space, like all that Frederick destroyed and all that Katharine concealed, an emptying of our history, which we can only try to fill with something different and new.

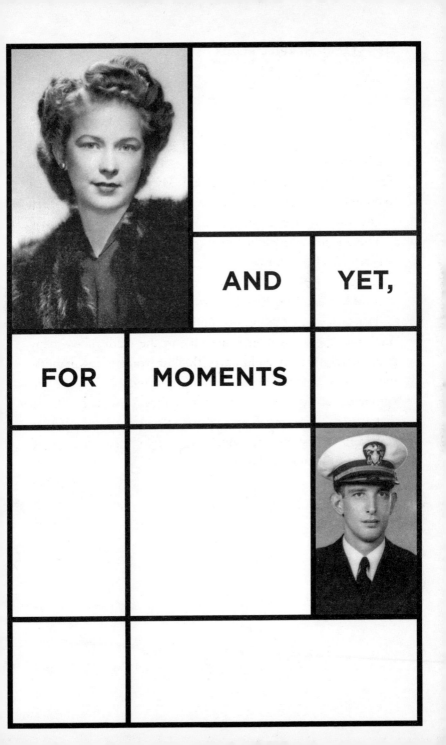

AND YET,

FOR MOMENTS

On a July day in 1989, my grandmother looks at the fire she has made.

This time, she burns all the pages. Simple as that. The paper burns; his words burn. Why should she expect it to be otherwise? Isn't this precisely the point? Yes. The point is that they are only words. One night, years and years ago, she had read those pages and let herself think that they were something more.

But, of course, they weren't enough. He wasn't enough. Not to hold her, or our family, from the senselessness of what happened.

She thinks of when she once saw a sparrow fall from a high branch of one of the trees in front of Echo. Down he fell, like overripe fruit, the collision of his tiny head with a rock soundless to her. He spasmed there, and never moved again. The moment happens and then it passes. Simple as that. Living things die. Paper burns. What had seemed timeless ends. He is gone, and now the pages he wrote are burning.

And yet. How is it that, despite all, the idea of another life persists? How is it that after all the ways he failed her, after all the effort with which she has tried to deafen herself to that history, the heart-boom of a first touch, forty-five years before, can echo even still?

Another life, one in which their love would have been enough, one in which their words would not have failed them.

Maybe it is true that sometimes, and only for moments, that other life had been theirs.

My grandmother closes the door to the Franklin stove, and the embers inflame. Within moments there is nothing left of my grandfather's pages, nothing at all.

Outside, treading the tepid lake water with my mother and brother, I notice that the chimney has started smoking again. I wonder about the fire, what my grandmother has burned, and why.